OUTLAW WOLVES

HEATHER LONG

For every single fan of Willow Bend who has patiently waited for me to get this book out there and for every person who has ever found themselves trapped by depression.

You are not alone.

INTRODUCTION

When I sat down to write this book, I knew that the heroine wouldn't be the most popular. She's been an antagonist for nearly three-quarters of the Wolves of Willow Bend series. Yet, I believe firmly every character has a story and I invite you to spend time with Rayne and Luciana then judge them for yourselves.

It's a new day in Willow Bend and Three Rivers.

xoxo

Heather

Rogue Wolf

Salvatore & Margo

Bayou Wolf

Lincoln & Serafina

Untamed Wolf

Dylan & Chrystal

Wolf with Benefits

Matt & Shiloh

River Wolf
Brett & Colby

Single Wicked Wolf
Giovanni & Murphy

Desert Wolf
Cassius & Sovvan

Snow Wolf
Diesel & Ranae

Wolf on Board
Jake & Mimi

Holly Jolly Wolf
Collin & Rory

Shadow Wolf
Mitch & Amelia

His Moonstruck Wolf
Hugo & Lesley-Anne

Thunder Wolf
John and Hadley

Ghost Wolf
Julian & Dallas

Sign up for Heather's Newsletter.

U.S. PACK TERRITORIES

WOLVES OF THREE RIVERS

Luciana Barrows – Former Alpha of the Three Rivers, mate of Rayne

Rayne Barrows – Alpha of Three Rivers, Mate of Luciana

Dani Reagan - Transplant from Hudson River, twin sister of Jami, younger sister of Louis.

Louis Reagan – Formerly of Hudson River before he went Lone Wolf, now the owner and cook at the town diner.

Jami Reagan - Transplant from Hudson River, twin brother of Dani, younger Brother of Louis

Mark Kenner – Hunter, and Rayne's Third, formerly of the Yukon Pack.

Jackson Barrows – Rayne's Second, and his brother.

Eddie Connors – Hunter, one of the five Hunters Rayne trusts implicitly.

Misty Conroy – Bubbly matron wolf, not quite submissive, but very low dominance.

Ramirez - Former Sutter Butte, post adolescent, late teens.

Arturo Libre – Formerly of Delta Crescent before he went Lone Wolf, now a transport and truck driver.

Della Maxwell – Formerly of Delta Crescent before she went Lone Wolf, now a transport and truck driver.

Willow Bend

Mason Clayborne—Alpha of Willow Bend, mate of Alexis.

Chrystal Royce - Omega of Willow Bend, daughter of Dallas Dalton and Julian, mate to Dylan Royce

Dylan Royce - Hunter of Willow Bend, mate to Chrystal Royce.

Enforcers

Julian – Chief Enforcer, most senior Enforcer for the U.S.

Dallas Dalton – Mate to Julian. Former Hudson River wolf, cousin to Brett Dalton, Mother of Willow Bend Omega Chrystal.

Mitch Jackson - Enforcer, Second to Julian, Western Region, mate to Amelia

Amelia Sullivan Jackson - Enforcer in training, Western Region, mate to Mitch and turned wolf.

Hadley Sexton - Enforcer, Formerly assigned to the Pacific Northwest. Originally from Willow Bend. Mate to John Nelson.

John Nelson - Enforcer, Formerly assigned to the South Eastern region. Mate to Hadley Sexton.

Hudson River

Brett Dalton - Alpha of Hudson River, mate of Colby. Cousin to Dallas Dalton.

Colby Dalton – Healer of Hudson River, mate of Brett. Formerly latent wolf.

Luc Danes—Second to the alpha. Brett's best friend.

Seven Hills

Salvatore Esposito – Pack Alpha, brother of Luciana Barrows, mate to Margo Montgomery Esposito

Margo Montgomery Esposito – Former Enforcer, southern region. Mate to Salvatore Esposito

CHAPTER 1

*R*ayne Barrows didn't know if he'd been done an honor or served up a threat. Sitting across from the most senior Enforcer in the United States—now the newly minted Alpha of the seventh pack—was not the most comfortable situation Rayne had ever found himself in. The wolf's ice blue eyes revealed nothing of his mood nor did his scent. If anything, he could be a ghost—except ghosts didn't radiate lethal power.

It didn't help that the man's mate was out roaming Three Rivers, unsupervised. To insist on an escort would have been insulting, even if the last thing Rayne wanted was the notorious rogue Dallas Dalton running around his pack. He didn't know why she'd been forgiven nor did he care, but he'd heard stories about her for years.

She wasn't to be trusted.

"You seem distracted," Julian said as though to pull his attention back to the room. Rayne didn't need the reminder. He was very aware of the other man's presence, just as he hadn't missed how every member of his pack had slipped off the streets the moment Julian and his wild mate arrived.

The unexpected drop in had been designed to put him on his heels. Adapting, however, was Rayne's strength.

"Not distracted so much as uncertain as to why you're here and what you hope to accomplish." Allowing that show of vulnerability was a choice he'd normally avoid. "I would offer you my congratulations, but the idea of Enforcers as a pack flies in the face of tradition."

"As does allowing rogues to form an unsanctioned pack," Julian responded with a faint smile. "We all have to get used to disappointment."

The dig struck. "Three Rivers is no longer unsanctioned or on probation." It had been the result of Rayne's first act. He became Alpha, and it removed the blade from their throats. Three Rivers was no longer beholden to anyone. Except perhaps for whatever retribution it was the Chief Enforcer sought. "We have a seat at the table."

"You do—because you defeated your mate." Disbelief coupled with frank disgust echoed within the words. "Another first. Perhaps Three Rivers should embrace more tradition rather than breaking every single one."

The man was granite. Unforgiving. Unyielding. "Traditions have their place in *their* packs. This is mine." If Julian expected him to justify anything to him, then he'd come to the wrong place. "Your mate is taking the nickel tour on her own. You wanted to talk to me. So—let's not play games and talk."

Instead of responding immediately, Julian merely raised his eyebrows. "As you are aware, you've had observers in the pack since discovery."

Yes, their fucking Hunters and Enforcers, coming and going all the while unaware of what was happening in the background. "They've also been leaving and returning to their own homes for the last week. Coming by to make sure none have come over to the dark side?"

The corner of Julian's mouth quirked. "No, I'm here to discuss our role going forward. As the current Alpha of Three Rivers, it's expected that you will be the one contacting *me* about issues requiring our intervention and enforcement."

Was the man serious? "I don't want your help. No one here does." The Lone Wolves who'd come to accept Luciana's initial offer had been treated as rogues and second-class citizens no matter their origins since the formation of Three Rivers. If they'd managed to track he and Luciana down before settling in Nebraska, they would have cheerfully killed him and returned her to her brother. For the length of several heartbeats, he'd awaited the bullet from Margo Montgomery's gun that she'd pressed to his skull. There would have been no avoiding that shot.

"That's a short-sighted approach for an alpha, and you're aware of that. You may not *want* our help, but you do *need* it. Normalizing relations requires active communication and interaction on a national scale—not just your half-built ramshackle little village." The cool judgment radiating in every syllable raised the hairs on the back of Rayne's neck.

It was bad enough to be stuck with Julian, worse with Dallas roaming the town and pure hell that Luce wasn't even talking to him and he hadn't seen her in since the afternoon of the day before. The last thing he needed was Julian patronizing him. The sooner they got this over with, the better.

"Fine." He waved a hand and leaned forward. They could just ignore the veiled insults. Julian didn't have to like him. In fact, if the man hated him so much maybe he'd stay far away. "Our laws are simple. Secrecy is sacrosanct. Borders are to be respected, our major offender isn't with us anymore so that won't be a problem."

It was only a moment after he said it that he realized the

3

unintended dig landed. Julian's mouth flattened and his gaze grew chillier if that was possible. The man was granite. "Chrystal is no longer your concern."

"No, she isn't." Then Rayne sighed. "I never had a problem with Chrystal. She was a good kid, a little confused and shy, but she was appreciated here. I admit—I didn't realize she was an Omega until too late. That's on me. I accept the fuck up. No other wolf will ever face that negligence on my watch."

He'd lived with omegas; he understood the precious resource squandered and the near miss Chrystal experienced. It could have gone so much worse.

The Chief Enforcer studied him for a long moment, then he nodded and his expression relaxed. "Good. Now let's discuss what you need."

"Time." They had their issues, but the pack was entirely viable. Projects were already underway to finish rehabbing their town. His wolves were sorting themselves out both personally and within the power structure. They'd been under a tremendous amount of pressure from all sides. "Stop crawling up our asses, take your observers and go. Let the healing happen, and if an issue comes up—you have my number and I have yours."

"The other packs have generously offered their experts and specialists..."

Rayne cut him off with a shake of his head. "I appreciate their generosity." Even if the word turned to ash on his tongue. Of all the alphas he'd dealt with so far, the only one he came close to trusting was Serafina. She seemed to want very little to do with them. "We need to do this on our own."

Julian proved impossible to read. The man gave away nothing. "Very well, let's discuss supplies. Trade between the packs is important to all sides. You haven't been receiving goods through any of the established routes."

4

If he had to keep turning him down, he would...

"Before you tell me no, you want to do it on your own this isn't about underwriting you, it's about continuing a thriving process that benefits every pack." Julian's frankness was appreciated. "Currently, Serafina and Brett control most of the trade coming in through the Eastern seaboard and the Gulf. Storms not withstanding, moving their imports out and onto the roads is a vital proposition and they need purchases to help keep the flow of goods up. Willow Bend provides a tremendous amount of produce and wheat as well as electronics, Sutter Butte—well they provide infrastructure, construction and specializations."

Interesting. "And the Yukon?" Because what the hell they could possibly get out of the bowels of Alaska and northern Canada he'd love to know.

"Diesel buys, he doesn't sell."

Of course he did. "I appreciate it, but we're still..."

"Yes, you're still rebuilding. You have some wolves—Arturo Libre and Della Maxwell—both are truck drivers. They were popular on the runs. Their work would suffice as a trade for the first six months, after you can negotiate prices. It gains you the time you need and your people some amenities that they can enjoy while participating on a grander scale. Trading on the expertise of the wolves within the pack is fairly common and benefits everyone."

The other wolf was serious. Six months of food and other goods shipping in could go a long way towards easing the harsh conditions. They'd finally gotten the power grid stabilized, rehabbed several houses and apartments. The businesses were slow to get off the ground but this could...

"Let me discuss it with the wolves you mentioned. And I'll do a call for volunteers from any of the others familiar with the routes and the trucking requirements. Once I have the names, I'll send them over to everyone. They'll have full permission to cross pack lines?"

"Standard procedures, they notify the seconds when they cross into the territory, and they'll receive the name of who they need to meet with." Something in his manner seemed to relax as he leaned back in the chair.

Rayne had done time on the docks during his training as a Hound. He remembered the trucks coming in, but he hadn't made the leap. "Excellent. I'll get you an answer soon. What else do you have in that offer bag?"

Maybe dismissing the assistance wasn't such a good idea. The packs were talking more now than they ever had when he was younger. Maybe there were trades and deals that could be reached to benefit the pack and help them grow stronger.

They could all use a win.

"Offer me some coffee, and we can discuss it seriously."

Fair enough. He had been rude, but he hadn't wanted the Chief Enforcer or his mate present. The fact the Chief Enforcer hadn't minded in the least when his mate wandered off to explore spoke volumes about his confidence. Rayne hadn't objected because he really hadn't wanted to deal with the question of why.

"Let's take it to the kitchen," Rayne suggested as he stood. The office was too much of Luciana, and every minute spent there reminded him she wasn't. He hadn't made his mark on it because he didn't want to erase her presence. "We can actually get food with the coffee. Hope you like gravy and sausage stuffed biscuits."

Rising, Julian allowed him to go first. A notable concession, but he would accept it as graciously as it had been offered. Maybe the visit wouldn't be so bad after all.

. . .

6

*W*ind raced across the grass, sending ripples out like an ocean wave coming in, but never retreating. The land around them—so flat and ordinary—reflected the weather like a tidal sea, relentlessly surging. In the distance, a black thunderhead climbed into the sky, darkness rumbling behind it. The flashes of lightning held Luciana Maria Esposito Barrows captivated.

Of everything she'd experienced since leaving Italy and coming to the United States, she would never tire of thunderstorms and their wild demonstration of nature's might.

The *Enforcers* were still in *her* town. Sitting in *her* office. Meeting with *her* mate.

The *new* Alpha.

Every single word grated and her wolf lashed inside of her. Three Rivers had been her dream, her goal to build a better pack, a home for every wolf who'd been turned out or abandoned. The American curse of Lone Wolves always being alone seemed a cruel and vicious joke on everything it meant to be a wolf.

Wolves needed family. Friends. *Pack*. Even the old veteran who retreated to his farm in the distance hills, as far from civilization and other wolves as he could—he was still important to the pack. It was their duty to see his needs were met. Even if those needs were solitude.

Closing her eyes, Luciana sighed. In her hand was a cell phone and on the screen the contact information she'd sworn never to use. Yet, she still sat here on the edge between everything and nothing, seeking a solid reason to make the call—a reason not born of anger or grief or even loneliness.

She was not *alone*.

Alpha. Mate. Enemy. Two of the three words she would never have applied to the man she loved. The man who

7

betrayed her. The wolf who kept her hostage. The individual she'd turned her whole life into a crusade to support. Rayne would never let her go.

Ever.

Once more her wolf snapped and snarled, but all that escaped Luciana was a long sigh. The Americans were a passionate people, but they tempered their passions with cold pragmatism and the oddest sense of morality. Loving and loathing someone or something in the same breath was not a new sensation for her.

Just one she would never have applied to the mate she and her wolf had adored without measure.

The wind raced passed her, tangling her hair and pulling it across her eyes. Shaking her head, she glanced at the phone in her palm. Her thumb hovered over the call button and she still couldn't bring herself to press it.

"Luciana Esposito Barrows," he vocalized her full name. Salvatore hadn't used her full name since they were children. "I repudiate you. Seven Hills is closed to you and yours. Never darken our land, never call to us for help, never invoke us to your need. You wished to be alone, so shall you have it. We do not know you."

Pain sliced through her. An unexpected agony as it cleaved her heart.

"She is yours," he told his mate, the bitch Enforcer, Margo. "The Enforcers may do as they will, I withdraw my protection and free you from the promise you made."

Skating her thumb away from the call button, she elected instead to shut the phone's screen off with a squeeze to the button on the side. Seven Hills repudiated her, but only after she had repudiated them first. It had taken her months to accept her brother's censure. Months to understand Salvatore had no other choice, but to let her go.

She couldn't call him. She could never call him for help. All they had built, all that occurred—the town, the pack, even her mate—had been her choice. Unshed tears burned behind her eyes and her throat went scratchy. Still, she would not let them loose. Pride straightened her shoulders and stiffened her spine.

A hushed whisper of sound, and a crunch of grass or maybe it was the slide of foliage against leather, but she sensed the presence of other before she scented it. Twisting, she glanced behind to find a woman with a lean, athletic form and shrouded in her own power approaching. Shrouded because it was so contained, yet beneath the cool façade crackled an alpha in her own right.

Long dark hair flowed as she moved, the wind tugging at it as it had Luciana's. She strode with purpose, and strength seemed to resonate with every step. The woman also had a familiar look to her—only where Luciana had seen similar features before had been on a far more delicate, and seemingly fragile frame. Chrystal was no longer Three Rivers, the wolf having chosen to follow her mate to his pack even as she broke from Luciana's.

"Dallas Dalton," she said by way of greeting. "Or has the Dalton changed now that you have mated Julian?" The Chief Enforcer had no surname that Luciana was aware of, nor had she asked him on the three occasions she'd met with him. The wolf was as prickly as her brother Salvatore on a bad day.

"Doesn't matter. Dalton is fine." The woman prowled with a kind of deadly grace. It would be a mistake to think of her as anything, but dangerous whether she was with her mate or alone. She'd let Luciana hear her coming, and Luciana recognized the choice. Distraction left her vulnerable.

A mistake she wouldn't make again.

When the other woman dropped to sit in the grass next to her, Luciana returned her attention to the oncoming storm. If she'd wanted to attack her, she'd had ample opportunity.

"I expected to see you at the meeting." Dallas said without preamble. The wolf's reputation as the fiercest Rogue in North American pack history didn't do her credit. Luciana had little use for the ways of Lone Wolves and the separation between packs—Seven Hills bound their packs together. They were all one; even the most minor pack had an ally to call upon and Salvatore...

No. She shook her head. Wandering down that path, even in her thoughts could have treacherous results. It mattered little what the woman thought, so Luciana let the statement brush by.

"Have you elected a name for your pack?" The last she'd heard they were merely the seventh pack, and whispered about as though a scandal all their own. Three Rivers had its share of former Lone Wolves, and transplants who came from other packs including Hudson River and Sutter Butte. Only a couple came from the Yukon—though the Shaw twins were most welcome.

None of which mattered, but the Enforcers had formed their own pack. What hadn't been made clear was whether the Lone Wolves were a part of it. Did it matter whether they wanted to be or not? The North Americans were a canny group.

"Did you pull Three Rivers out of a hat?" Question. Counter question. Despite the chill in the air, and the promise of moisture on the wind, Dallas leaned back on her elbows. The indolent pose was an act. Nothing about the woman read as relaxed or idle. Luciana debated whether this would turn into real battle. She was older, but age only mattered so much when it came to a true battle. Julian's mate wore her confidence like a banner for everyone to see.

"Did you grow tired of the meeting and decide to

wander?" They could do this all day. Interestingly, Dalton appeared to have been wandering alone. Though they had limited resources, they did have plenty of wolves to act as guards and escorts. Had she slipped them?

Laughter floated upwards on the breeze, and Dallas leaned forward mirroring Luciana's posture. Crossing her legs into a yoga position, she pointed at the storm. "That's moving swiftly."

"They often do—but it is only wind and water." The torrential force of these storms appealed to Luciana on a soul deep level.

"So it is..." Dallas trailed off and the silence stretched until it became unbearable.

Forcing herself to rouse from the meditative state, Luciana cut a glance to the side and found the woman studying her. "Did you want something?" Curt to the point of rudeness would have appalled her mother. Yet she'd not spoken to Mama since settling in the states. Salvatore cut her off, and it seemed their mother agreed with his ruling.

"Yes," Dallas answered, her eyes offering no clues to the enigma of her presence. "I wanted to see you."

The question of what did she see curled unspoken on Luciana's tongue. Instead of giving voice to it, she merely raised her eyebrows.

Finally, the other wolf said, "You didn't take care of my daughter."

Of course. Chrystal. "No," she admitted. Failing to recognize the omega for what she was fell wholly on Luciana's shoulders. The nascent bonds of pack, the weight of them, had tangled around her and she'd been fighting to sort out disparate personalities and balance them even as she wrestled with her own demons; demons that seemed to take on a life of their own. Her failure, however, had been her own. "I didn't."

She made no pretense of defending her actions. An alpha took care of their pack; they put the needs of their people above their own. For all her considerable skills, Luciana refused to abdicate how complicit she'd been in what could have happened to the young omega had she not found her mate when she did.

"Huh." The grunt surprised her. The other wolf transferred her attention to the storm in the distance. Though she said nothing, the air seemed to vibrate with all the unspoken words rustling in the grass between them.

The blanket of quiet settled over them, muffling the world as the rush of wind blotted out sound. The restlessness of her wolf demanded she challenge the woman for being in her territory, for being in her presence, for…breathing. The droll thought silenced the beast's objections. As yet, Dallas hadn't proved herself a threat. *Nor has she proven herself otherwise.* Luciana didn't see the point in borrowing another fight. Her resources were utterly tapped to manage the battlefields upon which she already waged.

"You really aren't what I expected," Dallas injected into the hush.

"Should I apologize for disappointing you?" It would be a cool day in hell when she did so, but it didn't hurt to ask.

"No…you really shouldn't." Rising abruptly, Dallas took a step away but the weight of her gaze remained a prescient thing. It pressed in on her, searching and demanding answers, but Luciana refused to be pressed into a discussion she neither sought nor desired. Chrystal had been a gift she'd barely understood and lost before she could appreciate. Just another black mark in her book.

Tingles of awareness prickled along her spine. Rayne was coming. He was downwind or she would have scented him already.

"Keep your chin up," Dallas said abruptly. "And if you

change your mind about needing someone to talk to, I've been known to be a very good at keeping secrets."

Then the woman was simply gone. Twisting, Luciana tracked what might be her passage through the field across the way, the grass there was taller than most men. They hadn't cleared it yet.

Surprising offer aside, she had no interest in seeing Dallas' mate or her own for that matter. Luciana rose, and scanned the horizon—he was close but he wasn't there yet. Sliding her hands into the pockets of her skirt, she set off down the dirt road and headed for the incoming storm.

CHAPTER 2

Thunder rumbled like a drum line marching on the town. Lead gray clouds blackened the sky and brought the hammer of night down upon them early. Lightning split the sky; the forks arc upward and blinding in their brightness. Luciana still wasn't back.

"So the offer is supplies and funds if we run some truck routes?" Arturo sat on the arm of the sofa while Della leaned against the back of it. They were grizzled, older wolves with stern visages—at least when they were talking business. Rayne liked both wolves well enough. They were both more go along to get along types.

"More or less. Julian indicated you were both regulars on the old truck routes—before you migrated here." Rayne had spent months getting to know each and every soul who arrived in Three Rivers. Acting as more of an emissary and peacemaker, he'd tried to balance out Luciana's more militant responses—responses he hadn't understood entirely at first. She had expectations, ones he was almost certain none of them ever lived up to, and maybe they never could. His wolf rested still, and watchful within him. They studied the two in front of them, measured their responses and reactions to each syllable.

"Cher, I've been driving since I was a teenager," Della's accent carried the rolling tones of the south, and home. Her dark eyes kindled with amusement and her smile was easy. "Used to do it for Papa back in the day, it's where I got my start."

Papa—the name they'd used for Old Man Andre when he was still alpha of Delta Crescent. A squeeze of pressure tightened against his heart, an old and long accepted grief. Rayne spent many years serving as a Hound, proud of the relationship he'd had with the alpha and the others in his service. "When did that stop?"

"Oh, fifteen—sixteen years ago?" Della shrugged. "I didn't keep count. Went Lone Wolf more for the experience I 'spose. I enjoyed being away more than being at home. Frays the connection." She didn't have to explain further. All wolves in a pack needed some contact with their pack mates and their alpha; it reaffirmed their commitment, their ties to each other around and through the alpha. Long distances could begin to weaken those ties until they all but fell away. "Still got family down in Shreveport, and I went back every couple of years or so—check in on them. Liked my life on the road."

Folding his arms, Rayne canted his head. The note of longing in her voice, a wistfulness tugged at him. "Then why come here?" If she'd enjoyed her freedom so much, why come to Three Rivers?

"Started out as curiosity, stayed out of pure pigheadedness." She shrugged, then a quick smile warmed her expression. "Now I kind of like you prairie rats."

A chuckle broke loose inside of him, even as Arturo threw his head back laughing. Hard not to enjoy Della's frankness. "I hear you," Rayne said, and he did. "You're in?"

"Oh, hell yeah, I'm in. I like the folks, but I do miss the road. I'll come back regularly—I'm assuming our routes will bring us through enough to check in, spend a night or two and then head out again?"

Good question. "I haven't nailed every detail down. I wanted your takes on it." Julian had been full of suggestions, but like every leader—he had his own agenda. Rayne wanted his people's viewpoint, and their expertise before he made any final calls.

"Then I'd say, most routes take anywhere from seven to ten days to drive between the packs with a packed rig. If we alternate and vary our routes, that would give us the opportunity to be back here, what every twenty to twenty-two days?" Della glanced at Arturo for confirmation.

The wolf scratched at his bristly chin, the corners of his mouth turning down as he considered her question. When Rayne first met him, he could only ascribe the surliness to him as though he were permanently in a bad mood. Over time, though, he'd come to realize Arturo just didn't smile, nor did he make a move until he thought it through. His choice to join Three Rivers had been far earthier than Della's curiosity. A woman he was fond of joined them, and he'd followed her.

"Thereabouts, maybe—depends on if we're driving the Crescent to Hudson River or the Yukon for that matter. Willow Bend and Sutter Butte are both closer." A good point, and something to think about.

"Then we make our plans contingent on getting you home at least once a month." In addition to renewing pack bonds, spending time with the pack fostered healthier relationships. It would also let Rayne assess his people, and make sure they continued to thrive by resuming their drives. "Provided you're both willing."

"You're not ordering us to do this?" His cagey expression

17

didn't betray much, but Arturo pushed. The unease in the pack since Rayne's unceremonious usurpation had brought them all out of the woodwork. The restructuring of dominance in a pack plagued by unrest and disillusionment from the beginning led to many confrontations. Too many hotheads in one place.

Expression unchanging, Rayne fixed his gaze on the other wolf. He refused to stand and loom or use his bulk to try and intimidate the other man. One thing Papa stressed in his leadership, power and authority that had to be delivered at the end of a fist wasn't leadership. *Real leaders take the hits, light the path, and demonstrate civility.* Nothing else would have been acceptable in Delta Crescent.

Shaking away those thoughts like a wolf shedding water, he waited Arturo out. The man wasn't going to get an answer. He'd already demonstrated he wouldn't give the order. Better for the wolf to comprehend Three Rivers was not Willow Bend, Hudson River, Sutter Butte, the Yukon or Delta Crescent. They would be a little bit of all of the above, how could they not be considering where all their people came from? Yet, at the end of the day, Three Rivers would be Three Rivers and they started blazing that path *today*.

Finally, Arturo lowered his gaze. It wasn't a full surrender, but rather a withdrawal of challenge. Della chuckled, her breath releasing in shaky, explosive puffs. "Well now that we've settled that, I'm going to get some grub. C'mon Arturo." With two sentences, Della deflated the lingering tension in the air. She dipped close to Rayne long enough to brush a kiss to his cheek. "We'll see you later, yes?"

"Always," he assured her, giving her hand a squeeze as he rose. Arturo hesitated a split-second before offering his hand. The minute pause and quick clasp saying more for the troubling landmines ahead. The wolf wasn't the first and wouldn't be the last to consider testing him. Arturo may have given in for the moment, but it was more like relieving the pressure for the moment.

It was far from over.

Then the pair of wolves left Rayne alone with his thoughts and the empty house. Scrubbing a hand against his jaw, he stood before the window and looked out over the prairie beyond. The angle of the windows in the office meant one side overlooked Main Street, while this one gave him a wide view down the street the turbulent skies crackling with flashes of lightning and ominous black clouds.

Hands in his pockets, he rolled his head from side to side. The vertebrae in his neck cracked. He might have succeeded in allaying his wolves' tension and concerns, but not his own. Julian's visit left him with a lot to chew over and he had a call with Mason and later with Brett the next day.

Damn alphas were being painfully helpful and direct. They may not be certain if they wanted him to succeed but they were keeping their boots firmly on his throat. No pressure. Really.

Nothing moved in the fields beyond. At least nothing which drew his gaze. The wind lashed against the tall grass—which would be hayed soon—on one side of the road, and the wheat on the other. Hopefully the storm wouldn't flatten it all. He still needed to make some sales to help refill their rapidly depleting coffers.

And just like that, the headache behind his eyes became a rapid tattoo of thuds. Leadership required balancing pack funds, pack resources, and pack temperaments. If he could do anything at all...he'd go back in time to the night he and Luciana lay in a tangle of limbs beneath a full moon in the hills above her mother's vineyard in Italy. He'd tell himself they would stay there, and that her inspiration to gather together all the *disparate* wolves was insane.

A part of him had believed in it—believed in her. He'd let his overwhelming love for her blind him.

Now, he stood as alpha of a pack he'd never wanted, never dreamed about and mated to a woman he adored, but who hated him.

Banging his forehead lightly against the glass, he growled as the lightning flashes grew more frequent and thunder shook the house.

The woman could ignore him from the safety of their house.

With that in mind, he strode out of his office and toward the doors. His mate may not want to speak to him or see him, but she'd never be able to hide from him.

And like with everything else in his life currently, he'd take what he could get.

*H*air plastered to her head, Luciana continued her long walk. She'd left the fields behind and followed a sopping path. The route was familiar to her, weaving in and around slight rises and falls in the land's rather seemingly flat architecture. The mud sucked at her bare feet, water swirling at her ankles in some spaces. Despite the chill in the air, she didn't turn toward town. Her clothes clung to her, having been soaked through. If she did get cold, she'd just shift and let her fur warm her.

The lightning flashed revealing the old abandoned farmhouse, which served as her destination. From the moment she and Rayne decided to settle the pack here, the house had drawn her. It was old, three stories, and backed into a thick mound where they'd built a root cellar. Several bedrooms made up the upper floors with only one bathroom, and a huge family room on the main level. The kitchen was archaic, and if one dismissed the peeling paint, broken windows and stripped carpet—it was only waiting for the right amount of love.

The sagging porch creaked under her feet as she padded across it. The main door stood slightly ajar, but the porch roof kept the rain from going inside. Once inside the dark interior, Luciana made her way to where the stone fireplace. It was probably the most solid part of the structure, and the centerpiece around which she wanted to rebuild the home.

Bracing her hands against the cool stone, she bowed her head and leaned there. The house silent save for the patter of the rain against the roof, and the wind twisting around the building. There was one spot where the air's passage seemed to be a song. Tonight, it was a moan, like the building suffered.

From abandonment.

From neglect.

From loss.

A part of her wanted to leave—this place, this pack...her mate. The first two, she might be able to survive. The last? How did she repudiate him when he held her heart?

Even though he'd been the one to shatter it, too.

Curling the fingers of her right hand into her palm, she resisted the urge to punch the stone. A familiar scent teased at her nostrils, and she whirled to find Rodrigo

"*Principessa*." Rodrigo Mazzanti stood framed in the open doorway, the lightning flashes creating a back lighting where he was left in shadowed relief.

"What are you doing here?" She relied on her English, rather than Italian. It was a little rude, but she'd discovered her native tongue let her vent her temper too easily. She had to demonstrate greater control, and avoid the pitfalls of emotional upheaval.

"I've been here a while," he told her, taking another step

into the room. Though the Centurion was smart, he didn't approach too closely.

"My brother?" Was it too much to hope Salvatore had left her an escape route? Did she even want to hope for as much?

"No, Principessa, Giovanni made the arrangements." He inclined his head as he spoke, and though the Centurions were all nearly equal in power, he didn't challenge her gaze.

Not once.

Was he cosseting her as she sulked in her rundown dream house? The disrepair a perfect metaphor for her life.

"Of course he did," she said with a sigh, and folded her arms before leaning back against the stone. Giovanni Conti was one of Salvatore's oldest and closest friends as well as being a Centurion. "To protect Salvatore no doubt." The ache in her heart told her that despite it all she had hoped it was Salvatore, that perhaps, just maybe they could make right what had gone wrong.

"I do not ask such questions," Rodrigo admitted, and he took another step toward her. Unlike she, he wore a coat and heavy boots as well jeans. His pants weren't quite soaking wet, so that suggested he had a vehicle. "I go where I am bid."

"So you've been here for how long?" Was Giovanni spying on her? She could hardly strike at any Italian pack from the center of the American heartland.

"A few months."

Well, he might not have meant to wound her with his answer, but the blow landed nonetheless. "All that time, and you've avoided all of our guards?"

Avoided her? Avoided Rayne?

A flash of other foreigners in her home only a few months prior burned the backs of her mental retinas. They'd come with dark threats and the power to deliver on them, leaving her to choose between two equally regretful options.

"You must excuse their lacking, Principessa," Rodrigo said

with a slow smile. The bastard was definitely patronizing her now. "Your wolves are not so coordinated as yet. And I mean you no harm, I keep my distance from all and just monitor you."

Did that mean he knew...?

"I saw what your mate did."

Shame flooded her and she jerked her attention off the other wolf. If he told Salvatore... If he told anyone.... They would all know her wretched failure. Her abysmal lack of... to her horror tears burned in the back of her eyes and she had to swallow to keep from shedding them.

Rodrigo closed the space between them, then his heavy jacket settled around her. Still warm from the wolf's body, it chased away the chills shivering over her skin. Yet it couldn't do anything for the wreck of her heart.

"Forgive me, Principessa, I am older than many of your wolves. They would have to know to look for how we can hide ourselves." A raw, unvarnished truth. Her brother gathered powerful wolves to his ranks. Every Centurion could be an alpha in his own right, yet they chose to serve him as the alpha of alphas in Italy and protect all the packs. Of course he could mask his presence. "I do not wish to cause you further distress. I would not have even revealed myself now, but your pain called to me."

Her pain.

Her shame.

When he slipped an arm around her shoulders, she let herself rest against his chest for a few, weak seconds. His scent, both familiar and comforting, teased her senses and soothed the jagged edges of emotion cutting through her. He reminded her of the orchards in summer, and the vineyards in spring—a heady cocktail and the source of some of the best wines.

Inhaling a lungful of the nostalgia, she pushed away from

him and then shrugged off the jacket. Catching it, she handed it to him. "You have caused me nothing, Rodrigo. Thank you for revealing yourself to me."

Gathering what she could of her composure, she faced him. An attractive wolf, Rodrigo was more broad planes, and long nose. He had a harsh, blunt look—like he'd taken one too many hits in a fight. At nearly two meters, he towered over her. The thick muscled arms bespoke of hard work, and training. A distant part of her mind acknowledged he had to continue his training somewhere nearby to maintain his physique.

How pathetic and weak had she left her pack? The Centurion had spied on her and her pack. The Hunters and Enforcers kept them contained. Still, they stood and they would continue to stand.

"What can I do for you Principessa? Tell me how I might serve you?" Strange choice of words.

"You cannot *serve* me, because you are my brother's. What I should do is send you home."

The corner of his mouth kicked into a hint of a smirk he didn't even try to disguise. "You may send me away, but I will remain close by. You are not alone Principessa."

With a sharp shake of her head, she pointed a finger at him. "Then go, Rodrigo, and skirt my lands as you wish. I cannot stop anyone from overriding my wishes. That does not mean I must welcome your company."

"Do not be angry with me, I will do as you ask…but know I am here. If you need me, I will be there."

The offer confused and tempted her. No way could she request his assistance, and yet the headiness of having one ally amidst the rubble of her choices was an offer she wasn't sure she wanted much less would ever take.

"I will not be asking," she told him, and kept her tone sharp. Even considering leaning on what he could do for her meant she should reject it. More, she wanted to reject it. Rodrigo should *not* be here. "Go, I require no company this evening."

If given an inch, he might press the advantage and life of late had not been kind to her. After a half-bow, Rodrigo disappeared out into the rain—a shadow as he'd been when he arrived. The wolf moved on too silent feet.

She'd been a fool and she'd grown far too complacent. No wonder Rayne had been able to best her in battle—that and she'd found it impossible to believe her mate truly had challenged her. Only too late had she come to accept the truth, and by then he'd won and she'd lost her pack, her place in it, her sense of self—and her mate.

He had tried to explain his reasons as he'd called them. From that moment forward, she'd avoided all contact with him. She hadn't moved out of the house in town they'd claimed upon founding Three Rivers, but she'd not slept one night under its roof since the loss. Not if she could help it.

Scrubbing her hand over her face, she turned to face the cold, empty hearth. No, there was nothing to be done about the past. Only the future and Rodrigo's temptation aside, she couldn't go back either.

No...she had to find a way forward. Find a way to...

A thump of booted feet on the porch aggravated her. The wind must have changed because she didn't detect a scent. "I told you to go Rodrigo..." Pivoting, she faced the door and her stomach sank.

Rayne stared at her, his beautiful, charming face utterly devoid of any emotion. "Who the fuck is Rodrigo?"

CHAPTER 3

*R*ayne ground his teeth, his jaw threatening to cramp or snap at the tension turning the muscles rigid. Anger coursed in his veins, pumping something dark, bitter, and dangerous through his body. Dripping wet, clothes clinging to every sensuous curve, his *mate* glared at him. The air in his lungs turned to lead. His mate had called out another man's name and told him to go away.

His mate, soaked from the rain, may even be hoping he couldn't detect the unfamiliar masculine scent in the shambles of the house. How could he not? A wolf who didn't belong to his pack had been sniffing around his mate. Not an Enforcer or a Hunter—they were no longer in Three Rivers. Julian and his mate left earlier in the day, Rayne had seen them off. Neither possessed this scent.

Gunpowder filled his soul. She was the match.

"I won't ask you again," he said into the silence where only her fury lashed at him. His earlier question still hung in the air *who the fuck is Rodrigo?*

Nothing in his soul prepared him for the possibility yet

all the reasons bubbled within him like a barrel full of boiling pitch.

The sweep of her dark lashes downward hid the soft brown of her eyes. Those gorgeous eyes had captivated him from their first meeting. He'd thought them doe eyes, sweet and unassuming—beautifully innocent.

God, he'd been an utter fool and besotted by the sheer beauty of her.

It took time for him to recognize the cunning beneath the gentility, the intelligence embedded in the innocence, and the fierceness in her delicate frame. All of which only made him love her more—even when he wanted to throttle her.

"It matters not," she answered, finally when he refused to remove his gaze. The uncertain shift of her stance and the way one of her shoulders drooped should have given him a measure of satisfaction. She didn't challenge his authority, at least not with her body language or her tone. The content of her response, however, was something else entirely.

Not that anything in their current situation pleased him on any level. He should just take her home, get her warm, and make sure she had a meal. Maybe then she would speak to him again.

"It does damn well matter," he ground out despite his every other intention. "You're out here, far away from our *home* and you're talking to wolves who do not belong." His chest clenched, his heart giving a painful wrench.

She uttered one of her famous Italian curses, the spitting of her voice turning the word unintelligible. Not that he needed a translation, the dismissal in her expression said all he needed to hear. Worse, it confirmed his dark suspicion.

"Rodrigo is none of your damn business. He has nothing to do with you or the pack you took away." As if she were no longer a part of it. "So you will leave me here...*this*..." She extended her hand to sweep the shambles of their surroundings. "This place is my home, it is all that you have left me, so why don't you leave again and give me peace."

The jagged claws of guilt sliced through his veins, shredding tendon and muscle without leaving a mark. It threatened to consume him, to thrust him headlong into that desolate hell once again, the one that he had often found himself in before he ever met her.

"This is *not* your home," he warned her, narrowing the gap between them. God, all he wanted to do was kiss her, pull her into his arms and rebuild the connection they once shared—before it turned toxic and threatened to destroy them both. "Your *home* is *with* me."

Her scoff struck him like a physical blow. "As if." The snort of disdain did little to settle the near panic swirling into the maelstrom of terror-frenzied anger twisting his soul. "Go away," she said, deflating and pivoting away. "I don't want to see you."

Surrender was not in her, anymore than it had ever been in him. Her warrior's spirit infused him with the courage of their mission in the first place. Their mating had been like the storm raging outside, tempestuous, wild, and unavoidable. Not once in the last two years since he'd first laid eyes on her had he a moment to regret the compulsion drawing them together or the treasure he'd discovered in her.

Arm snapping out, he wrapped it around her middle and dragged her back against him. Her claws dug into his arm, but he took the pain. He owed her that much. Pressing his face to her hair, he inhaled her scent. The woodsy notes of cedar combining with jasmine, black pepper, and hints of amber. If he closed his eyes as he took her in, he transported back to the vineyards outside of Tuscany on a hot afternoon when she'd strolled past where he'd been working.

Hot day.

Sexy wolf.

His fate had been sealed, but it would be another few months before it became a reality. Now it seemed eons since those lazy afternoons, the long walks, the laughter, and the stories.

Would he ever even see her smile again?

"Are you done with me, Alpha?" The cold cutting tone sank its teeth into him. The rancor in her voice, all the venom in her bite—he deserved it. He should have been with her when it mattered. Should have been there when she made that decision. Instead, he'd been tied up in pointless confrontations with Hunters and Enforcers surrounding Three Rivers.

She had needed him and he hadn't been there.

"I will never be done with you," he swore against her hair. "Never. You can hate me, you can slash me, you can fight me every step of the way, but I will never be done and I will never walk away." He would never leave her again. Then because she wished it, he gave her a gentle squeeze before releasing her. Luciana pushed away from him and crossed to the broken hearth. The distance was negligible, yet it was a chasm he couldn't cross.

That close to her, he couldn't miss the notes of the other wolf. Not so close as to be pounded into her skin, but enough to know the male was interested in her and he didn't know him. An interloper in his lands—near his mate.

"I will always be here for you whether you will it or not," he finished, straightening as he tested the air for more of the male's scent. He tracked her every movement, the way her shoulders pushed back, and the defiant tilt to her chin as she straightened. Battered and bruised pride aside, she would not show weakness. Not to him.

Never again.

A price he would have to pay, no matter how noble his intentions. It was almost his turn to scoff. Nothing about his intentions had been noble—they'd been primal, purely focused on saving her to the exclusion of all else.

Estranged was better than dead. Or at least the mantra was what he told himself.

The silence stretched out between them, crowded with every word they didn't say. "Are you done?" she demanded finally.

"Never," he murmured, then slid his hands into the pockets of his jeans. Better to keep them occupied or he would drag her to him again. Kiss her until they were both too lost in each other to remember the anger and the loss.

Maybe.

But she radiated *stay away from me* and there were some boundaries not even a mate should cross. He would merely have to soak in the sight of her and let it satisfy his need for her.

She was alive.

She was still here.

A huff of breath, then she turned an exasperated look on him. "I meant with this conversation, *sei duro come il muro.*" Blockhead, more or less. It was the nicest thing she'd said to him in months and he'd certainly been called worse.

"Come back to town," he murmured. "There's a car outside, you can ride in it and I will walk. You should be in the house where it is warm and a meal is waiting for you."

Her gaze lifted to his, a spark of recognition shivered through his wolf. Like the man, however, the animal waited. Their prey was hardly toothless. Then throwing her hands up, she stalked past him to the door. "Fine, I will take the SUV, and you will walk. Satisfied?"

She didn't wait for his answer and Rayne didn't offer one. Instead, he stayed in the house. Eddie had ridden out with him, and the loyal wolf was one of the five Rayne trusted most. If he couldn't be at Luciana's side, then he'd keep those wolves he trusted close to her.

Of course, she'd shaken her protection several times. They would just have to get smarter. He waited until the engine of the SUV faded into the distance. Outside the rain continued to hammer against the roof and the thunder rumbled, a growl to match his own.

He tested the male's scent and searched for any place he'd touched.

Rayne had some hunting to do.

*L*uciana wanted to slump in the back of the SUV. Until she'd reached the running vehicle, she hadn't even realized Rayne had brought backup. But of course he had, the wolf thought three steps ahead of most. He planned for contingencies. Though she teased him about his paranoia, she had to admit—it came in handy sometimes. Like now, when she could sit in the back of the car and let someone else do the driving. When she could escape her mate by accepting her mate's offer.

It was also inconvenient, because she could show no weakness to these other wolves. These wolves who had been *hers* to save and now served her mate. She was merely the odd wolf out. Eddie had given her a friendly enough smile and a nod. He made no comment on her condition and didn't ask where Rayne was. Once she climbed inside, he'd put the vehicle in gear and headed towards Three Rivers proper, the tires bouncing through the thick puddles as it traversed the uneven landscape.

No, she didn't dare reveal the depth of her feelings to

any of them. Until the moment Rayne had taken the pack from her, they were supposed to be her pack—her charges. Hers.

Hers, not his.

Not one had stood for her. Not a single one had shown her the loyalty she had pledged to them.

Now they were only her caretakers and if they looked at her with pity in their eyes, she did not want to see it. Schooling her features took every effort. Her scent would reveal very little; none of the wolves here could truly read her save for Rayne. Not even the way she could mask her scent had seemed to affect him in the slightest.

The corner of her mouth tugged and her eyes had a suspicious burn, but she blinked it away. His reaction at the house, layers of distrust and raw possessive fury contained behind an expression devoid of all emotion warned her that the restless, soft spoken, and easy going wolf she'd grown to adore was long gone.

"We're here, ma'am." Eddie's slow rolling accent drifted over her and pulled her attention to the present. He didn't exit the front of the SUV, and only gave her a quick look in the rearview mirror. At least, she only got a glimpse of his eyes as they flicked to her. He'd pulled right up to the two-story they'd converted first as they'd settled into the town. It was right on the corner in the middle of the main strip. The veranda surrounding it and the white clapboard gave it a rustic air even if they had utterly refurbished everything inside.

Pushing open the door, Luciana stepped back out into the rain. Though few drops reached her. Eddie had pulled into the carport behind the house. Squaring her shoulders, she paused at the driver's side door and waited for the wolf to lower the window. "Thank you for the ride." Though she'd rather swallow acid, she continued, "You should return for

Rayne now." Command etched below the words, but she added no heat or fire to them.

Eddie dipped his chin, as if in acknowledgment, but his eyes held hers a beat longer than normal. It wasn't her dominance or his respect for her causing his gaze to lower. No, the wolf was wholly Rayne's and he showed her courtesy out of respect for *his* alpha. "My orders are to stay here, ma'am. But this storm is going to get worse before it gets better and you should be inside."

It may have been a suggestion on his part, but the steel in his gaze told her he wouldn't flout the orders he'd already been given. If Rayne wanted to walk back in the storm, she had no choice but to let him.

Let him? Reality crashed over her with the thunder echoing its force above. She had no choice in anything Rayne did any longer. He'd seen to that.

Pivoting on her heel, she strode to the back door of the house and let herself into the kitchen. Her nose told her a split second before her eyes she wasn't alone. Misty turned from where she stood at the stove, a warm smile alighting on her face. Despite all the changes, Misty Conroy hadn't adjusted her manner in the slightest. The bubbly wolf adored everyone, and wasn't remotely shy in how she showed her affection. Even when hugging—or maybe especially when hugging. She was forever putting herself in the path of others and volunteering to help.

Rejecting her was akin to kicking a small animal, and no one could tell her to stop invading their space. The surliest of the wolves among them would take time to give her a kind word or caress. Since Rayne toppled Luciana for alpha? She'd become a permanent fixture in their home.

"You look like a drowned dog!" Misty exclaimed, and there was too much heart in her manner to take it as an insult. "Goodness, you go upstairs and get out of those wet clothes, then into the shower. I've almost got the stew ready and there's fresh bread in the warmer. I'll put together a tray for you."

Not giving Luciana a moment, she grabbed her arm and hustled her toward the stairs. It was go with her, or yank her arm back. Her wolf snarled internally at the interference. She didn't want to be touched, but she wouldn't wound the other woman.

"I'm fine, Misty." She went for simple reassurance with a measure of demand for obedience. Carefully, she extracted her arm from the other wolf's grasp. "I can come back down for the meal. You should get home before the storm grows much worse." Then with a certain amount of mischief, she added, "Eddie's outside, and I know he won't let you make the walk in this weather."

"Oh…" Conflict flickered in Misty's eyes as she hesitated. Nothing about this woman's emotions or thoughts filtered through a mask. They played out on her face like a live performance. "I told Rayne I'd be here for you if he didn't make it home tonight…"

So Rayne didn't plan to come back to their house. Luciana told herself she could live with that, even as her gut tightened and her kneejerk response was to demand where would he be spending his night if not in his bed? It wouldn't be in hers regardless, those privileges she'd revoked the moment he'd turned on her. Not when she'd avoided even entering the house or sleeping there at all. So she had no right to even an ounce of jealousy or question. Nor did she want to experience either.

Not snorting in derision took every effort. Again, Misty wasn't at fault and as long as Luciana reminded herself of that over and over, she wouldn't make the mistake with her that she had with Chrystal. The other wolf wasn't an omega nor was she a submissive, but she was as close to the latter as she could be while still possessing some dominance.

"I'll be fine and I'd rather be alone. I'm tired. Just turn the heat off under the stew on your way out and let Eddie take you home." The not so gentle verbal nudge had the desired effect. Misty's eyes brightened and she enveloped Luciana in a hurried hug before she could avoid it.

"Thank you and oh, you are wet, go take a warm bath. The stew will be plenty hot for some time." Then she bussed a quick kiss to Luciana's cheek before she hurried back to the kitchen. Less than a minute later, she was out the back door. Luciana remained in the hallway, and listened.

Eddie was out of the SUV the moment Misty exited the house. His deep timbred voice questioning, but Misty radiated so much cheer and insisted she was going home and didn't want to be a bother to Miss Luciana, that Eddie relented and offered her a ride.

The Hunter might have orders from his *alpha* but he would no sooner send Misty out into the cold rain to walk the long block than Luciana could. The corner of her mouth twisted and she walked up the stairs slowly. Her bare feet had dried sometime during the stay in the house and the ride back to town. Mud splattered her flesh, staining it as though the remnant of every bad decision she'd ever made.

At the top of the stairs, she turned away from the hall leading to the master suite—his suite. She'd taken the smaller bedroom, with the smaller tub and the single bed in it. The room his brother Jackson had occupied when they'd first come here. A room she'd evicted him from when Rayne...

Shoving away those thoughts, she continued into her room and stripped off the wet clothing. Her—the house was silent save for the storm rattling the windows and the rain pounding against the roof. The scent of bread and stew almost masked the rich masculine scent, which seemed to thread through every fiber of the structure.

Yet, he wasn't here, and she could take some comfort in that and allow herself to be surrounded by him even as she didn't have to face him. The scent served as both a torment and a comfort. And alone—alone she didn't have to hide from the reality of each.

In the bathroom, she ran the water and added a small bath bomb. The vanilla and jasmine scents would soothe her restless wolf, and perhaps act as a balm to the rest of her nerves.

Her phone buzzed with a new message, and she padded out to retrieve it. Turning it over, she stared at the number she didn't recognize, but the message in Italian told her exactly who it was.

Sei così bello. Se potessi essere lì, vorrei accarezzarti la pelle e lavarti I piedi. Stai al sicuro, mia principessa. Ti troverò presto.

Rodrigo overstepped. Turning her head, she glanced at the open uncovered window and lightning illuminated the buildings beyond and the figure standing atop the one across the street.

Nudity was nothing to a wolf and it had ever been so with her. Not once in her life had she been ashamed of her form. She recognized the value of her own beauty and accepted as she did her wolf—a product of her birth.

So why then did she want to close the blinds and hide herself away in the bathroom?

Chin lifting, she resisted the urge and yet a cold tremor raced over her flesh. Why the hell was he watching her so closely and who the hell did he think he was promising to stroke his hands over her?

Dropping the phone, aware he observed, she returned to the bathroom with a slow, deliberate walk. She had no time for his messages or his interest.

He needed to obey her and keep his distance.

Even if he claimed to be on her side.

Once inside the bathroom, she closed the door and leaned against it.

Despite her pride, her heart raced and her skin went clammy. Eyes closed, she counted to a hundred as her bath finished filling and for once, she was grateful there was no window in the bathroom.

Tomorrow, perhaps she would buy curtains.

CHAPTER 4

*R*ayne only returned to his home near dawn. Searching for the interloper occupied a huge chunk of the evening, yet it was not the only reason. The storm abated a couple of hours earlier, but his jeans clung to him like a second skin as did his t-shirt. He'd made a full circuit of the lands closest to the town, and then struck out to any outbuildings nearby that might be used for shelter.

He found no sign of the foreign wolf. In the pre-dawn hours, he alerted the wolves he trusted most amongst the pack to be on the lookout for anything out of the ordinary— scents, faces, or names. Refusing to give more details, he checked with Eddie. The wolf had remained outside of their house keeping watch over Luciana after taking her home. He'd left her only long enough to take Misty home, but indicated Luciana remained in the house.

It was almost as if he had to erect walls around his mate to contain her. The very idea nauseated him. A block from their corner lot, he ducked into the diner rather than finish the trip. The last thing he wanted to see was the rejection in her dark eyes or the ice in her manner. His mate hated him, but she couldn't leave. He adored her, but he couldn't let what had been happening stand nor was he strong enough to let her go.

They were both consigned to this hell.

If he wanted her in their home, he could let her have her peace until the inexorable draw forced her to seek him out this time. In their tug of war, she'd only come to him once and then it had been to glare stonily in his direction as she informed him that she would no longer share their bed nor would she allow him to touch her. They might be mated, but they would never be intimate again.

Ultimatum delivered, she'd stormed away and it had been four agonizing days before he had to go and find her. So far, five days had been the longest stretch and even then his wolf had gone insane wanting to find her. As long as the feral demand rode his animal, he didn't dare let it go too long. Luciana didn't deserve the kind of madness that might lead to, particularly as he sat in the center of an unstable pack.

The bells over the door jingled as he pulled it open. The scents of fresh coffee, grilling bacon, and sweet waffles swarmed around him as though attempting to chase the scents of disappointment and regret away. Fortunately, it was so early only a couple of people were already settled into the diner. It had been the second building and business they'd reclaimed upon settling in Three Rivers. For the first three months, nearly everyone ate here with Rayne and Luciana covering all the costs. Gradually, as they firmed their economy and developed more sources of income, they'd transitioned the diner to Louis' capable hands. He loved cooking for everyone, and once the embargo lifted from the other packs, his whole family had come west from Hudson River.

"Coffee's fresh," Louis said by way of greeting. The big man looked more like a lumberjack than a chef, but despite his fierce appearance, he preferred caring for the general needs of the wolves around him rather than fighting to defend them. That didn't mean he wouldn't fight, but as Louis liked to say—he was a lover, not a fighter.

Tapping the side of his nose, Rayne spared the man a smile. Growling and stomping around would only upset the delicate balance they were beginning to find as a pack. If it meant tucking his bleeding and ravaged heart out of sight of everyone, then he would do exactly that. His first duty had to be to protecting the pack he shouldered.

Once seated at the counter, Rayne stretched his legs out. His hair had flattened under the weight of the rain, but it was already curling as it dried. The jeans weren't the most comfortable, but they would do. Dani Reagan, Louis' baby sister slid a cup of coffee in front of him. The wolf was barely eighteen, and should be going to college but she'd elected to take a skip year in order to help her family settle in Three Rivers. Her twin brother Jami decided to attend virtual classes and had every intention of going into software design. Which reminded him...

"Dani, where's your brother?" Then Rayne grinned faintly. "Not Louis."

The younger wolf laughed, her gray-green eyes dancing. "He's snoring at the moment, he was up all night playing some new game that released and he doesn't have to pull his weight at the diner today." The last she delivered with an eye roll.

"Not that he does much more than the dishes, right?" Rayne deadpanned. It wasn't the first time he'd heard the complaint between the twins. But he enjoyed their freestyle energy and they were good for the pack. Put too many damn loners together and no wonder they'd had all the problems. The Reagans gave them a central family at least, Louis, Dani, Jami, and their parents Angela and Frank—or Pops as he preferred. Pops had been a construction worker, and he was invaluable to the rebuilding effort. Angela a teacher, and she'd already volunteered to start working on a school. Three Rivers didn't have a lot of kids, hell they didn't have a lot of anything, but the two high school age kids they had needed to do online classes while the single elementary age child was being home schooled.

Someday, Rayne promised himself, someday they were going to need that school and it was better to get started now.

"Nope," Dani said, her grin widening. "He's useless in the kitchen and Louis banned him last week after he nearly set the deep fryer on fire."

Yeah, Rayne didn't want any part of that. "Good to know. Tell him I received word from Vivian Buckley, and she is more than happy to provide him with career advice, and we can arrange a video chat for first introductions."

Mason's second AJ had been on the fence about adding onto his mate's considerable workload. Their twins were at the crawling and into everything stage, while Vivian also had her own work, but she'd graciously agreed to mentor the younger wolf in the field of study she already excelled at.

Dani's expression lit up. "He's going to die."

"Or be insufferable," Louis called out, and when he caught Rayne's eye, the chef pressed a fist over his heart in thanks. Rayne nodded to him. It was a small thing, arrange an intro-duction, facilitate a mentorship—but it was for one of his wolves and hopefully be the first of many such opportunities. Negotiation with the other alphas required patience, and diligence. Every wolf in his pack came from somewhere else, they'd all been born into other packs, following other alphas before most went Lone Wolf, then later came to Three Rivers. Very few fell into the category of the Reagans, wolves who willingly transplanted from one pack to another.

So far, those alphas all seemed to be invested in helping Three Rivers succeed. It had taken time, and nearly cutting out his own heart to earn the investment. But a cub had to walk before it could run.

Rayne wanted to race to the wind, but he had to move as swiftly as the slowest member, which meant they would crawl until everyone found their footing.

"Once he masters his craft, I know he will give back to the pack." They all would in some way, it was how all packs thrived. They donated to the pack funds, offered their expertise, or services. They helped each other.

"That he will," Dani agreed swiftly, and for all her snark about her twin, pride shone in her eyes. "Now, what would you like for breakfast, Alpha?" The breathless note of admiration on the last two syllables squeezed his heart. The pulse of pack bonds tightening.

They were a long way from where he wished them all to be, but Rayne smiled. Each inch of success warmed future efforts. While he'd planned to go home, and check on his mate, the warmth invading the café and the tingling of the bonds so newly familiar to his pack warned him to stay put. He had to nurture them all and as much as he hated to believe it, Luciana probably didn't want to see him.

He'd have to content himself with their interaction from the night before. The brief moment was like a drop of rain to his parched soul even if her calling out to another man—another wolf left him furious. Loosening his grip on the coffee mug, he forced a smile to his face even as he shoveled his fury into a dark corner of his mind and barricaded the door. If he didn't, he would risk upsetting the wolves already present and those on their way.

Dani's smile didn't diminish by a single watt, so perhaps he'd been successful. "What's the special?" At his question, she bubbled to life once more and pressed a hand to his arm.

The gentle affection settling the raging wolf inside him from growling to grumbling.

He'd check on Luciana after breakfast.

The promise quieted his wolf some.

Ten minutes later, the diner had filled with more wolves. Most were workers who'd taken jobs outside of town. They would tackle the ninety-minute commute via carpools. If they were surprised by Rayne's presence, none showed it. In fact, as they entered, one by one, they pressed a hand to his shoulder, another to his arm. More than one shook his hand.

He knew them all, knew their stories, where they'd come from, why they'd gone Lone Wolf, and why they'd elected to come to Three Rivers. There were still more men than women, nearly all adults, and one post-adolescent, barely nineteen years old who'd been eighteen when he'd latched onto them.

Ramirez had been part of Sutter Butte, and he'd struggled in the tyrannical structure, which by all rumors had begun to change. He'd not only gone Lone Wolf, he'd run away, but he didn't do well on his own. The boy was so much a beta it wasn't funny, but fear, as Rayne was well aware, was a powerful motivator. So Ramirez grasped onto he and Luciana at their first meeting.

Like Chrystal.

The mere thought of the omega left Rayne's stomach churning despite the excellent breakfast. Dani flitted about the place, taking care of her customers, filling coffee cups, serving food, and all with a smile and a gentle hand. She had a near healer like quality about her. Dani, like Chrystal before her, drew Ramirez like a moth to a flame. The young wolf said very little to her, but his manner and demeanor brightened whenever she ventured near. She'd loaded his waffle with strawberries and whip cream, settling it in front of him with a flourish and playful grin. Ramirez's ears went bright red and he ducked his eyes. Rayne sipped his coffee to hide his grin, soaking in every action.

"Hey boss," Mark Kenner dropped onto the stool next to him. The Hunter had moved up the ranks swiftly, and now stood third after Rayne's brother. Though based on his attitude and the fact Jackson wasn't terrifically interested in leadership, Kenner stood a solid chance of rising to the Second—but only if Jackson wanted to step down. Rayne wasn't prepared to see a true battle between the pair.

"Mark," Rayne greeted him. "Breakfast?"

"I'm good, ate at my place. Came in for coffee...and because we need to talk." Though he kept his voice low, too many sharp ears in the diner caught the undertone of seriousness in his voice. A thread Rayne had no interest in pulling while surrounded by so many.

"Let's get cups to go," Rayne said, with an easy smile. "I need to do some inspections." While true, he needed to check on the status of repairs to other buildings in town, it wasn't high on his list for today.

There was still a foreign wolf in his territory. His mate seemed to at least know the wolf, and she hated Rayne. None of these were acceptable to his wolf, and while he wouldn't take his rage out on Luciana, he could and planned to deal with the foreign wolf with extreme prejudice.

Dani prepared the to go cups, and handed them over. She tried to wave off Rayne's money as he paid for the breakfast, and left her a tip. Cupping a hand to her cheek, he silenced her protest. With a quick brush of his lips to her temple, he said, "I'll see you later."

Her smile warmed him, then he was heading to the door where Mark waited patiently. Rayne took his time on the exit, a handshake here, a shoulder squeeze there. He made sure to pass by every wolf present. Reaffirming the nascent bonds which were still fresh, and ragged—though they were far stronger than they had been. Pulling his thoughts away from that dark and dangerous path, he motioned Mark out ahead of him.

"Let's walk," he informed the wolf, diverting down Main Street to the section still under reclamation. What had been a feed store, and next to it an old bookstore were currently being rehabbed with living quarters above. Eventually, Rayne would like to see homes stretch outside of the direct area in town, but that would require growth of the pack. They were few enough in numbers, they actually had room for most of the wolves already, though some were doubling up in the apartments they'd finished. By the time they completed the town rehab, every wolf would have their own place, and only share if they chose to.

Then they'd have room to grow. First they needed to heal, then they could grow. But he'd take what he could get.

Dawn had come while he lingered in the diner. The overnight rain left the day cloudy, and gray light filtered through. The hints of moisture in the air remained strong. The storm wasn't done with them yet.

No hammers echoed from inside the construction areas, tarps had been spread to keep the interiors dry where the roof needed patching on one building and where windows were missing on the other. Likely they would start later in the day if the weather permitted.

If not, there was plenty more to do to fill in the hours.

Rayne drifted through the feed shop. None of the doors were locked, and the interior had been stripped down to the studs. It needed new insulation, new walls, and flooring. It would serve as a clothing and shoe store. One of the later arrivals also had skill as a seamstress and Jackson had done work as a cobbler of all things in their spotty youth. It wouldn't be a department store, but it would provide them all with access to new clothes. Dress the part to play the part.

Mark trailed him silently; the only sound the occasional sip of his coffee. The wolf's presence at his back was a comfortable one. He was one of the few Rayne trusted, but he didn't know as well as he should. The wolf had come from the Yukon Pack before he went lone wolf, and there were hints of Native American or maybe First Peoples as they were called up north in his features. Relatively quiet in his demeanor, Mark was no pushover.

With no one else around, Rayne faced the other wolf. "What do you need to discuss?"

To his credit, Mark didn't look away or hesitate. "Your mate."

His mate. Their former alpha. The reason their pack existed. Rayne merely raised his eyebrows. He wouldn't assume anything from the single statement. Taking a sip of his coffee, he waited the other wolf out.

Mark didn't keep him waiting long. "The pack isn't sure why she stayed."

The pack, huh? "The pack? Or you?" Not explaining himself was a luxury most alphas enjoyed. Rayne wasn't most alphas, and he'd held his position for a tenuous short number of months.

The other wolf had the decency to grimace, and then he spread his free hand as he extended both arms. Surrender echoed in his posture. "I'm not saying this to piss you off. I have heard others ask the same questions I have myself in hushed voices. No one wants to upset you, and more than you may think actively support the choices you've made."

"But...?" The last thing Rayne wanted was to drag the words out of his third, but the wolf brought it up for a reason. Better to face it head on than ignore it or pretend anything else.

"But I can't imagine a world where a defeated alpha stays in the pack." What he didn't add was most defeated alphas died in the transition of power. "She's miserable, and isolated. No one sees her except Eddie and occasionally Misty. *I* know she doesn't sleep at your home every night, and some days she doesn't even return to town."

His wolf unfurled within him, rousing to study the man across from them. Not one ounce of untruth passed the other wolf's lips, but he wasn't saying all he knew. In fact, Rayne scented more and his focus brought Mark's wolf to the surface, his eyes flashing golden.

"Rayne, I apologize if I'm offending you. Her presence is upsetting to a lot—fuck it, her presence is upsetting to me because I choke on the dark cloud surrounding her, and what it's doing to you." Honesty echoed in every syllable. "I thought she'd leave when you forced her to yield and spared her life. A lot of us thought she'd return to Italy and her brother. Maybe it's a hell of a thing to say..." His throat convulsed as he swallowed and his gaze dipped away. He didn't want to say whatever words were coming next, and maybe he had the good sense to be afraid. "We're all grateful the two of you formed this pack, it's...home now. A home I plan to support and defend, and she may be the reason we came together. But she's not the reason we work. You...you did it, and you did it to support her, as her second and her mate, but she didn't return the favor and then the Volchitsa..."

Slicing a hand through the air, Rayne silenced him. "Do not bring up those Russian bastards. None of you know the story of that and I won't share it."

"As you wish, Alpha." No one referred to him by the honorific and Mark's wolf offered no challenge. The concern he wore like a second skin. Were there really other members of the pack who didn't want his mate to even be a part of their pack anymore?

The thought made him sick.

"As for the rest, Luciana is mine and I *want* her here." It should end all arguments, but it wouldn't. How could it? Luciana didn't want to be there or with him and to be honest, he couldn't answer why she hadn't left him yet. Or maybe he did...maybe she had been trying and that was why the foreign wolf was present.

Maybe it was Rayne who refused to let her leave.

No maybe about the last. He refused to lose her, but he wasn't sure how to hold onto her.

"Then we *have* to make her feel more welcome," Mark said in a solemn voice. "I will deal with the others who whisper..."

"Let them vent," Rayne told him. Silencing objectors would only lead to more resentment. "The fault is not all one sided." Ignoring dissent could lead to other problems.

Raking his fingers through his hair, he turned away from Mark and paced across the empty room. The scents of wood and sawdust tickled his nose. The other wolf remained where he left him and beneath the confidence lurked unease and worry. Mark hadn't wanted to offend him; at least he'd been as honest in sentiment as he had been in his words. He'd said what Jackson would never broach with him.

Another tick in the column suggesting Mark would be a better second. Fuck, he didn't need to deal with it now. His mate supplanted as alpha, his brother removed as second. He might as well alienate everyone he loved.

"Let them say what they need, hear them, and respond. Do not encourage their rancor, but let's lance the wounds and let them drain." They didn't have a damn healer yet, but they needed to do something or what festered in their pack might end them sooner rather than later.

"Alpha... Rayne," Mark said, then paused. His troubled expression gave way to sympathy. "I know you want to keep your mate, I can't imagine... I can't imagine what happened that drove you to challenge her. None of us can. To stand against your mate in that way, it's inconceivable. That you were able to... I thought maybe it's not a true mating. Perhaps... perhaps it would be better for you to repudiate her and let her go. Better for you. Better for her. Better for the pack."

Fuck. That. "Thank you for telling me," Rayne told him, ignoring the advice. "It took balls to say all of that to me and I won't soon forget it." The courage and the advice, but he left both unspoken. The last thing he planned to do was repudiate Luciana. Too many had failed to believe in their mating—Salvatore and Margo to begin with, but they'd accepted it. Everyone else needed to learn the same truth. "If the whispers grow to something more, tell me." He wouldn't sanction sedition against himself or his mate.

"On my honor," Mark said, then put a fist over his heart. "With your permission..."

Rayne waved a hand, dismissing him and then waited until he'd left before he dropped his chin to his chest. The hell of it was, he had no idea how to fix this damn nightmare. None at all.

But it was his job.

He was the alpha.

The buck stopped with him.

CHAPTER 5

*G*ray light crept around the corners of the blind. Colorlessness illuminated the day. Luciana didn't want to open her eyes. For these tremulous moments, she could imagine all was well. She could linger in the hazy dream of a world where she and her mate were still close, where the zing of adventure filled their blood, where salvaging a pack from the disparate and abandoned of the North American packs gave her purpose. If she could simply lie there a few seconds longer before the cold, awful reality intruded... yet those seconds were all too fleeting.

Eyes open, she sat up. Her body ached from the hard mattress, and her mouth was dry. The house around her was absolutely silent, not even the distant clatter of dishes or vacuuming to suggest Misty had returned to handle the housekeeping. The other wolf only came a few times a week, and today, blissfully, did not seem to be that day.

After shoving away the blanket, she stood and stretched her hands to the ceiling. The vertebrae along her spine cracked, and popped. The decades since she'd been born had been kind to her, far kinder than the last two years.

Had the world been simpler then? The quiet parties, the quilting her mother hosted, and the long political discussions all seemed a half-formed memory, like something she'd read from a book. The war came, and it destroyed so much of their holdings when the fascists rose to power. Other wolves tried to invade...and their papa murdered while covering their retreat. Those dark days were like the shadows a nightmare, half-forgotten in the light of day and yet still capable of making her heart race and her skin clammy.

Without the handful of photographs her mother had saved, she wouldn't even know what her father looked like. Raking her fingers through her hair, she padded across the barren room toward the bathroom in the hall. Only the master bedroom had an ensuite, another sacrifice she made in trying to leave Rayne. A snort escaped her; she'd made it so far with barely a house much less a bathroom.

As quickly as she tried to dismiss her thoughts, they trailed through her again. Her father, all she had of him were stories told by her mother and by Salvatore. He'd been nearly a man when their father fell and she a little girl. The war years were a lean haze of hunger, darkness, and grim whispers. After... after they found their laughter again, and the light, and companionship, but even living at the vineyard in the big stone house with its sweeping walls and gorgeous artwork, something had always been missing.

They were all haunted by a ghost—her mother by the mate she'd lost, though she'd proven fierce and a survivor. Salvatore ruled the packs, bringing them under one umbrella once more, one by one. He and his Centurions, while their mother ruled their home and Luciana. She'd never been safer.

And she'd never been more caged.

Disgusted with her wandering thoughts, she pushed into

the bathroom and turned the shower on. She needed to wash it all away, clear her head and figure out what to do today. Halfway through her shower, the door downstairs closed with a gentle, but firm thud. Determined steps echoed across the wood floors below.

Dammit. She'd slept too long and now Rayne had returned to the house. Maybe he'd go into the study and she could slip out the window. It was a short drop to the ground outside, and she'd almost made escape an art form.

Five minutes later, she wrapped a towel around her hair and another around her torso. She'd failed to bring clothes in with her, so she had to walk back to her room and change there. After plucking the lotion from the counter, she paused at the door and took a deep breath, centering herself. Shedding the unease and distress, she grasped together the ragged elements of her self and drew them over her like fur sliding over her skin. Her wolf responded, her power a pulse beating in time with her heart. Composed, she let herself out and made her way to her room.

The hushed quiet of the house trailed after her, a whisper holding its breath. Settled on the corner of the bed, she ran lotion over her legs, then her arms. A quick wipe to her hands then she stood and pulled the towel from her hair. The damp tendrils clung to her shoulders and back. Normally, she'd take the time with some conditioner, and a comb, but who the hell did she care to impress?

Dropping the towel from around her to the floor, she paced over to the closet to find clean clothes. The sliding doors provided her some camouflage from the wolf now standing in the doorway to the hall. The squeaking of the stairs had betrayed his soft steps. Aware of his scorching gaze running over her, she ignored him as she stepped into a pair of panties, and then reached for a tank top. She didn't need to wear a bra and if she needed to change, the damn thing got in the way. The soft cotton slid over her skin raising tingles along her spine.

It was the fabric and not the wolf staring at her no matter what her rebellious body might want.

Though she preferred a skirt, she selected pants. Running shoes or boots? Deciding on boots, she choose a flared leg black pant to step into. A hiss of breath escaped between her observer's clenched teeth as she dragged the pants upward. Let him look at what he couldn't have any longer. Tossing her hair back, she turned and met Rayne's laser stare. The lines around his mouth were tight, and a muscle twitched in his jaw.

"Yes?" She raised an eyebrow, but he said nothing so she moved back to the bed and sat to pull on her boots. Rayne's gaze tracked her each and every motion. Only when she was done did she stand, then make her bed. Still the wolf at the door said nothing.

Tidying her living space came second nature; her mother had drilled that into her from a very young age. Scooping the towels from the floor, she spared another look at the obstacle standing between she and the bathroom.

"Luciana," Rayne said, his voice a ragged, low whisper dragging over her senses to tug uncomfortably at her belly. The heat spooling there, coiled around her spine in a slow, sinuous stretch. Pinching off the thought before it could take root, she erased the expression from her face and stared at him. Protecting her thoughts and masking her scent were also second nature, trained by Salvatore. As his sister, there had always been the thought she could be weaponized against him. In the early years after the war, it had been paramount she protect herself if he could not be present to shield her.

Hard to manipulate or track a wolf who could mask herself. A skill she'd used to great advantage to reach where they were now... Poor recompense, she supposed.

"I'm waiting," she reminded her former lover with a verbal jab and his expression tightened. For far too brief a second, something akin to longing gleamed in his eyes and then it too vanished. He turned sideways, allowing her to pass but she'd have to brush him to do so.

Bastard.

Accepting the challenge, she glided past him and ignored the way her skin prickled when his flesh touched hers. The heat he shed didn't wrap around her or encourage her to lean close. There was no haven in those arms no matter how thick, and full they were. He was the past.

They were the past.

Their relationship died the same day he'd challenged her. Even if she'd won... they would have been over. Aware of him shadowing her every step and his breath warm against her bare shoulders, she took care of her damp towels and made sure the bathroom was neat before pivoting and coming face to face with him again. He occupied the door, blocking her into the all too small room.

"Where are you going?" He rasped, his accent all but vanishing under the harshness of his tone. Stubble shadowed his cheeks, and gave him a rough appearance. His clothes were dirty, and his hair stuck up in different directions as though he'd run his hands through it repeatedly.

If he didn't stink of a dozen other wolves, she'd wonder if he'd bothered to speak to anyone at all in the last few hours. A distinctive perfume clung to his shirt, one she recognized from the diner. So he'd been there and flirted with the young Reagan pup.

Good for him, maybe he'd let her leave sooner or rather

than later. Her stomach twisted at the thought and her wolf raked her claws against the inside of her skin, but she refused to focus on either reaction.

"Downstairs," she retorted, and gazed at him with a patience she did not feel and calmness, which was in and of itself a bold lie.

A sigh escaped him, and he lifted a hand as though he intended to cup her cheek. She flinched her face away, eyes narrowing. Rayne dropped his hand, and then pivoted to the side giving her even less space to pass him. Not hesitating, she pushed through the slim space only to bump against the doorjamb as his arm came up in front of her, and the other behind her, caging her in.

"Don't run," he warned, and she didn't turn to look at him.

Lifting her chin, she issued her own challenge. "Or what? You'll issue a challenge and attack me in front of the whole pack? Oh wait...you already did that." Damn tears heated the backs of her eyes, but she refused to shed them.

His fingers dug into the drywall and it came away in flakes. "Dammit, Luciana, can't you spend five minutes and just talk to me?"

"No," she told him, without hesitation no matter how it rent her heart. "You had the same options, and you chose this path for us. Now you live with it." The words telling him to go to hell as she severed herself turned to ash on her lips. No matter her fury, no matter the betrayal—she was not ready to destroy the last precious thread between them even if he'd all but abandoned it for power.

"I did try to talk to you," he ground out between his teeth. "Over and over, but you let that fucking Russian have your ear, and you refused to hear what I was saying."

Luciana closed her eyes, the verbal swipe having scored blood. Yet, she dared not let her guard down and reveal the hit. The fucking Russian in question had been a Brit, and he'd done enough damage and she hadn't been able to kill the lap dog soon enough—the sacrifices cost them all, but the true price was one she could tell to no one, least of all Rayne.

It was a small comfort, albeit a comfort, that the bastard would not be able to inflict harm on her mate and had never been able to. She'd accomplished that much at least.

"Then you should have tried harder." Her voice didn't quiver as she managed to mask all emotion from it. "Or perhaps your challenge was your last attempt, but it was the worst one. It matters very little now."

More dry wall flaked away and his claws dug into the wall itself, leaving deep grooves. That would need to be repaired. "Fucking hell, Luciana. I want to talk to you—we *need* to talk."

"No," she said, and left it there. If he didn't let her go soon, she would have to fight her way to freedom and as he'd already proven, she couldn't beat him. Not when the last thing she'd wanted to do was harm him. The desire handicapped her severely.

Too bad he couldn't say the same.

Though in truth, the desire to protect him waned in the face of his continued to push at her.

A portion of the frame tore away and then Rayne dropped his arm, effectively opening the cage. She strode past him and then descended the steps maintaining an air of absolute calm even if her agitated wolf wanted to either flee or fight. Her beast didn't understand the strain she put them both through, or the conflicting emotions tearing them apart.

Her respite proved brief as he continued his pursuit down the stairs and into the kitchen. She'd planned to make coffee, but perhaps she'd just head out and let him trail her across their territory. Eventually, he had to get bored and leave her be, right?

Then in a fit of pique, she turned to the coffee maker. The previous evening's stew sat on the stove, untouched. The rich meaty scent of it, despite having cooled, tempted her but her stomach rolled at the thought of eating anything.

She took her time, grinding the coffee beans. A triple shot of espresso would be delicious. Rayne settled against the counter, his arms folded as he regarded her. As long as she kept him out of her periphery, she could ignore him, but not the tremors his stare left eddying across her.

Unfortunately, he remained too near the espresso machine itself so she couldn't miss the traces of earth, bacon, coffee, and grease from the diner and sawdust—likely from one of the construction projects—underscoring a particular note of juniper and berries.

Dani Reagan.

Resentment tangled with the barbed wire of jealousy, sinking deeper under her skin where the bloody marks wouldn't be visible.

Giving a hard twist to the handle, she started the hot water flowing through the grounds to make her espresso. The dark, rich scent did little to blot out the scent of the female on his skin. Had he spent the night with her after sending Luciana home like some errant child? And if he wanted the little bitch, why couldn't he simply let her go?

Why couldn't she dismiss him?

Once she'd pulled the three shots, she lifted the cup and stepped away from him. She needed to drown out the nauseating ideas conjured by the wolf on him. She scented others, many others, but only Dani's scent came through clear and distinct. Closing her eyes, Luciana took a deep drink of the espresso.

"You can pretend and ignore me all you want," Rayne

said, his tone softening from the earlier harsh rasp. "We can't stay at this impasse. It's not good for the pack. It's not good for us. It's not good for *you.*"

"The pack?" Her upper lip curled. "Really? I thought you wanted to be alpha for the good of the *pack.*" Wasn't that his whole damn excuse for the challenge in the first place?

"And I wasn't *wrong.*" He matched her tone for tone. "We were losing ground and if you continued to consort with those damn Russians, the other packs would have destroyed us...destroyed you."

The snort escaped her before she could give it a second thought. "No they wouldn't have. They were too busy chasing shadows and fighting for a reason to not destroy us. They had multiple opportunities and the only two alphas among them powerful enough to issue such an order were *outvoted* by the softer, younger ones."

"Serafina is neither soft nor young and she was on the fence, she was gauging our success. If she caught even a whiff of what you were doing, she would have sided with Diesel and Cassius."

There had never been any question about which alphas were the most dangerous to their cause. If Julian and his Enforcers had been a pack then, the danger to them would have increased.

"And it doesn't matter, what I did had nothing to do with them and everything to do with protecting the pack, not that you would know." She sucked in a breath, trying to stamp out the furious anger roiling through her. "Whatever...enough. I will not debate this with you. The Volchitsa are gone. You are alpha. The damn pack is secure, you have your wish." She punctuated the sentence by slamming her empty cup down before she pivoted to stride to the door.

She made it two steps before Rayne grabbed her arm and dragged her backwards. Instinct warred with preservation, and she drove her elbow into his gut and her boot onto his bare foot. The distinctive sound of bones snapping preceded his fingers releasing their bite against her arm, and then she faced him and they both glared.

If she'd realized he wasn't wearing shoes, she probably wouldn't have stomped so hard. Probably.

Then again, he should learn that his privilege of touching her had been revoked.

Permanently.

"You have your position, you have your pack—but never forget, you do not have *me* or any rights where *I* am concerned." It physically pained her to say the words, a sharp, jagged thrust to the gut.

His eyes flashed and his wolf glowed in his eyes. He narrowed the space between them until his heat rolled over her, but he laid not one finger upon her. "I have every right where you are concerned. You are still *mine.*"

"A hollow claim for an even emptier promise. You can put whatever name on it you wish, but I will never belong to you again." No matter how much it ripped at her heart or left her wolf wounded to hear it. Still her other half roused to brush against the inside of her skin, incensed and ready to snap.

They both bit when wounded.

Pain flickered across Rayne's face, too swiftly to be tracked and then a granite mask settled in place. "Be that as it may, you can dismiss whatever you want, but you are mine and you will allow no other near you. Nor will you leave, do you understand?"

The demand for obedience struck her, his dominance over hers. They were too evenly matched in some ways for her to acquiesce to his control. It crashed against her like a heavy wave upon rocks. She might be permanently stuck, but the water would not dislodge her.

"Whatever helps you sleep at night." She'd heard the

phrase often enough in the past months, and she'd never found a use for it until now. The barb struck, striking like flint against his stony exterior. His jaw flexed and the grinding of his teeth echoed in the harsh space separating them.

They stood there, bound in the vicious jaws of their mated trap. Neither looked away, and neither gave in. His wolf all but snarled at hers, and hers bristled, hackles raised. They hadn't wanted to hurt him before.

He might not be so lucky a second time.

Finally, Rayne's eyes bled back to green and he exhaled a long breath. "Do not leave our territory."

It was as good as a by your leave as far as she was concerned and she strode for the door. She needed air, any kind of air…and to clear her nose of the scent of the wolf clinging to him.

But she also needed to rid herself of his scent, all dark, musky and powerful. Alpha suited him, though she would be loath to admit it aloud. It was the same power that attracted her in the first place. Power tempered by gentleness and warmth.

One foot out the door and his last words slammed into her. "Stay the fuck away from that Rodrigo bastard, Luciana. Trust me, I will know and I'm already planning to kill him. Keep going near him and I'll make sure I skin him first."

The words jolted her, and when she spun to retaliate, she found herself alone. He'd left the kitchen before she'd made her escape and he'd had the last word.

She had no damn interest in Rodrigo even as a possible tie to her former home. The wolf took too many liberties and she hadn't forgotten his spying the night before.

Pain ripped through her middle, and she forced herself away from the house, away from Rayne and farther, away from the town. She bypassed the main street and headed out into the fields, blindly walking as fast as her legs would carry her and she refused to lose it there. No one would see her weakness, or her loss.

She made it a full mile before the first tear fell.

And a second before the sobs broke from her throat.

CHAPTER 6

*E*very fiber of his being leaned in the direction Luciana disappeared. His wolf, stretched, almost out of step with him as though the animal could follow their mate without him. The animal snarled when he remained planted. Curling the fingers of his left hand into a fist, he forced himself to take several long breaths soaking in the scent of her lingering in the room.

The hints of amber, cedar and black pepper were almost drowned out by the jasmine floating around him. He wanted to roll in the scent until it coated every inch of him. Pathetic.

Closing his eyes, he slammed his fist into the wall. The plaster and drywall gave way as his fist sank through it. Dust plumed up to dance in the sunlight. The farce of fairy magic wasn't lost on him. Blood marked his knuckles, and he barely acknowledged it before he drove his fist into the wall again, widening the hole. Pain vibrated along his forearm, fragments of the wall pierced his numb flesh. The third strike filled the air with copper as the blood ran freely down his hand and arm. The white drywall had turned a faint crimson and the hole looked more like a partial dilemma stretching across three and half feet.

Across the wall, a framed picture of the Tuscan Valley where he'd met Luciana in the first place swung drunkenly, then just fell. The shattering of glass as it struck the floor along with the splintering of the frame seemed a suitable punctuation mark to the last several minutes.

A swift knock on the front door followed by the door opening to admit his brother were the last things he wanted to hear or see. At least he closed the door behind him. Jackson's scent, as familiar as his own, preceded him as he strode into the kitchen. "Fuck," he said softly. "What did she do this time?"

"Don't," was Rayne's only answer. Bad enough he had Mark talking to him about the pack's concern regarding Luciana. Jackson's opinion had never been high, but he'd accepted her—until the moment he didn't.

"You're the one bleeding." His brother crossed to the sink and ran a towel under cold water, then he tossed it over. "And destroying a wall I finished two months ago." He didn't look at Rayne as he studied the hole. It would have to be ripped out the rest of the way and reset, then plastered again.

It was a damn mess.

Just like everything else.

Rayne wrapped the cold towel around his brutalized knuckles. The pain didn't help distract him from the way his wolf wanted to bay or the ragged pieces of his heart trying to cobble together the will to thump. If he discovered he was slowly bleeding out, it wouldn't surprise him. How much blood loss could a wolf survive?

Maybe he could test the theory.

"I'll take care of it later today," Jackson said, sparing him a half-glance before he sniffed at the dregs of coffee in the pot. Rayne wouldn't drink it without some antacids. Apparently his brother agreed because he diverted to the fridge and pulled out a couple of beers.

"It's barely nine in the morning," Rayne told him, but it didn't slow Jackson popping the lids off the bottles and handing one over.

"It's five o'clock somewhere," was Jackson's only comment. "You done bleeding? I figure this is a conversation we need to have in your fancy office."

"Or we can never have it," he warned his brother. Jackson stepped up when they'd gone to him, he'd signed onto this pack idea earlier than most. Yet unlike anyone else, he'd come for Rayne alone. A fact Rayne understood, and even appreciated. They had no other family; it was just the two of them. Their parents had a son before them, but he'd died in a drunken dominance brawl when Rayne was young. Jackson had never known him.

That day, Rayne had gone from protected, baby brother, to only child. He'd loved the day Jackson came along, and swore to protect his brother the way Rene had once protected him.

Only I can't disappear on him. The thought staunched his soul's bleeding, and his wolf settled onto its haunches with a grunt. Neither man nor animal was happy, but they'd given their oaths and they would die before they betrayed them.

Again... a dark little voice whispered in the back of his mind.

"If I thought we could get away with it Rayne, I'd let it go." Jackson had never been confrontational. He lacked what most in the pack would label alpha potential. Though most Lone Wolves seemed to have the potential in spades, Jackson was a true beta. He *needed* someone to follow, someone to protect and be protected by. He did better in a pack, and when Rayne went Lone Wolf, he'd isolated himself and drifted along the fringes of Delta Crescent. His girlfriend—a human—had known who and what he was, but their relationship dwindled in Rayne's absence.

Epic fail on my part. Not the loss of the girlfriend, relationships were fluid among most wolves, all except family and mating. Mates, then family, then pack, it was the way of things. Alphas most of all looked upon the pack as their family, and it elevated them all.

God, he'd fucked up so much on this damn quest, and now he stood in the center of a pack he'd never desired, but he could not fail while losing the one woman he'd turned his life upside down to please.

The old alpha of Delta Crescent, Papa used to say if they wanted to hear God laugh, they only needed to make plans.

Taking a long pull from the bottle, he studied his brother as the other wolf watched him. His shoulders were back, his chin up and his arms open and loose. He hid nothing, and offered no deception. Concern etched into the lines of his features, and his worried eyes tracked Rayne's every movement.

Fuck. First Mark, now this.

"Speak," he told him, bracing for the worst. "Tell me."

"You don't need me to tell you, Rayne." Jackson didn't mince his words. Instead, he motioned to the hole in the wall then to Rayne's own bloodied knuckles even though the wounds were already closing. "You *know* already, I just have one question."

"And that question is?" Even if he could guess it, better to let his brother say his piece.

"How much longer are you going to do this to yourself?"

If he could have managed a laugh, he would have but all Rayne could do was shrug. "I will not repudiate my mate." The thought left him sick at heart and soul. As miserable as he was in the moment, Luciana was still there and her presence meant they still had hope.

Maybe crumbling, dusty, and shredded hope—but hope nonetheless.

"Dammit Rayne," his brother sighed and his shoulders slumped. "You're going to tear yourself apart trying to hold onto her."

"I don't care," Rayne answered, the staccato force behind every syllable striking as though fired from a weapon. "She's *mine*."

"And if she declares herself done with you? If *she* repudiates *you*? What then?" The horrifying prospect fused with a red haze across his vision. Though they'd fought, she ignored him, shut him out, and oftentimes disappeared—she'd yet to directly break their bond. The claiming went both ways, and while it had been a true mating, and he loved her more than his next breath—if she wanted to be rid of him, he could not hold her.

At worst, he'd fade and maybe it would be for the best.

While he wanted to be out there, tracking his mate, and pledging himself to her again, he had to protect what they'd built, and pray time would earn him a measure of forgiveness though his presence seemed unable to accomplish a breath of it. "Then it happens. Where are we with pack funds?"

A glance at his hand showed the wounds had all closed, and he dropped the blood soaked towel into the trash before leading the way toward his office. Jackson's heavy sigh followed him. The conversation was over for now.

Still, Rayne's gaze went to the window and the town beginning to bustle beyond. Luciana should be out there, and not alone in whatever field she'd gone to hide herself. She should be building, guiding, nurturing or just sitting beside him and working with him to figure their future out.

Even as Jackson began to talk, Rayne barely heard the words passed the rushing in his ears. Challenging Luciana had been to save her as much as the pack, but she only saw the betrayal.

How the hell did he repair the damage he'd inflicted?

*T*wo days later, he was no closer to an answer than he'd been during his discussion with his brother. Jackson had already torn out the rest of the wall. Somewhere along the way, they'd reheated a stew Misty had left and eaten it all. Instead of tracking down his mate, Rayne spent the day on issues cropping up between the wolves in the pack. He'd let James "Jami" Reagan know about Vivian agreeing to mentor him.

When they'd run into wiring issues for the Wi-Fi and computer systems, he'd spent hours with two specialists working on a way to make it happen and to improve their wireless connectivity for the town. Of all the things he'd imagined as an alpha, infrastructure and tech troubleshooting hadn't been high on his list.

With those issues resolved, he worked with Della and Arturo to set them up for their runs. They also agreed to take any potential volunteers on the road trips to train as drivers. The hours of the day filled quickly, and he slept in snatches here and there. Loath as he was to admit it, he only returned to the bedroom he'd once shared with his mate to use the master bathroom for a shower, a shave, and to change clothes. If he slept at all, it was on the sofa in his office.

The bed in their room was far too lonely.

Yes, he checked the guest room she'd claimed for herself more than once. His mate was never in it.

By day three, however, he'd reached the end of his leash and the tension snapped within him. He needed to find her, particularly when not even a whisper of her lingered in the town. Not only had Mark and Jackson gone silent on the topic; so had all the other wolves.

If not for the tenuous connection still stretching out from his soul, he might be disappointed to believe she'd gone for good. Yet, the very thought of her could send his senses zooming to the thread tangling them together. The mating bond might be stretched, frayed, and fragile, but it remained.

Misty had shown up to do some cleaning, but he ushered her out and sent her to work with the others on the refurbishing rather than worry about his place. With what little he ate being at the diner, there was little in the way of mess. He could fold the one blanket he used and Rayne had long since mastered the art of doing his own laundry. A quick shower, a shave, and fresh clothes and he braced himself to go hunting. Not letting his gaze rest overlong on his bed, he left the room but paused at the top of the stairs.

Glancing down the hall separating him from the guest bedroom, he fought against the inexorable pull. The need to be with her, even if only in passing imagination gradually overcame his resistance. Nudging the door open, he leaned against the doorjamb and took in a deep, heady breath of her scent. It lingered everywhere here, though diminished by the passage of time.

Fingers trailing over the wall lightly, he paced across the spartan room to the bed. The blankets had been tugged up, and the pillow straightened with nary a wrinkle to suggest she'd made use of it since the morning of her exodus. Fists clenched, he studied the whole room. Very little of her personality had even touched this room. It could be any empty room anywhere in the world, and yet his awareness of *her* sharpened. Not giving himself anytime to think about it, he scooped up the pillow and pressed it to his face.

Memories rolled over him, thunder chasing the lightning across a storm-tossed moment. The way the sunlight curved over her dark hair. The tangled eroticism binding them in the heat and scent of a vineyard in Tuscany. Their first dance at a club in Rome, and the way she teased his body not quite touching him as they moved together. The decadent liquid warmth of her laughter as he regaled her with tales of his youth.

The moment fire kindled in her eyes when he brushed his lips to hers, and the way they went incandescent when he stepped away, determined to leash his wolf's desires. He was a guest and she was sister to the alpha. He was overstepping his bounds.

Crushing the pillow to his face, he sank down against the blankets. It was the closest he'd been to reveling in her scent surrounding him than he'd been in a long time. He let the memories crash over him as he lingered against her pillows. It wouldn't mark him as thoroughly as he'd like, but he rolled in her scent and let it rest against his flesh.

Mark, Jackson, and the rest wanted to forget he belonged to her and she to him.

It was the last thing Rayne wanted to lose.

There, for a few moments, he could lose himself to the feeling of her arms around him. How she nestled into his side as if carved perfectly to fit him. Soft and supple, silk and steel, she was everything to him. The day she'd seduced him —or maybe he'd seduced her—he'd become more who he should have always been. Putting a smile on her face filled a measure of the void within him. He'd never understood the sense of loss and dispossession he'd experienced when he left Delta Crescent until the day Luciana became his.

Never again to be lonely. Never again to be lost. He'd wandered, and he'd been found. The day he'd challenged her, he'd shattered everything they'd built and the foundation upon which he'd rediscovered happiness. Tears marred his vision as he lowered the pillow and stared up at the ceiling.

In choosing her safety over her trust, he forfeited any right to demand happiness from her and yet... Rayne could not let her go. But maybe he could still give her time, time to adjust, to acclimate to the changes he'd demanded of her. How else could he justify such choices?

Pushing away from the bed, he set the pillow and blankets to right. She should move back into their room and he could take to sleeping in the office. It may mean nothing, but the gesture, no matter how small, would see to her comfort. If that was all that was left to him...

His phone rang, and the weight of the cell phone in his pocket seemed more an anchor holding him back from drifting away with the tide. Swiping his hand across his eyes, he drew upon the mantle he'd chosen for himself before he pulled his phone out.

The name on the screen gave him pause. Swiping his thumb across the bar to answer it, he let himself out of Luciana's room. "Mr. Dalton," he said by way of greeting as he made his way down the stairs. "To what do I owe the unexpected call?"

"I told you to call me Brett," the Hudson River alpha said, his voice easy and relaxed. Of the five—wait six—other alphas, Brett Dalton of Hudson River and Mason Clayborne of Willow Bend were the easiest to get along with—surprisingly enough. Not even Serafina Andre Buckley offered him the same relaxed manner. Course, he had history with Serafina and his encounters with the other pair of alphas began after he removed Luciana.

So maybe they were grateful to him.

It didn't change his innate distrust, and wariness over their changing their minds. His pack was not in a position to challenge theirs—or anyone's for that matter.

"I recall," Rayne told him, keeping his tone neutral. "However, I was brought up that first names were for friends and we're not quite there yet."

A beat of silence, then Brett chuckled. "Very well, I can accept that, Mr. Barrows."

It may seem a small thing, but the measure of respect in the Hudson River alpha's voice settled some of Rayne's disquiet. Once in his office, he closed the door and checked the street out front. Old habits died hard, and Hounds trained for situational awareness.

"I would appreciate it, Mr. Dalton. Now, what can I do for you?" He didn't offer help as a matter of course, preferring to maintain a healthy distance until he could weigh his options regarding whatever the other alpha wanted.

Another moment of pregnant silence, then Brett sighed. "I have an odd request, and you may turn me down without any fear of insult or reprisal." How generous of him to offer as much. "That said, I feel like if you do turn it down it will say more about your pack than mine." Of course, it would.

Rayne said nothing, and waited. No matter how intriguing the proposal might seem with such a lead up, the best traps were equally as enticing.

A low chuckle, and the squeak of leather as though the other wolf leaned back in a chair. "I wouldn't have responded to whatever ass said that to me either. But one of us is going to have to give an inch somewhere and I'm willing to be the one at the moment. I would like to send a couple of wolves to you, as visitors, in part to render some assistance and in part to provide some necessary training."

No matter how he tried to decode the statement, Rayne couldn't work it out. "Send them to me to join the pack?" Was he trying to pawn off wolves he didn't want?

"No," Brett answered swiftly. "A limited visit, no longer than ten days. Preferably less than five."

Interesting. "What do you think these wolves can offer me that I'd be willing to grant safe passage for such a visit?"

The diner had a lot of foot traffic. Lunch time. Rayne checked his watch and shook his head. He'd lost track of the day, but then a broken sleep schedule would do that.

"Because during our last conference call, you informed Mason and myself you had no healers." Straight and to the point. "Healers remain scarce in many packs."

"Except Sutter Butte." A fascination for many of the other packs, but then the violent history of Sutter Butte would suggest a need for such talents.

"Except them of course," Brett conceded. "You may or may not be aware that Hudson River lost our primary healer a few years ago."

Rayne heard the rumors. The mad wolf. The murders. Anyone who attacked a healer had to be insane. Wolves were protective by nature, but healers engendered the need even more. Perhaps a matter of evolutionary self defense, Rayne wasn't a specialist in such matters. "Yes, I did and for that you have my condolences." The dead healer in question had been Brett's grandfather. A double loss for the alpha.

"Appreciated. During the intervening years, Willow Bend sent a healer to us, a younger one, to fill in the gaps and she's divided her time between Hudson River and Willow Bend." Brett gave him a moment to absorb the fact. "It's a gift which can never be repaid, however, as was recently pointed out to me... it can be paid forward."

"So you want to send Willow Bend's healer here?" That was a risk. Willow Bend remained the closest pack to their borders and they hadn't had the best relationship with them and what they shared now was a tenuous if fragile peace.

"No, their healer remains in Hudson River, she's apprenticed two wolves here and has graciously agreed to remain as a teacher and advisor until the oldest of the pair is in a position to take over full time." Okay, what the hell wasn't he saying? It seemed as though they were communicating on two levels.

"So you want to send one of your apprentice healers?" Again, it would help for Rayne to understand the magnitude of the offer. Sharing a healer *at all* was beyond a gift, and to send an apprentice... one still honing their craft, a generosity Three Rivers had not earned.

"Yes, at the request of both Willow Bend's healer," Brett tone tightened, a momentary glimpse past the jovial to guarded concern before it eased again. "And the apprentice in question. It's not unusual for apprentices to take the step into journeyman by visiting another pack and rendering aid. Most healers do not roam, as you well know." No, they didn't.

Young wolves, those fresh into their adulthood, but sometimes as old as their late twenties would roam either as Lone Wolves or as visitors to another pack to stretch their legs and figure out who they were before settling into pack life. Healers never went Lone Wolf, and they rarely roamed, but they did take the time to visit other packs and other healers.

"Three Rivers doesn't have a healer for your apprentice to work with," Rayne reminded Brett, choosing his words carefully. "While we would be honored by the gift of your healer's time, I worry this will not offer them what they would find in a more established pack."

"True, but as I said, we're paying it forward. This healer is very capable of assessing and treating injuries; she has the training as a nurse and recently completed her degree and licensing in addition to her healing gifts. While I would prefer she remain here, she has made this request and I cannot deny it. However, I do require that she be accompanied by a wolf of my choosing should you agree to her visit.

And as I said earlier, I will take no offense should you decline."

No, he wouldn't. Rayne left the window and dropped into a chair nearest the fireplace. From here he could still see those passing by on the street, but he wasn't as visible himself. It sounded more like Brett would be thrilled if he said no, which meant the healer in question was important to him.

All healers are important... Shit.

Brett Dalton mated a healer, at least that was what the Reagans had let slip. A latent wolf, one who came into her ability to shift and to heal late, but his mate nonetheless.

Brett Dalton was asking him to let his mate come to Three Rivers to *help* Three Rivers.

Fuck. Me.

He should say no, but they really did need a healer. Even one passing through, someone to offer some measure of comfort and reassurance. It could help settle nerves, and buoy spirits.

For the length of time it took Rayne to wrestle with the debate, Brett waited him out. The Hudson River alpha had to be as aware of his breathing as Rayne was of his. They knew the other hadn't hung up.

Finally, Rayne said, "I don't know if we're deserving of such an honor." If Brett didn't bring up the fact the apprentice healer was his mate, then Rayne would play along. "A visit from a healer would be most welcome and you may send whatever wolf you deem appropriate to protect them." Even if it meant they got a visit from Brett himself. A thorny proposition, but Rayne couldn't imagine sending Luciana to another pack without being damn sure of her backup.

The other man let out a long breath. "They would like to leave immediately, but will need three days to prepare before they arrive. Will that work for you?"

Yes, it would give him time to secure a domicile for them. Normally, he would invite the healer to stay in his house directly, but with Luciana...no better to give the healer and their protector some privacy. "I will make the arrangements here, and on my honor...I'll protect your healer, Mr. Dalton, with my life if necessary."

It was the right thing to say, and he'd have made the oath for any healer entering his territory.

No way could they fuck this up.

The visit could make or break their pack.

"In three days then," Brett spoke quietly. "And I will hold you to your oath."

With that, he hung up and Rayne leaned back in the chair. The world's weight had just increased a thousand fold.

Fuck.

CHAPTER 7

*T*he first night she stayed away out of pique. The second, she remained away because she'd lost anyone following her and crossed over into Colorado. Funny, of all the things Rayne and his Hunters had taken over, repurposed, or micromanaged away from her—they'd forgotten the little Kia she'd purchased because it was adorable. The car hadn't been parked in town, though. She'd moved it into a storage facility some thirty-five miles away in preparation for winter.

There it had languished, forgotten by everyone including herself until she'd walked away from Rayne, shaking with quiet fury and worse—tears. Not shedding them had been even more painful than an interrupted shift, but she'd used the pain to fuel her flight from town. Going overland took time, particularly when she didn't shift or run full out.

Time to think was what she needed. Time and distance.

It wasn't until she'd seen the storage place in the distance the rough idea began to form. She had options. She'd always had them, and she didn't *need* Rayne's permission to leave or anything else. Yes, he'd taken the pack, and yes, he was still her mate.

Pain flared in her mid-section. The word seemed anathema to how twisted and warped their bond had become. No matter the truth of it, Rayne could not *command* her. The only wolf whose command she'd ever obeyed had been Salvatore and when he repudiated her... Another frisson of pain lanced through her, though this was more of an ache than an agony. Her brother's absolute rejection of her choices and his cutting ties with her had been *brutal* at the time. Yet she recognized the need for it, and respected his decision even if she wished matters had ended on a happier note for them.

Matters...my brother no longer wishes to know me and I can hardly fault him. I made my choice and I believed *it.* The thought banged around as she keyed in her access code to the storage facility. The unit she'd rented had been a huge one, and she'd paid for two years at the time. It seemed a reasonable length of time to need the extra space while they got the town built.

It was located at the back of the facility and she keyed in her code to open the metal corrugated door. The interior was climate controlled, and filled with a few boxes, some select pieces of furniture—she'd arranged their shipping before leaving Italy and had them stored just outside of Washington D.C., sending for them only after they'd settled in Nebraska—her vehicle, and long rolling rack with dozens of fine dresses, and expensive outfits. All of them horribly out of step with the simple life they'd chosen here, but ideal for her life as a pack princess in Italy.

Pack princess. The snort escaped her and she shook her head. Yes, she'd been among the Americans too long. Words like spoiled, pampered, and princess were often equated with fragile, weak, and spineless.

Luciana was none of those things. If she had been... if her brother's repudiation hadn't destroyed her, then her mate's betrayal surely would.

Closing the storage room door, she took time to clean up from her long walk. It wasn't a shower, but she could find a hotel and get one somewhere... else. Not really making plans, she changed her clothes, then packed a small bag, before retrieving a hidden pouch containing a few thousand dollars American, along with two emergency credit cards, her ID and her passport.

Rayne's passport slid out from behind hers, and her heart stuttered. The blue cover was soft beneath her fingers and despite the lack of damage to her flesh, it might as well have scorched her. Closing her eyes, she took a long deep breath. Then another. And another. Again and again, until she had her heart under control and her tears banked. Tossing the passport back into the box, she closed her eyes for several seconds.

Keys. Cash. Clothes. Car. It was enough to get away. Within an hour of arriving at the storage facility, she pulled out of the gates and onto the quiet two-lane highway, heading west. Colorado and her national parks was only a couple of hours away.

Twenty-four hours after walking away from Rayne, she ranged through the natural hush of a national forest. The bracing cold air and fresh snow gave the landscape a pristine atmosphere. The perfect isolation—the trail she'd followed was considered difficult and few but the most dedicated hikers ventured upon it, and humans were unlikely to venture too deeply in the heavy snows normal in the region.

Luciana planned to get as far in as possible, store her gear and go wolf. She and her animal both needed the time. And maybe if she could find her peace here, she could figure out her best course of action.

Not that there was a best course of action. Forgiving Rayne didn't seem possible. Worse, even if she could find a way to forgive, she wasn't sure if she could ever trust him again. Shoving the thoughts aside, she concentrated on climbing the trail with a pair of snowshoes strapped to her back for when the snow grew too deep. Having hiked in the Alps (Italian and Swiss) over the years, she knew the value of bringing the right tools and supplies. Though at the steady rate of her passage, and the snow depth, she'd be shifted before it grew too deep.

Cheeks stinging from the cold, she sucked in deeper breaths of air. The storm she'd walked through only a few days before had been humid, loud, and wet. This air was so dry, the sun almost too bright, and the snow too white. She should have taken this trip a long time before.

Maybe Rayne and I should have taken this trip... Halting the thought before it could slide off the trail and descend into the rocky crevice of doubt and self-loathing, Luciana pressed onwards. The farther she climbed, the faster she went, the more she engaged her muscles and her concentration on the path, and survival.

As a child, she'd grown up in the stark contrasts of well to do loving family center and brutal, near starvation and hunted, war conditions. Sheltered she might have been from the true horror—Salvatore more than standing between her and the enemies, wolves and human alike, who would have thrilled to the success of killing any of them—she understood there was a thin line between their human and animal halves. A very thin line. If pressed, she could shift and her wolf would know what to do even when she as a child or a teenager or an adult struggled.

Basic instincts kicked in, and it was to these halves of their soul they owed the intangible piece marking them as healer, alpha, omega, beta, paternal or maternal. Their wolves didn't need schooling, deportment, or history classes —they simply knew.

The human half? Luciana paused at a crest in the trail and looked at the area spread out around her. The heavy trees, the scent of rich pine, and fresh snow. The forest had its own predators, mostly cats and the occasional bear. Nothing recent on her trail though, no territory she infringed upon. The smaller game would also keep its distance. Despite the riot of confusion tangling her in knots, she was a predator in her own right. The other creatures would know it, and most wouldn't deem it worth the blood loss to challenge her.

As long as they weren't defending their young or their territory.

Like the alphas of the U.S. They were predators and I definitely infringed upon their territory, without apology or regard. I relished the challenge they would bring, or at least I'd thought I did.

The truth of the thought draped over her like a heavy wool blanket, and dislodged one of the stones digging into her soul. She had known exactly what she was doing and no amount of artful pretense could deny otherwise. Rayne explained it time and again, and she'd told him... "It will be fine, my love. They are entrenched in their beliefs, but even they cannot deny this need or why would there be a need for the so-called Enforcers."

Her mate, though worried, didn't dispute her logic or her confidence—or maybe better put, her over-confidence. In Italy, all the pack alphas answered to Salvatore. They had many packs, and many strong leaders, they had even stronger Centurions and all answered to Salvatore. They were intertwined, and the strongest of them would always stand for even the weakest.

It was how they had survived both World Wars. What had the American packs survived? An economic crisis? A few attacks on the sovereignty which didn't tear apart their cities?

Stop. Comparing the two was not productive. *Basic fact, I knew what trouble I would cause. Also basic fact, I didn't expect them to unite* against *me.*

There was a harsh truth. Their divisions should have been an opportunity to build alliances, and yet at every turn, she found the normally isolated packs working together.

More, they ended up unifying with the damn Enforcers.

What didn't I see?

Running a hand over her face, she winced at the contrasting barbs of cold. It was time to shift, the temperature continued to drop and she needed the warmth of her coat. Her wolf needed this run. They both did.

They needed the basics.

She *needed* them.

Scanning the area, she found a good spot to strip her gear and secure it in the waterproof pack. She'd lash it high enough to keep away ground vermin, and out of sight should she run into any human hikers—despite her doubts or lack of any trace of them on the air—better to plan for the worst and hope for the best.

The minute she began stripping, shivers raced over her skin. It was almost too cold to get down to bare skin. Shifting in clothes offered other dangers and discomforts—not to mention ripped clothing. Dancing from one foot to the other, she concentrated on getting everything stored in the pack and the pack lashed to a tree a half dozen steps off the trail itself.

Her toes burned and her nipples were as hard as stone. Shaking her hair back, she reached for her wolf. The surge of fur sprouted over her even as she blended from human to animal with swift alacrity. In mere moments, she stood braced on four legs rather than two and the cold no longer bit at her. Shaking off the tingles still rippling over her, she settled into her wolf or maybe her wolf settled into her. Nose lifted, she scented the air.

Yes.

Wild land, trees, small animals, and the hints of other predators, she savored each fragment undertone striking her. Dancing over the snow, she let herself go. Within moments, she stretched into a run. Winding through the forest, she raced across the snow. The world narrowed, shaving off agendas, politics, and hurt feelings leaving only the wolf, the wind, and the woman to run.

Pausing at one outcropping, she threw back her head and howled before she darted off again.

Hours melted away as she ran. Startling a rabbit from the safety of its burrow, she managed a snack. Stalking larger game, she brought down a young buck. The hours continued to tumble aside as the sun dipped low in the sky. A series of crevices provided shelter from the wind, and finding no other predators laying claim to the partial cave, she settled in for the night.

Stomach full and muscles burning pleasantly from exertion, she curled into herself, back against a wall and tail wrapped around her legs. The wind howled as a new storm rolled in. The change in the air promised even more bitter chill, and fresh snow.

Eyes drooping, Luciana drifted. It was the most relaxed she'd been in months, isolated, free, and without the care for anyone stumbling upon her or demanding more than she had. No one could stick a knife in her back if her back wasn't there and her mate couldn't ambush her with guilt.

All of those harsh, lonely thoughts bled away.

She and her wolf were enough and sleep brought the first warm dreams since she'd encountered the British wolf on the edge of Three Rivers territory.

Luciana roused with the first hints of dawn in the morning. She ate some snow in lieu of water, then followed her nose to a trickle of a stream desperately trying to escape the frost. From there, she hunted and found a breakfast. Then she roamed again, only slowing when another storm seemed in the offing to scout a place to shelter.

Three days she languished, and neither wolf nor woman was ready to return. She was miles from her clothes, her keys, her car, and her life. The wolf had no need of such things; they had everything they could want or desire in the alpine forests. Twice she turned her nose to the east, to where she'd left her things and twice, she turned away.

The fourth day turned brilliant, the storm clouds departed, the sun shone and the magic of an ice and snow covered land became her playground. The night's shelter had been a copse of trees, gnarled and twisted around each other and she'd slept in the middle, buffeted against the winds and cold. Her claws clicked on the ice.

A half-dozen steps out of the trees, and she caught the taste of cat on the breeze. Large cat. Everything within her went still as she canted her head, testing the air once again. Ears flicking, she listened. It was early, the sun barely higher than the horizon. Her breath frosted in the cool air.

Movement to the left. Clicking claws on ice. A low thrumming growl.

Ears pinned, Luciana turned and faced the largest cat she'd ever seen. The beast wasn't even trying to mask its sound as it walked across the frozen ground. It definitely outweighed her, and the wicked unsheathed claws were enough to give her pause.

Pause.

Not retreat.

Lips peeled back, she released a low warning growl. It was a majestic, stunning animal and she did not want to be pushed into the position of killing... him. The cat moved a step to the side, his mouth opening as he let out a yowling growl of warning as well.

As the cat tried to circle her, she pivoted to keep them face-to-face. Hackles raised, she matched the low whining volume of the cat's challenge with her own. Yes, the cat was larger, but she would be faster. It had a longer reach, but she could go lower on the ground.

It was an animal protecting its habitat; she was more and would fight to continue to survive.

Even as the cat continued its circle, he didn't lunge in or try to narrow the distance. The cat's volume dialed down a notch, an entreaty suggesting the cat didn't want to fight. He didn't want her there, and he wanted her to know it.

Keeping her growl steady, she let the sound vibrate out of her. The rumble warmed her insides, almost a war chant, gearing her up for battle. Never letting her eyes leave the cat's, she didn't miss the moment the cat looked away and yowled again before he bounded a few steps farther, widening the distance between them.

First round of the battle went to her.

They repeated the maneuver for a few more refrains, but when the cat didn't retreat Luciana stepped forward. The cat startled, a hissing cry rising and falling like a modulated recording being warped.

The cat gave more ground.

Good, he was a damn beautiful creature.

Again and again, they repeated it until the cat finally bounded away—perhaps ceding the battle such as it was. Then again, she didn't let her guard down. It had taken time to drive the cat off, and he may simply be waiting for her to let her attention wander. A split second distraction could leave a weakness open to exploitation.

A fact with which she was painfully and intimately famil-

HEATHER LONG

iar. It would serve them both for her to remain wary. Testing the wind, she studied the landscape and listened. The cat had gone downwind, which allowed him to keep track of her scent but limited her senses.

Fine, a good choice.

She diverted east, following the sun. Her claws clicked on the ice as she scampered over the top of the crusted snow. The mixture of snow and plummeting temperatures left a harder surface. Heading for the deeper bits, she trusted her weight and balance to keep her moving across the top of it.

The density of the cat would sink in the heavier piles. Unless the cat took to the trees, and though she spared a glance upward as she continued, she didn't expect the cat to pursue her. No sign of the tawny fur, or sound hinting he followed.

Adrenaline fueled her passage and she took the time to put distance between she and the cat as she wandered in the direction of her clothes, and her car. It wasn't until the sun was high overhead she accepted it was time to return. The unconscious decision drove her for hours, but recognition of having made the choice didn't slow her steps. Hunger tugged at her belly, but she longed for a hot meal, some espresso, and warm clothes. The wolf didn't care about those items, but she was also content with their destination.

In her wanderings, she'd taken only what she absolutely needed from the land to survive. It had been both a freeing and humbling. Luciana didn't require a huge home, a pack, or even family to survive. She survived on her own, and found peace in her solitude. But surviving did not equate to thriving.

Instead, she existed in the nebulous space between decisions. A place where life happened *to* her instead of life being what she *made* happen. Trapped in limbo not by others, but by her own failure to act.

No longer.

When she returned to Three Rivers—huh, she was indeed returning—she and Rayne would make the decisions, which needed to be made.

Then, perhaps she would take a leaf from the American playbook and go Lone Wolf...or journey to Europe. Not Italy, that path was closed to her.

It neared sundown before she reached her clothes. Tired and hungry, she had avoided hunting, but perhaps she shouldn't. Shaking off the negativity, she trotted to the spot where she'd stored her bag. It remained where she'd left it, though snow clung to it. Shifting would not be terrifically comfortable, not with the level of cold and her current state of fatigue. Still, she had a relatively short hike down to her car—another hour or two and there were rations in the bag to tide her over.

Decided, she reached for herself and let the wolf recede. Her shifts were smooth, smoother than many she'd seen. It was like shedding water as the fur vanished and she straightened to stand on two legs. Her skin steamed in the cold, and she was grateful for the lingering warmth of transition as she reached for her bag.

Tired, isolation, and the gathering dark however were no excuse for missing the approach of another until a too familiar voice slunk out of the darkness and curled against her skin. "There you are...*bentornata bella.*"

What the hell was Rodrigo doing here?

CHAPTER 8

*B*y the end of the third day since Luciana vanished from town, Rayne's grip on his temper crumbled. He'd kept his focus on the multitude of tasks required to continue the town's rebuild, facilitate training for some members of the pack—either through mentorships with older wolves or negotiating trade to put them in touch with specialists in other packs. Della and Arturo were on the road, handling their first runs and Three Rivers received a shipment of fresh lumber, tile, huge tracts of carpeting, and nearly a hundred gallons of paint in three different colors: white, light tan, and more surprising, red. Among the shipment were other materials and tools for rehabbing the various buildings.

Jackson inventoried all of it, and declared they had more than enough to finish two full houses, and a section of four apartments over one of the unfinished shops. A feeling of success surged through the pack at the pronouncement and they were all pulling together in an effort to get the work done.

They needed roofing materials, but for now they did

patch jobs. The winter weather wasn't conducive to stripping roofs off buildings. He had time to work on acquiring those materials. In the midst of all of this, he made arrangements with the Reagans to help in hosting the visiting Hudson River healer and the protector coming with her. He half-suspected it would be Brett himself, and ran the risk of insulting the alpha by giving the host duties to former members of his own pack rather than in a private home, which was why he had Jackson focus on polishing one apartment fully. They could let the visitors stay there, in their own building without close neighbors. The Reagans would be near enough to be gracious, but far enough to afford privacy.

It was splitting the difference.

Fucking politics. Rayne pinched the bridge of his nose. He hadn't slept in days. In between all his negotiating, managing, and planning sessions, he'd continued to hunt for the wolf who didn't belong in his territory.

He'd found a campsite, old, likely months old. It had the faded scents of at least two wolves. Neither had been Luciana, thank God. While he accepted it as good news, the bad news was it meant there were at least *two* strangers in his territory. Maybe more.

Was it the damn Russians, again?

He'd kept the tales of the Volchitsa action in Three Rivers to himself, not revealing it to either the pack or Enforcers. He'd definitely not told the other alphas. It was no one's business. It had been handled.

Or had it?

The last thought worried him more than any other. Rodrigo wasn't a Russian name, but then what did it matter? Three days, and no sign of Luciana, no word of her and not even a whisper from the pack.

Another, deeper cause for concern. Jackson and Mark had both taken the time to mention their thoughts on his continued mating. The fact they deemed him weak enough to need that advice or worse, Luciana dangerous enough they fear her presence, left him on the defensive. Frankly, what worked for Three Rivers seemed to really be working. Measured success could be gauged everywhere he looked, except in his own home.

Three. Days.

Had she been injured? Taken captive?

Run off with a lover?

The last thought cast a red haze over his vision, and his wolf snarled. The rake of the beast's claws against the inside of his skin proved so fierce, it surprised him when bloody score marks didn't appear on his flesh.

His wolf wasn't jealous of the idea, no. Instead, a low simmering anger throbbed through his soul. His wolf was furious with him for even entertaining the thought. Recognizing the wolf's blind loyalty didn't do him any good, however. The last thing the man wanted to believe was Luciana would betray him...

Then again, she probably never believed I'd betray her either.

Round and round in circles he went, endlessly chasing his tail and what did he have to show for it? A pack on the cusp of stability and a mating disintegrating. It was as though he could only succeed at one—his mating had been solid while the pack floundered after all.

His wolf clawed at him again. Three days since they'd seen their mate. Three. Long. Damn. Days.

Aggravation struck the flint of fury, and he walked away from the building crews and weaved around the other wolves on the street—some heading home, others heading out. Slow and steady, they were building a functioning community and trust. Rayne ignored them all, he went straight back to their house.

Though he hadn't expected to find her there, his disappointment at the presence of only her fading scent pierced him. *Pathetic.*

Find. His wolf ignored the jibe. *Hunt.*

Hunt? Where the fuck did he start? If he'd gone after her in the first damn place, maybe he'd know where she was, but instead, he'd let her go. For months, she'd taken off for one or two days, but she always came back.

What if this time she'd truly left?

Find. The wolf's impulse echoed through him like a shout cried out from the mountaintops.

Luciana wasn't in town. He didn't need to search it to know, but he couldn't risk not searching. His wolf didn't dispute the assessment. Rayne had been all over there town the last three days and detected not even a whiff of her delectable scent.

Pressing the contact information for Jackson, he waited less than a beat after his brother answered to order, "Organize a quiet search party for Luciana. Everywhere in town, and beyond within a five mile radius. If she's found, don't approach just call me. No questions, just do it."

Not willing to hear Jackson's derision over his choices he disconnected the call.

The house she frequented was outside the five-mile radius. Outside, the sky darkened. Winter storm warnings had gone into effect earlier in the day, but they didn't expect the storms to truly arrive until the next day.

His next call was to Louis at the diner as he gathered what he'd need including heavy coats if she were at the ramshackle house when the storm hit.

"Hey man," Louis said by way of greeting when he answered the phone.

"Louis, have you or any of your family seen Luciana at all in the last three days?" Of all the wolves in Three Rivers, the Reagan family unit drew even the most disparate among them. A tight knit family among misfits. They offered a display of stability unlike their alpha pair who seemed to continually fail.

"I wish I could say yes." Sympathy hung heavy in the other man's tone. "She hasn't been inside in months to be honest. Even when we do see her, she crosses streets to avoid contact." The wolf's compassion turned to sorrow. "I know she's hurting, we all do. We want to help, we just don't know how."

A wolf who wasn't telling him to get rid of her. A wolf who cared about their former alpha, and their current alpha's mate. Or maybe he was just Louis, and he cared about everyone.

The knot of tension in his chest loosened a fraction. "Thank you, Louis," he said, more relieved than he wanted to admit. "I appreciate you looking out for her."

"Of course, she's still pack..." The other wolf quieted, and the moment elongated before he said. "I know there are some who do not think she should be here anymore, but they are acting from a place of fear. We need to act because we choose to act, not because we are afraid of what will happen if we don't act."

Strength existed within Louis' logic. Rayne could apply the same to the issues he and his mate currently faced. He wanted to act, but he was also afraid of losing her or driving her further away. Granted, he would never let her go, not willingly. But could he, in turn, shackle her if she wanted her freedom?

Everything was such a fucked up mess.

"Thanks, Louis. I mean it."

"Always. I'm preparing a welcoming meal for the Hudson River healer."

Crap. Dammit. Shitballs. He'd allowed himself to forget they were expected later that evening even though he'd... "I'll make sure you know when they've landed and head this way."

An Enforcer would be escorting them rather than one of Rayne's own Hunters. They were landing at a private airfield several miles outside of Three Rivers' territory after they paid a visit to Willow Bend. He had no complaints about the Enforcer escort, healers got all the protection and the Volchitsa incidents were far too recent and too raw to take any needless chances.

Overkill would be the new norm for a long time to come. *Of course, I don't know where my mate is at the moment, so perhaps I should try approach something resembling normal before I decide on such broad statements.*

He hung up with Louis and carried the gear out to his SUV. They had a different collection of vehicles, but the big SUVs were standard. They could fit inside in wolf form, and they doubled as shelter if they were on the road too long. Rayne, like most wolves, didn't much care for hotels.

They reeked of too much cleaner and too many other bodies.

Ugh.

He checked the time on his phone. If he left and drove straight for the ramshackle house, he take the few hours to plead his case and convince her to return with him before the healer and her escort arrived.

Plead my case?

The thought gave him pause. A mate shouldn't have to plead with their mate—shouldn't, not couldn't or wouldn't.

Plead because he chose to plead.

Apologize because he chose to express his sorrow at losing her trust.

Entreat her for another chance because he chose to court her…

Court her. A slow smile spread across his lips. That was

exactly what he should have been doing all this time. It was how he won over the hot-tempered and wild wolf when he'd met her in Italy. Although, to be fair, she had pursued him at first and then she'd played coy.

Luciana had wanted to be courted, to be chased, and more for the wolf who wanted her to earn the privilege. In challenging her and all the subsequent fallout, he'd backed off and let her lick her wounds. He accepted her anger and her rejection as his due and told himself when she calmed down he'd...

Fuck, I'm an idiot. In choosing the pack over his mate and his mate's ultimate safety over trusting and loving her, he had damn well betrayed her. Then by not acting, but letting her stew and staying away to 'protect' her, he'd done even more damage.

Idiot.

Enough wool gathering, he needed to find her now. He needed to court her. The first step, win her smile. Her smile could melt the ice in his soul and free him from the arctic chill of isolation. The next step? Win back her trust and affection. None of the steps would be easy. In all likelihood, they'd promised to be damn near impossible.

But he'd grovel if he had to.

Luciana was worth it.

With fresh purpose, he pulled out of the carport, and headed for the road. His phone had been painfully quiet. The town of Three Rivers was by no stretch of the imagination large. Jackson and the others could search all of it swiftly. If they hadn't called him, it was because she wasn't there.

Even though he expected as much, it still left his soul twitching.

The quick drive to the ramshackle house didn't let him brood for long. No sooner did the house come into view than he recognized she wasn't there. Still, he forced himself to park and explore it with his own senses. His wolf agreed wholeheartedly with this plan and the force of pushing him to find her alleviated, but the respite would be brief. The need to be with his mate was a compulsion he didn't want to ignore.

Before, he'd satisfied the desire by simply looking at her, or picking a fight with her even when he didn't want to fight. To see the anger flash in her eyes, to hear the cutting note in her voice—they'd been a balm for him, let him reaffirm the bond between them no matter how tenuous and frayed.

Pathetic.

Nothing about those interactions truly satisfied him, but he wasn't sure how to bridge the chasm he'd helped to dig.

The scent of snow followed him as he made his way across the dilapidated porch. The first time they'd found this place, Luciana had been immediately enchanted. She'd seen the potential in the falling down wreck which probably should have been condemned decades before, as it had been abandoned.

Yet his mate laughed away his objections, then told him to look with his heart and not his jaded eyes. To imagine with his soul and not his cynical mind. Rayne grew up in and around New Orleans, he'd spent years moving along the Gulf Coast, he knew all about history, and loss and rebuilding. Sometimes you couldn't save a building and the best thing was to tear it all down then build something new.

Luciana snorted. *"What do Americans really know of historical? Your country is still a toddler. In Italy, we have structures thousands of years old and we do not tear them down because they are damaged...we repair, we curate, we enhance the legacy."*

Then she would kiss him to take the sting from her words and her dark eyes would kindle with clever humor and teasing warmth. No, she would not allow anyone to tear the house down. She wanted to take it on as a project, to see it flourish once more. In fact, she wanted to move here and perhaps build out into the countryside and add farms or vineyards, maybe livestock. All of it seemed so fanciful, she'd practically grown up in a series of wealthy Italian villas and vineyards.

He thought it a pipedream what she imagined, but as he made his way through the house he tried to see it as she did. The paint peeled from the walls, the wooden floors bowed, and pulled away. The brick crumbled around the fireplace. The light fixtures were long gone in most rooms, leaving only a tangle of abandoned and lonely wire to hang from the ceilings.

In truth, Rayne didn't see what she did, but he didn't have to believe in the house.

He had to believe in her.

Fingers curling into a fist, he stalked from room to room. Images of her dancing ahead of him as she described her vision haunted him. Traces of her scent lingered in the main room only, so faint he had to question if he only scented her because he wanted it so badly.

Though the trace of the male he'd scented that night also lingered and he sure as fuck didn't want to scent that bastard. At least *Rodrigo* hadn't returned to the house, a small mercy.

Or maybe she's with him somewhere else entirely, where we can't find her.

The thought earned another sharp dismissive rebuke from his wolf. Luciana was their *mate* and mates didn't cheat.

Mates don't challenge their mates for leadership either. Yet he'd already done that.

Stop.

Stop.

Just stop.

Rayne halted, forced his fists to release and took one

steadying breath after another. Chasing his tail was unnecessary. Finding Luciana was the goal.

She wasn't in Three Rivers.

Deep breath.

She wasn't at the house she loved.

Release the breath.

She hadn't been seen in town since walking away three days prior.

Deep breath.

She'd walked west.

Release.

Walked.

Inhale.

Wolves could cover a lot of ground on foot, but it was easily fifty or more miles to the next anything in that direction. A storage facility on one of the two lane roads; and another thirty plus miles to a town of any size.

Exhale.

Storage facility.

Rayne pivoted and strode out of the house without a backwards glance. Luciana had rented a storage unit months before, back when they were first getting settled. They'd shipped a lot of her items over before leaving Italy, all a part of their plan. They hadn't had anywhere to bring it, and she'd rented the unit specifically to keep the furniture, clothing and more fragile items...

And her fucking car.

He didn't have time to drive all the way there, just for clues, and perhaps get back before the healer arrived.

Politic or not, he didn't care.

It was about damn time his mate came first.

He was halfway there when his phone rang. He used the voice system in the car to answer it.

"Mr. Barrows," Brett's voice came through the console.

Knuckles white on the steering wheel, Rayne exercised all of his control to keep his voice calm. "Mr. Dalton."

The other alpha chuckled, "I look forward to the day we can skip the formalities, in the meanwhile, I wanted to let you know my healer has been delayed here for a few hours longer. The weather has been rather inhospitable and they are threatening to ground flights. I'd prefer she wasn't flying right into a storm."

Relief pumped in Rayne's veins. More time to find his mate. "It's looking like snow here," he said, proud his tone sounded measured and agreeable. "I think giving it a time is the best plan." The sky had darkened considerably as he drove farther west. "We're ready to welcome her, so we only need a few hours notice."

"Thanks for understanding," Brett said, his tone gracious but the undercurrent of steel remained. He didn't really give a crap if Rayne had understood, his healer his rules and Rayne respected it. "I'll be in touch."

"Until then." The call disconnected and Rayne pressed a button on the steering wheel. "Call Pain in my Ass." It was the contact name for his brother.

Jackson answered on the second ring. "No sign of her and I've checked everywhere twice, myself."

"Thanks, I've got an idea of where she is and I'll be out for a day or two, hopefully not longer. Call me on the cell if there's anything otherwise, keep the teams working. If the storm grows worse, shut it down and tell them to stay inside and stay warm. Hudson River's healer is delayed with storms back east, so it could be a bit before she's here."

"Got it." Jackson was silent, but the dead air seemed ripe with unasked questions Rayne had zero interest in answering. Finally, his brother said, "You'll be back before the healer gets here, right?"

Protocol would demand his presence. The healer would

be under his protection, and it would insult the hell out of Brett and his pack not to mention running the risk of borrowing far more trouble than he had the credit to cover. "I'll be there."

With or without his mate, and his wolf growled. The animal didn't like it, but since the man didn't either, his wolf couldn't really bitch.

"Stay safe," he ordered Jackson. "Keep the peace."

Not waiting for any more comments, he ended the call.

Three damn days. He had no idea what he expected to find at the storage facility, but when he arrived and let himself in—thankfully he still had the codes—he found items missing from her unit, most prominently her car.

Rage vied with worry and despair at the discovery. Then he ground his teeth and focused. Long before he'd been a Lone Wolf and met his match in a fiery Italian wolf, he'd been a Hound, and a damn good one for the Delta Crescent pack. Tracking was in his nature and his training. If he couldn't us his nose to follow her, he'd use technology.

Her car had a navigation system, and a security feature they'd been sure to upgrade to, just like his. Pulling it up on an app on his phone, he entered the passwords and security questions.

The car was in Colorado.

Dammit.

Setting the phone back into the holder and adding the coordinates to the GPS in his car, he got back on the road.

He would find his mate and heaven help anyone who got in his way.

CHAPTER 9

Shock tumbled right into anger. Why the hell was Rodrigo *here*? Five days since she'd left Three Rivers, if her accounting of time held. With darkness rapidly approaching, she would soon be at six days. The run had given her a measure of peace, letting her escape from both herself and the crushing disappointment of the multiple failures in her wake.

It was time to return to Three Rivers. She was ready.

What she wasn't prepared for was the dark, almost possessive gleam in Rodrigo's eyes as he skimmed over her naked body. Steam still rose from her skin, the heat generated by her transformation warming her despite the frigid weather. Nudity was normal for wolves, an everyday occurrence and they didn't leer at each other. They didn't appraise another's body. Jerking a shirt out of the bag, she ignored the snow cooling her feet and glared at Rodrigo.

The rake of his gaze continued to linger on her curves before rising to her face. A slow smirk curved his lips, and it was definitely a smirk. No other word described the calculated pleasure he seemed to be enjoying at the moment.

"I asked you a question," she reminded him, and made no attempt to mask the hostility in her tone. "What the hell are you doing here?"

"Protecting you," he said after too long of a pause. He continued to stare at her, gaze drifting to her breasts and lingering there. The tautness of her nipples seemed to fascinate him, and she dragged the shirt over her head, foregoing a bra for now. Then she pulled out her pants and dragged them on. Rodrigo huffed a little, his breath coming out in little cloudy puffs. "You are safe with me."

Somehow, his assurance made her altogether warier. "I do not *require* your protection nor did I invite you on this excursion." Dressed, she stuffed her chilled feet into boots. The snow clinging to them would melt and probably make the walk unpleasant, but she armored herself in the fabric. If nothing else, it kept his nauseating eyes from staring any deeper.

"I am here to protect you, I do not require your permission, Principessa." He spread his hands, and no matter how open his manner seemed—he didn't retreat from her space. If anything he crowded closer, and she could taste his breath from where she stood. Her jacket was in her hands and she dragged it on, another layer of defense.

"Step back, Rodrigo." Command filtered into every word. The wolf had forgotten himself. Yes, he was a Centurion, and like all those who served her brother, he was a powerful wolf. Every single one was an alpha in their own right, only they chose to follow Salvatore. They were *power* and they radiated dominance. The force of his crashed against her, but she didn't bow her head or retreat from it.

The curve of his lips deepened, and he narrowed the gap between them farther. What the hell did he think he was doing?

Then he put his hand on her cheek, a caress, possessive

and intimate. Luciana dropped the bag, and seized his wrist with one hand. The violent wrench she used to dislodge him only worked because she took him by surprise. Rodrigo was larger than she was, but she was faster.

The bones beneath her hand crunched. His swift indrawn breath served as the only reveal of the pain she inflicted. Locking her gaze on him, she forced his arm away from her. Applying force, she pushed his elbow to an uncomfortable angle. Teeth bared and clenched, he glared at her.

"You do *not* decide you can touch me," Luciana informed him, pinning him in place as she applied more pressure. A million hectic thoughts raced through her brain, battling for dominance. None of them she let out to intervene in this battle. "You do not touch me, at all."

Quiet fury reflected in the darkness of his eyes even as a circle of gold illuminated them. For the first time since she seized his wrist to remove his hand from her face, he exerted his own pressure to relieve his arm from the vicious hold she'd put him in.

His physical strength versus hers, she lost ground as she slid in the snow. Not all the force she brought to bear on his wrist prevented him from straightening his arm. Then he wrenched free and seized her arm instead. One yank, and he hauled her back to him. Twisting, she let her back strike his chest and in one continuous flow of movement she slammed her elbow into his solar plexus and stomped her booted foot down on his. Neither individual maneuver was enough to dislodge him, but combined it rocked him and his grip on her lightened.

Tearing free, she swung the backpack, and it clipped Rodrigo's brow. One of the metal buckles sliced a cut, which immediately welled with blood. His eyes went from brown to pure gold, and his expression tightened to something feral.

"Back off," she ordered him, filling her voice with every

ounce of dominance and power at her disposal. Centurions, however, had never been hers to sway.

"Or what?" He raised his brows, daring her to complete the challenge.

Or what? She could run. Her familiarity with the landscape would definitely give her a head start. Running would concede the advantage to him, and while the offer of an ally might have held some faint appeal before—she wasn't interested in whatever game Rodrigo wanted to play.

"Or you and I will have a very different kind of problem," Luciana said, masking her scent. No way she would allow him the headiness of her very real fear. She was far from Three Rivers, far from any kind of backup—not that any of the wolves there would leap into the fray to protect her. Not anymore.

A distant part of her mind called bullshit. There was one wolf who would still come for her, and fight at her side. Her wolf knew it and didn't give a damn what she thought about it. As it was, they were both sizing up their opponent, cycling through everything they remembered about Rodrigo.

"Do tell, Principessa." His voice took on a silky tenor, seemingly unperturbed by the idea of bodily harm. Or maybe he thought her weak since her own mate had toppled her?

The wolf moved with an economy of motion, yet he favored his left side. He always lead with his right, he often stood with his right side forward even in face-to-face discussions. Even now, it had been his right hand he'd used to stroke her cheek. His right wrist she'd broken. They healed fast, but it was still an advantage.

When she said nothing, he smiled. "You can say anything you like to me, after all I told you I was here for you."

Here for her. Right. Not just in a supportive capacity then. Was he there to take her back to Seven Hills? Because that wouldn't happen, nor could it. Rodrigo was not high on the list of Centurions; he'd only been one for twenty or twenty-five years. He'd often been assigned to her mother's vineyard and their region. She'd known him for years, so why was he...

"I don't *want* you here. I didn't *invite* you here. Technically you're trespassing and violating the laws of the North American packs." Yes, it was absolutely rich coming from her. Had she not violated all of them?

Apparently Rodrigo agreed with her as he chuckled. "You worry too much bella, I can take care of both of us. Though the land we're on currently is claimed by no one...and you are far away from the pack that treats you so poorly."

She cursed mentally. "I'm not going back to Seven Hills." Miraculously, saying the words aloud bolstered her confidence and consolidated a belief she'd had for months. One she hadn't even admitted to herself.

Seven Hills was no longer her home. Nor did she want it to be. Yes, she missed her mother and her brother. All their differences aside, they were still family. But Three Rivers...

"No, bella, I understand." Then he touched her face again, the touch fleeting before he gripped the back of her neck and hauled her forward. His fingers bit in her flesh and her wolf roused, cold determination flooding her veins. "We will make our way elsewhere...there are so many opportunities. South America, Asia, perhaps even Northern Europe. As much as I love Italy, I knew you would not want to return and I will not go without you."

Keeping still, she resisted him drawing her closer. Instead, she let her claws grow. Partially shifting her hands was child's play. His eyes burned, the gold color having utterly obliterated the brown. She wasn't talking to just the Centurion any longer, but also the wolf. An angry, dangerous wolf who didn't seem to give a damn about what she wanted. Only satisfying his own twisted desires.

Apparently what he desired was her.

Killing him would open a kettle of trouble between Three Rivers and Seven Hills. Not killing him would leave her in a dangerous, and precarious position. Her wolf didn't give a damn about politics. Once upon a time, the woman would have agreed. Her mother once called her *la collera*, the rage or sometimes, *la tempesta*, the storm. No restraint, no filters, and all action. If someone pissed her off, she called them on it. If someone challenged her, she didn't hesitate to use every tool in her arsenal to take them down.

One of those tools was no longer available...or was it?

"Do you truly believe Salvatore will be all right with your actions? Or have you broken with Seven Hills?" They did not have Lone Wolves in Italy. All wolves whether they lived alone or within the precincts of a pack, they were all one larger pack. They all needed and looked out for each other. Time alone was something to be provided when solitude was required.

Rodrigo answered with a shrug. "For you, I will go. He should never have allowed the American to take you."

"He hardly *took* me." The scoff slipped out before she could think twice about it. Rodrigo tightened his grip on her neck; her wolf grew restless with her allowing this treatment. Their clothing was loose enough if not for her jacket, then she could shift and tear him open in a matter of moments.

Or she could simply disembowel him with her already formed claws. It would ruin her clothes, and it likely wouldn't kill him. Not immediately. But he would be down until he could shift a few times and it would be make for an effective point.

"I *chose* him," she reminded Rodrigo. Honestly, was there a more stubborn or self-involved creature than a male wolf with alpha tendencies? Their biological imperatives seemed to make everything their choice, their call, their claim or in her particular case, Salvatore should have stopped Rayne as if she had no say in it at all?

Yet, no mating *could* happen through force. No matter how much they wanted to say they'd won their mate or claimed their mate. The mate had to claim them in return or it was merely a painful empty promise.

She'd wanted Rayne.

She'd *chased* him.

"You were blinded by passion, *la tempesta.*" He sounded so smug. "Do not fear. I will eliminate the problem for you and make you free once more."

Possessive rage flamed hotter. "Do *not* speak to me as if you have that right." He would *not* touch Rayne. Done with his grip on her and his intimations, she struck. Her claws left a stripe of blood up along his side, carving through his jacket, his shirt, and his flesh. Hissing, Rodrigo's grip shifted and he flung her away from him. The backpack slid from her fingers as she crashed into the side of a tree.

Pain flared along her side, the back of her neck ached where he'd dug his fingers in. The bruising force of his hand and the collision with the tree lit her up. Heat radiated from those spots, and it fueled her wrath. Rodrigo stormed toward her, but Luciana moved.

He was not her mate.

She would not hold back.

In a fight with a larger, stronger wolf—the only advantage she had was speed, agility, and ruthless determination. She had all three in spades. Her wolf surged beneath her skin, and then her vision changed, sharpening despite the gathering gloom. The other wanted to hurt them, or at the very least, control them.

Not. Happening.

In this, she and her wolf were in perfect sync. Rather than

waiting for Rodrigo to get to her, she rushed him. He braced himself, angling his body for an attack from below. She was smaller; it made sense. But she didn't go low, she launched herself, one foot colliding with his upper thigh, as her knee slammed into his chest. The momentum carried her upward, and she dug her claws into his shoulders as she completed the flip.

Catching him off balance, she hauled his bulky ass backwards and dropped him in the snow. Tumbling clear, she landed on light feet and pivoted. Rodrigo didn't stay down; the speed at which he lunged to his feet and closed on her took her breath away.

Adrenaline surged as he struck with his right fist—the one with the broken wrist and she narrowly twisted to avoid the hit while grabbing his arm. Digging her claws into his injury, she wrenched downwards. The break extended up his forearm, and she used his momentum to throw him.

Not waiting for him to rise this time, she launched herself onto his back and stabbed her claws through his coat and into the heavy meat of his lats. He roared, and jammed an elbow back the blow glancing off her chin. Blood filled her mouth as her head snapped to the side. Then he shook her off as he rose to his feet.

Pure, unadulterated anger distorted his features. Crimson scattered over the snow and his fists turned into claws. So she wasn't alone in her partial shifts. Made sense...though Rodrigo was still younger than she. Rolling to the balls of her feet, she went low this time even as he went to seize her and angled to hit him in the groin with both fists. He adjusted his stance, and he took the blows to the thigh.

Swearing, she had nowhere to go as he seized her, one clawed hand on her throat and the other catching her right arm.

White-hot pain lanced through her as her wrist snapped,

and her vision blanked when he broke her elbow. His claws pricked her throat, and heat swelled as blood dribbled down her neck.

"I love that you have a bite," he said, closing the distance with his gaze zeroed onto her mouth telegraphing his intent. No, she spat in his eyes even as she curled her free hand and dragged her claws across his face. Red welled from the score marks and his roar damn near deafened her. Then his hand on her throat tightened, cutting off her air. Spots danced before her eyes and she clawed him again.

Injuries, bites, and bruises she could handle, but deprived of oxygen, her muscles went lax and her vision decreased. She warred against unconsciousness. She couldn't fall here. If she lost, he would take her and that was a defeat she could not accept.

Would not.

Lashing forward with her leg, she managed to catch him in the groin and he gurgled a wet, miserable sound. The abrupt release dropped her to her knees in the snow. The world slowed, and her limbs went sluggish. She had to get up. She had to fight. But she couldn't do more than gulp in air.

The backhand he delivered to her cheek sent a burst of pain through her face and left colors sparking against her vision. Were her eyes open or shut? She'd landed face first into the snow. The cold delighted her skin, and helped numb the injuries, but it didn't bring her dazed brain back to focus.

A sharp blow to her side lifted her out of the snow and she flew to the side a few feet, stopping only when she hit a tree.

"You must learn your place," Rodrigo said, stomping toward her, a relentless slash of darkness in the gathering night. She couldn't bring his blurred form into focus, and then his foot struck her side again.

Something in her chest snapped.

It had already been a struggle to breathe, and she couldn't get air into her lungs.

Those wicked boots stopped right before her face, and it was now or never. If he struck her in the head, she would collapse.

He would win.

No.

Just no.

He lifted his right foot, and she rolled, twisting with every ounce of force and speed she possessed, ignoring the starbursts of agony from her abused arm, and chest. Her face had gone thankfully numb. She got both of her legs wrapped around his left. Off balance, his kick hit her hip with bruising force, but she locked her knees on his and rolled—inexorable force against a potentially weak joint.

His howl of rage and pain split the air as the joint *popped* viciously, and then she scrambled away on one hand and her knees. Her right arm screamed when she tried to put her weight on it, and she fell just a few feet away.

Get up.

The vise around her chest squeezed.

Get. Up.

The unnatural angle of her arm kept her from pushing up easily and left her struggling one handed.

Up. Up. Up.

Downed wolves were dead wolves.

The air around her changed, electrifying and the silence hit her like a blunt instrument. A deep rumbling growl interrupted the perfect canvas of nothingness. Knowing even before she turned her head what she would see, Luciana's heart rate accelerated as it tried to claw its way from her chest.

Rodrigo had shifted. The powerfully built wolf, perhaps a

third again larger than her own glared at her. Nothing human reflected in his eyes... only rage, agony, and the promise of retribution.

Her wolf pressed against her, and they both braced. Her shifts were fast, but she was wounded and still dressed. So many variables, then the wolf charged at her.

No.

No time.

No.

She swore the scorch of his hot breath rolled over her face, and then Rodrigo vanished with a yelp. It was his turn to land against a tree, and a broad shouldered wolf took up position between she and the mad Italian.

Rayne...

CHAPTER 10

*B*y the time he reached Colorado and her abandoned car in a lot near the trailhead, his mood had descended from bad to worse. The need to find her pulsed with every beat of his heart. Another car parked next to hers—a rental. He didn't know the vehicle, but based on the time of year and the weather, only the foolhardy would hike in these conditions.

Making a note of the rental information on the small tag on the back, he left it for investigation later. Frustration, worry, and something indefinable warred within him. The first two nagging emotions left him twisted inside, but the third? The third tore at him, like a savage beast determined to shred him apart.

After placing a single phone call to verify all was as well as could be expected in Three Rivers, Rayne informed Jackson he would be unreachable for a couple of days, and left instructions on how to handle any eventuality.

Two days.

Two days he could carve away from the pack to track his mate. Two days before he'd likely hear from Hudson River if not sooner. They would call his cell phone first, and that phone would remain in the car, along with the rest of his gear. A day to return the call would be acceptable, two days? It would push it. Therefore, he could only allot two days before he had to return here and at least check in.

With a narrow time frame in mind and the continued darkening of the skies, Rayne elected to travel in his wolf form. He'd be warmer, cover a larger swath of ground, and his senses would be sharper. He also knew Colorado fairly well; he'd spent a couple of years in and around these huge ranges after he'd first gone Lone Wolf.

Winter was the worst time of year for tracking someone. The snow muddied the scents. The colder weather punished missteps, and the storms? The storms were a threat all their own. The first winter he'd spent out here, he'd thrived on the challenge and it was through ice and snow, he'd let himself be reborn. Decades of service to one pack, one ideal, and one family left him a little raw and worse, numb when he'd chosen to leave Delta Crescent.

In ranges like this, he'd worked to shed the Hound and figure out who Rayne was. And in other mountains on the other side of the world, he'd discovered who he could be. Shaking off the melancholy, he disciplined his thoughts. The dark tangle of emotions choking him wouldn't serve him or his mate out here. Here, he needed every ounce of the cunning he'd possessed as a Hound, all the determination he'd learned as Rayne, and all the power he'd consolidated as mate, and eventually Alpha.

Without a care for the cold or worry of being observed, he stripped out of his clothes, locked everything in the vehicle, and hid the keys somewhere safe before he shifted. His wolf rolled over him in a crack of bone and rending of flesh. What he lacked for in speed in his shift, he made up for in steadiness when the shift ended. His wolf was a large, ranging beast and he had stamina for days.

Testing the area around Luciana's vehicle, her scent was a hint of a memory. A more masculine scent—more recent— overlaid it and he tracked it back to the rental car.

The unknown wolf.

No wonder Rayne hadn't found him in Three Rivers, the son of a bitch was out here—*with* Luciana. The rage settling in his belly fired his blood and drove away any trace of the cold. His trail was far more recent than Luciana's, and as much as he longed to follow and deal with the interloper, Rayne wanted his mate more. His wolf didn't dispute the desire. Of one mind, they followed the traces of her scent and headed into the snowy, cold park.

By dark of the first night, he had to hunker down in the hollowed out remains of a downed tree. It provided him with a barricade against the wind. He subsisted on small game, even as he followed the winding track of his mate—and the places where the damned interloper's path cut across hers. Cut across.

Over and over the words repeated in his mind. Cut across. The wolf was smug. The interloper did not travel alongside Luciana. Their scents were differing ages, she passed through and he after her, but time had elapsed. The fresh snowfall diluted some of the trail, but each time he tracked them again, it reinforced his belief.

Luciana hadn't left with the male, but the male had followed her.

Possessive vied with protective, yet underneath it all remained a solid thread of demand. The wolf wanted their mate in their sight. They wanted to *know* she was safe, to scent her, and to touch her.

Then they would deal with the damn interloper.

Halfway through his second day, he'd lost the thread of

her trail and had to double back. She'd wandered, wound through the woods and along ridges, then down again with no discernible pattern. Time ticked away on him, pressing him closer and closer to the moment he had to call off his search and return to his vehicle. A part of him wanted to check to make sure her car was still there, and the rest of him warred against the instinct.

He'd already chosen the pack over his mate once, how dare he do it again?

Hours of sorting through different traces took him in circles. In a few places she'd cut back across her own trail, and sifting through the scents told him some were days older than the others. If she'd been trying to muddy her trail, the differences wouldn't have been so distinctive. Also, he didn't believe she was trying to lose him. The age on the interloper's scent was different again from hers.

Was he stalking her?

The fury in his gut went to ice. Was she aware of being hunted? Alone, isolated, and without any kind of backup in an inhospitable wilderness... If he howled... would she hear it? Or would it alert her pursuer to how close he was?

Worse, what if she heard it and chose against answering him or letting him find her? Unable to even contemplate the thought, he pushed it aside and kept his primary focus on finding her.

Find her.

Make sure she was safe.

Figure everything else out after.

The need to see her had grown unbearable, to merely run his fingers over her cheek or fill his lungs with her scent. Hell, he'd be happy with the swipe of her claws burning through his flesh.

Shifting gears, he made the conscious decision to wind toward the primary trail leading to where they'd parked. If need be, he'd venture down far enough to verify her vehicle's presence, retrieve his phone, check in, and then return to search for her.

He couldn't return to Three Rivers without her. He just... couldn't.

The time spent on the descent bled away precious drops of time. The doubt gnawing on his soul tore huge chunks out of him. The coppery scent of blood teased his nose and he paused. Head lifted and ears canted, he tested the air and listened intently. Fresh. Warm.

Wolf.

Not...not Luciana.

The interloper bled.

His mouth opened, a primal instinct to draw the other's scent, memorizing more notes of it. Pain lanced with hunger and desire marked the metallic taste. The first amused him, but the humor evaporated on the second. He'd already changed course to follow the scent, when a cry of pain danced across the snowy landscape. More, he tasted fresh blood.

Luciana's...

Redoubling his speed, he flew across the snow, leaping the drifts as he whipped through the trees. Muscles burning as the cold air stung his lungs, he didn't slow his pace. A jump brought him to a downed tree, coated in ice. The scene unfolding before him came straight out of a horrific nightmare.

Luciana down in the snow, blood leaking from a wound he could not see, but definitely smelled. Above her, shifting with ferocious speed, a foreign wolf and his eyes glowed with hell and the promise of pain. The wolf lunged at Rayne's mate, and Rayne pushed away from the icy log, trusting gravity and his own speed to intercept the blow.

He hit the large wolf from the side and knocked him into

a tree. A sweep of his gaze over Luciana didn't reveal any more about her injuries. Trusting her to survive, Rayne turned back to the other wolf, Rodrigo presumably. Not that he gave a rat's ass what the wolf's name was when he was about to be a carcass. The bastard had inflicted harm on Luciana, and seemed intent on doing more damage.

Not a chance in hell. Baring his teeth, he didn't waste time on a growl of warning as he streaked towards the other. The brute force collision knocked the breath from his body, but he didn't slow his assault. Teeth, claws, and muscles worked together to find purchase on the other in order to rend apart the enemy.

A bite sank into his shoulder, the pain a fresh hot bloom in the chill. A claw tore down his leg, and blood spattered against the snow. Rayne ignored the injuries, tearing a vicious strip of skin and fur from the other wolf's head. He savaged the ear and sank his teeth into the ruff around the wolf's neck.

It scrambled against him, and tried to throw him off. They tumbled, and hit the edge of crevice. Their combined weight dislodged the snow, and then the ground beneath them seemed to slide away as they fell over the edge. The other wolf took the brunt of their impact, and Rayne took advantage of the situation, sinking claws and teeth into the other wolf's back.

With a roar, Rodrigo dislodged him. Rayne struck a frozen rock. A rib cracked under the force. The bruises lit up along his left side, and his foreleg went numb. Snarling, he rose out of the snow and faced off against the other wolf. Rodrigo had a few pounds on him, but Rayne had fought bigger wolves his whole life. It wasn't the size of the wolf in the fight, but the size of the fight in the wolf.

In his case, Rayne wanted his opponent slaughtered.

Above, a low moan drifted on the breeze, a feminine sound crackling with pain.

Luciana...

His focus split, he lunged at the other wolf and Rodrigo wheeled, the snow flying as he bolted. Rayne wanted to pursue, and his wolf wanted to kill, then Luciana made another sound and he forced his attention back to his surroundings. He'd gone over an edge and he had to climb out, or circle around.

Worry skittered through him. Rodrigo had bolted, but if he circled back fast enough... No, Rayne refused to accept that as a potential outcome. He would make the climb. Ignoring the blood oozing from his side and leg, he found purchase in the icy stones, and inch-by-inch, he made his way up the wall. It might have been easier with hands, but then he'd have been more exposed to the elements. Luciana didn't have time for him to shift, and then shift again.

His paws joined the parts of his body aching and bleeding as he reached the lip of the crevice. With a hard jump and scrambling back legs he fought to get over the edge. Luciana seized him, her fingers sinking into his fur. Her counter weight and balance pulled him the rest of the way over until he was in the snow, leaning into her.

Pain contorted her features, and she held her right hand and arm at an odd angle. The harsh breaths she released steamed in the air beside him, but he straightened, running his gaze over her, then nosing at her side. The shirt had come away in strips; blood speckled her clothing and her flesh. Pressing his nose gently to the bruised and abused flesh, he ran his tongue over it.

No infection soured the scent, and he tasted nothing beyond her. A clean injury, likely one that shifting would heal. She hissed at the contact, and he leaned his head away, ears flicked toward her. To his eyes, she remained stunningly beautiful, if haunting in how tight her mouth had flattened to a thin line and how sharp the relief of her cheekbones. Battle, roaming, and a lack of food had left her honed down to her essentials and the wildness he'd been attracted to from the beginning.

A shift of her grip reminded him she'd grabbed ahold of him. Her fingers were still in his fur, and she stroked a hand upward, careful of where Rodrigo had torn into him. The bleeding had slowed, yet the stinging of the injury remained. She chased it all away, the tingling spread by her touch rolling over him.

When was the last time Luciana had actually touched him, much less maintained the contact long past when *necessary*. A sigh worked through him, he and his wolf basking in the contact of their mate.

"You're bleeding," she whispered, the low contralto stroked over him and he damn near sagged as he leaned into her grip. "How badly?"

Then she had a hand on the side of his face as though trying to get his attention. Maybe she had been, the world blurred for a moment. Focusing on her nearness and her scent, he let his jaw open in a hint of a smile before licking her nose.

The remote expression in her eyes retreated, and she grimaced. "It's too cold for that," she admonished. To his disappointment, she released him and straightened. Every step she took radiated pain. Unwilling to be parted, he padded after her. The rasp of his paws against the snow and the way the skin around his injuries pulled and threatened to reopen mattered far less than losing contact with her limping form. She climbed through the deep snow, almost wading but she didn't slow and he moved across the top of it, keeping a worried eye on her.

She claimed a backpack from the snow, then worked her

way to the trail. The snow was still deep, but only to her calves and not her thighs. Leaning against a tree, she pulled the strap of the pack over her left shoulder, then looked down at him as he pressed to her leg. The damp would soak through her pants, and a hint of blue around her lips worried him.

It was exceptionally cold. Her clothing was ripped, jacket and shirt, but she pulled them tighter against herself. His concern must have reflected in his eyes or his scent, because she pressed a hand to his head, carefully stroking his undamaged ear.

"I can walk, we need to get to the car..." Then Luciana hesitated, and her expression tightened. "Cars, I suppose. You followed me."

It wasn't a question and he wasn't keeping it a secret so he just stared at her.

"Of course you did," she said with a sigh, so much defeat echoed in the breathy sound and his chest tightened. "I was gone too long."

Way too damn long. He wouldn't apologize for his worry. Look at what he'd found when he got here.

Still toying with his good ear, his mate glanced at him from beneath her lashes. There, shining amongst the dark, was a regret and something other, both of which pierced him. It was as though her eyes spoke a different language; one he didn't have a hope of translating.

"We should go before he returns," she murmured, disbelief underscoring each word.

Head tilted, Rayne studied his mate. The advice sounded so incredibly strange coming from her. She was the first to leap into the fray and the very last to walk away. If anything, he expected to have to persuade her or at least block her from chasing down the wolf.

"Don't," she said, holding up a hand as if asking him for

patience. "I know you have questions, and you're judging me right now."

No he wasn't.

"And perhaps you have a right to some answers." Grudging as she may have admitted it, he didn't disagree with the sentiment. "I will...I will give them to you."

Good.

"But we should go...he's dangerous and now he's wounded, both physically and pridefully." She gnawed at her lower lip, the cold had left it chapped and a trickle of blood had dried at the corner. He wanted to inspect all of her injuries, not just his own.

With a nudge, he herded her to move and she took a step, then another all the while cradling her right arm.

Pain eddied in her scent.

The arm was broken.

Rage flash fired through him all over again.

Only the knowledge she was in pain and needed him— whether she could admit it or not—kept him planted at her side instead of hunting down the son of a bitch and ending him.

"I know you're mad," Luciana said, her voice so soft he almost missed it. "You are not alone in your fury."

Thankfully, he was in wolf form so his automatic response of *so* remained blunted.

"I needed these few days away," she continued, as if needing to fill in the silence as they headed in the direction of the vehicles. It was still a good hour's hike, particularly with the sluggishness of her pace and the way his chest tightened with every step. He kept reopening the wound on his leg and he couldn't take a deep breath.

Didn't matter, he could handle it.

And he wasn't sure he was in the right frame of mind to hear how she needed to be *away* from him or the pack. Since he couldn't respond verbally, he listened. Maybe, just maybe, he would find a kernel of direction.

After all, she was *finally* talking to him and God how he had missed her voice.

"I needed to figure out who I was…am…can be." Anguish discolored the words. "I don't like hating you."

Fuck. He didn't like that either.

"And I'm not even sure I can hate you."

Please say you can't.

"But I don't think I can love you anymore…"

It wasn't his broken rib, which kept him from breathing.

"I…I don't know where to go from here, but I do know we can't keep living the way we are." Silence followed the pronouncement, and attention divided between the trail behind, and the trail ahead, he couldn't really parse all her words.

She didn't want to hate him, and wasn't sure she could. That was a wonderful thing, a good starting point. Losing her love though?

Where the fuck did he go from there? Mating bound them, hearts and souls. It was as much an emotional bond as a physical one, and in some cases metaphysical. No one had ever tried to parse all the components of what made mates, at least none that he knew. Some things were simply accepted because they were. Mates found each other, either on first sight or through the development of a relationship. No one person could force another to mate. It had to be accepted on both sides.

A mate claim could be repudiated if one desired to mate another who didn't want to be mated *before* a claim could even happen. History and pack tales said it was a painful process for the repudiated party, but they could and did heal…in time.

What happened when a mate rejected the other *after* a mating?

Was that even possible?

And if she truly wanted to leave him, could he force her to stay? It was anathema to everything love and mating were about. The closer they came to the cars, the more he wished they'd stayed in the snow and the mountains. As much as he'd hated the silence, the indecision, and the loss—it was nothing compared to confronting the very real possibility Luciana intended to repudiate him and if he loved her as much as he believed he did, all he could do was let her go and keep her safe until she found her place.

Fresh pain splintered the shattered pieces of his heart.

Being Alpha *sucked.*

CHAPTER 11

*B*itterness and anger swarmed her soul like a dark, living and very hungry thing. Her physical injuries only slowed her pace as she and Rayne descended to where they'd both apparently left their vehicles. A large piece of her remained damaged, as though the wolf and the woman were fractured. Within, her wolf remained almost eerily silent. Every stumbling step she took demonstrated her gracelessness. Even her head ached, as though it had been overstuffed and insulated her from the sounds around them.

Or maybe it was the wind locking her away in a soundless tunnel. At her side, Rayne trudged along, always modifying his gait to hers and his damn leg kept trickling blood. The quiet between them was unbearable but she didn't know how to shatter it.

The throb in her right arm pulsed with every beat of her heart. Maybe it was the throb or the way Rayne bumped against her legs, or the depth of the snow, or maybe it was some combination of all of the above, but they'd barely crested the last slope descending to the parking lot, when her legs went out and she went down. A face full of snow wasn't the worst of her indignities. She tumbled, jarring her arm, shoulder and hip. The slices on her side opened again and she only halted when she hit a parking barrier at the bottom and her vision went white.

Her eyes jerked open, and her internal clock said she hadn't been out that long. Cold seeped into her, she was still in the snow, the concrete barrier next to her left shoulder, and the snow soaking through her clothes. At least the slush cooled the deep slices on her side.

"Luciana." Rayne's voice washed over her. The way he said her name—so reverent, like a prayer. Then he turned her over and she nearly blacked out again. There was bone poking through her right arm.

The sky rumbled overhead. Thunder to go with the snow. Could the day get any worse?

"I'm going to bind your arm," Rayne informed her, his tone solid, his words edged, and sharp. "Stay still."

It was all she could do. Every movement, even breathing seemed to jostle her. How the hell could a broken arm hurt so much?

Well, broken arm and wrist. Maybe a few fingers.

Her gaze dipped to where the fragmented bone stabbed through her flesh. Sickness roiled in her stomach, but she refused it. Heat flushed her face, and she was at once disconnected and too much present. The world swam in and out as her vision blurred, fraying along the edges.

A hand on her arm, murmured words, and then pain so wrenching she couldn't make a sound as her arm straightened and the bone was shoved inside. God she hoped he'd shoved it back. Her thoughts fragmented, splintering as though shards of bone themselves.

Time slowed to a lethargic crawl, so grotesquely stretched out, a minute became forever. More of them was unimaginable. Yet eternity stretched onward as pressure and pain vied for her attention and her vision blacked out only to white out, then return again. Black. White. Gray.

Black. White. Gray.

Clouds.

Rayne.

Black.

White.

Gray.

Pain suffused her blood and then the worst happened.

He lifted her from the snow.

Thankfully, blackness swallowed her before he took a step.

The next time she blinked her eyes open, she found puddles of yellow light cast by an old fixture from the hall. It was too dim for much more than a night-light. Wood crackled somewhere. Smoke.

Leather.

One by one the scents assaulted her as though lined up awaiting her notice. The last, the strongest, was Rayne.

They were home.

She knew this place.

Hall light...

Lifting her head, she squinted through fuzzy vision. Flames in a stone fireplace, it was similar to the one in the office downstairs, but this was on the other side of the house.

Dark wood furniture. A crimson colored duvet.

Their bedroom.

He'd brought her back to their bedroom.

Closing her eyes, she let her head sink back against the pillow. With more awareness came the thudding of hurt. Her arm was on fire, from the tips of her fingers to the socket where her shoulder joined. Her torso ached, as though even the exertion of breathing split apart the skin with each breath.

The longer she lay there, the worse it became.

Why the hell had she woken up to this torment?

Tears pooled across her already hazy vision. Even as one spilled over onto her cheek, the bed shifted and warmth came too close to her hell. She wanted to flinch, but she didn't dare move.

"I'm here," Rayne told her, his voice rough with sleep and fatigue. "I'm sorry love, I fell asleep." His fingers brushed against her cheek, and some of the pain diminished.

Alphas could take on some of the burden of suffering. Mates could take even more. The motion cooled the lava in her blood. Her shallow breaths deepened and her awareness swam.

Forcing herself to focus through the dizziness, she studied her mate. Tight lines marked his eyes, and his mouth was almost an angry slash, save for the hint of gentleness as one corner tipped upward. Pale, he wore his fatigue like a badge.

She hadn't been the only one injured.

"How long?" She managed to croak out the words, her throat raw and dry. Rayne didn't answer immediately as he stretched over her and by some miracle didn't rock her. Then a straw was at her lips and it took her a moment to remember how they worked. The first draw of tepid water offered bittersweet relief. The dryness went away, but the act of swallowing hurt more.

"How long?" She repeated, trying to organize her thoughts into some semblance of order.

"Less than a day." Disapproval radiated in every syllable and despite the harshness of his tone, he studied her intently. "You need to shift, but you wouldn't."

She wouldn't.

Alphas could order a shift.

Luciana closed her eyes; it was her only escape from the intensity of his hazel gaze peering into her soul.

"Drink more." He punctuated the order by pressing the straw to her lips once more.

As much as she wanted to deny him the command over her, she wanted the moisture more. She drank, though each swallow seemed more like glass shards scraping her throat than water. Enduring it, she knew her body needed the water.

"Now, shift. You're not dressed, nothing to impede you."

Not dressed.

Fantastic. She was grievously wounded, half out of her mind, and now naked in the bed she'd shared with her mate.

A bed she'd left the same day he'd challenged her.

"No," she told him. Exhaustion ringed her, but for the dull throb of pain everywhere, she'd have already capitulated back to sleep.

"Luciana..." Impatience colored his tone. Impatience and something more. Something she didn't want to examine too closely.

"No," she repeated. Then because he would likely assume she acted only in defiance of him—a not unfair assumption all things being equal—she continued, "The bone is completely snapped in two. The shift will not repair it...it could make it worse."

She'd seen a wolf injured in the fields, he'd had a bone sticking out of him and in his pain and agony, he'd shifted. It was the body's natural inclination to defend itself.

After running her tongue of her chapped lips first, she sucked in another long drink. The water helped even as it hurt.

"Think of Josiah," she told him. Josiah was one of their wolves. A Lone Wolf who'd originated in Willow Bend, they thought. The wolf didn't discuss his past. He'd been a Lone

Wolf for at least two decades, not because he didn't want to be among other wolves...but because he didn't believe he deserved to be. Her tongue stiff and thick made shaping words difficult. Sweat trickled along her face.

Hopefully sweat. If she had another injury she really didn't want to know about it.

"What about Josiah?" Fierce concentration reflected along with the firelight in Rayne's eyes as he stared down at her. It was hard to even look at him from this angle; she had to relax her neck. It kept pulling on her shoulder, which pulled on her arm...and right now she truly didn't want to pull on her arm. Flashes of pain struck like lightning, hot, fast, and sharp.

The sheets rustled, and the bed dipped gently, but not enough to disturb the support beneath her wounded body. Rayne circled the bed, and dropped to the floor in front of her. He could lock gazes with her and she didn't have to move her head.

"You look like hell," she whispered, the words slipping out before she could draw them back in. Of course, he looked like hell. He'd fought Rodrigo, been injured, had to drag her back to Three Rivers, and bore some of the burden of her pain. The taut lines of his expression were harsh, a fierce relief only emphasizing his strength. He'd never looked more alpha than he did in this moment.

The realization flowered with a bitter burst in her chest.

"What about Josiah?" Rayne asked again, seemingly ignoring her comment. And why shouldn't he?

"Josiah lost an arm through some accident, yes?" The wolf had never confirmed the *how* of it. "He left his pack, he wandered, he took odd jobs, and he kept himself isolated."

"Until you talked to him," Rayne reminded her, tracing a pattern against her hip with light fingers. "I remember, I didn't even half-realize he was a wolf, but you recognized him right away."

A flare of her pride roused from the ashes where it had lain in utter defeat. "Because he compartmentalizes everything. He was so very repressed, so very...it matters not what I saw, but I've known wolves like him. Wolves who are so very damaged by a physical injury we cannot simply heal from. It takes a truly traumatic injury to put us in that way. Difficult, yet not impossible."

Her throat went dry again on the last words. Difficult, absolutely. But her arm was a wreck. And if she could not shift to save it, she may not be able to save it at all. The cold reality sank into her damaged bones. Her eyes must have closed again because Rayne pressing the straw to her lips startled her.

"Drink," he commanded, but the order rolled off her like water striking rocks. It splashed, scattering the demand for obedience. Her wolf didn't disregard the command, her wolf wasn't even conscious. She accepted the offer not because he wanted her to, but because she needed it.

Then his hand brushed against her stinging cheeks, and it was too warm. She tried to move away from the caress, but it only jarred her arm, sending a new current of pain to throb against her already wrecked nerves.

"You're running a fever," he said, more to himself than to her. He wasn't even looking in her eyes. Instead, he scowled. "We can attempt a shift, if I can align the bone..." His scowl deepened. "Fuck, we don't even have a damn clinic."

Luciana let her eyes close again. It took too much energy to keep them open. If he could hold off her pain or help her bear it, maybe she could sleep for a while. In sleeping, she could avoid the very real truth her vicious injury would result in.

"I will find something—someone. Stay here," he added in

a hurried whisper, then brushed a kiss to her forehead. The motion, so natural and organic, sent a rivet through her. Yet, he was gone before she could react. When her eyes opened again, she was alone with the flickering shadows cast by the firelight. Relief threaded through the discomfort tugging at every nerve ending. Yet on the heels of that relief came...

She pulled her mind away from the maudlin thoughts. Her arm was a damn mess. As careful as she could manage, she adjusted her position to try and look at it. The limb lay awkwardly against her side, swollen, and swathed in bandages. Dark splotches stained the pale color, which went with the sharp coppery tang in the air.

As if summoned by the thought, she sorted through the scents in the room. Hints of Rayne overlaid her own. The blood she scented was definitely hers. If his injuries lingered in anyway, she couldn't detect them by scent. An odd tug in her middle reminded her it was a good thing. He'd been able to shift, from wolf to human—of course he had. If he hadn't, she would likely still be face down in the snow. So his injuries were either superficial or at least not so grave that a shift couldn't fix them.

Excellent.

A second pulse radiated from her mangled arm to her shoulder, then down again. Even in the half-light cast by the fire and the hall lamp, she couldn't mistake the mangled mess of her arm for anything else.

Open wounds could lead to infections.

Distorted bones could be crippling.

For one, long agonizing second, she tried to imagine losing the arm and her heart sunk. What had she said to Josiah? *You have more than just one arm, you have two strong legs, sharp eyes, a fierce mind, and a determined will. You are more than the sum of your loss, Josiah. Will you not run with us a while and share your bounty?*

She'd meant every word. Still did. Josiah had proven invaluable to the pack. He'd been one of the first to truly settle into the town, and he'd been kind to even their most disparate members...maybe someone who was always on the fringe, because they chose to be there, recognized when others drifted that way.

If she meant all of that, then losing an arm shouldn't diminish her in any way.

Some deep-seated primal part of her snorted. An alpha should be calm and controlled. They should soothe the turmoil and pain, forcing steadiness even when everything else raged.

She'd done that for Josiah.

Somehow, the idea of doing it for herself seemed anathema.

Sweat trickled from her hairline. Her stomach rolled, and the shadows above went wavy. Closing her eyes, she swallowed against the rawness of her throat. Had Rayne only been gone minutes or was it hours? The interminable drag sucked her down. She blinked, but her eyes didn't shift. Her night vision, as much a part of her as her wolf, didn't react.

Was she already fighting an infection?

No, Luciana couldn't concentrate on that. Her specialty wasn't healing. She barely knew any of the healers at home... Thoughts stuttering on the single word, she squeezed her eyes shut lest more than sweat slid down her cheeks. Her heart squeezed so viciously she couldn't suck in a deeper breath. Had Rodrigo cracked her ribs as well?

Lying here and feeling sorry for herself wouldn't accomplish anything. Her parched throat and dry mouth needed water and the rest of her needed a bathroom.

One breath.

Two breaths.

She sat up. Her vision damn near whited out for a moment.

One breath.

Two breaths.

Three breaths.

She swung her legs over the edge of the bed and turned. The spots in her vision danced, and the room wavered.

She gave it six breaths before she even attempted to stand. The world swayed as she made it to her feet. It took every ounce of discipline she possessed to not flatten her hand against the bed to help her stand. Her arm hung like a deadweight, like a deadweight soaked in kerosene and lit on fire. Swaying to the flow of the room, she maintained her stance until the floor quit buckling. Now she only had ten or twelve steps to go. Locking her jaw, she put one foot in front of the other, the water already forgotten on the side table.

Pee first.

Add more water later.

By the time she reached the bathroom, she wanted to simply curl up and take another nap. Sweat poured down her skin. It wasn't until she caught sight of herself in the mirror that her nakedness hit her. She could see every purpling bruise mottling her flesh, the ribboned claw marks on her torso, extending to her flank. The horror show of her arm, and not even the bandaging could disguise the awkward way it hung. There was more than one broken bone in there.

Leaning heavily against the door, she threw up. It was nothing but the water she'd drunk and some bile. The act tore at her already abused throat. Looking away from the mirror, she stumbled the last awful steps to the toilet. One good thing about her nudity—she didn't have to fight with her pants or how to remove them.

The moment she sat on the toilet, she sagged. Her whole being seemed centered in concrete and it was all dragging her down. She was still sitting there a minute—ten minutes, who knew?—later when a haggard Rayne let out a harsh breath in the doorway.

"Fuck, Luciana. What are you doing?"

She squinted at him. "Peeing...I think." Was she? Had she? God, it was all so humiliating.

"Stubborn, stubborn woman." Well it was better than stupid. He pushed away from the doorframe and crossed to her. Then to her utter shame, he took a moment to clean her up before lifting her off the seat and flushing the toilet.

"You used to like that about me," she replied. It was one the qualities he'd said he admired. The first time he'd complained about her stubborn refusal to listen to him, he'd done it with all teeth and smiles. Then he'd acquiesced to her demand of a picnic.

It was the same day they'd kissed for the first time.

"I still love that about you," he murmured as he carried her back to the bed. She returned far faster than she'd made her earlier journey.

"Liar," she groaned as he set her down. "Not much about me you could love anymore." Everything just hurt. Hell, her damn toenails hurt. Maybe they should just cut her arm off and get it over with.

"Shh, chère. I love so much about you." The admonishment in his tone stung, but of course he'd say it. He was Alpha. He had to care about everyone. Wasn't that what he'd told her over and over again? Personality conflicts had to be weighed against the needs of even the least of them. Salvatore... damn her heart hurt again... Salvatore always expressed his affection for them all. No one in Seven Hills doubted their alpha loved them.

Well none save the one who'd cast it off and been repudiated for her choices and her pride.

Eyes burning, she turned her face away from Rayne and

ignored the hell her act pulled on her arm. "Maybe I'll die and this will be better for all of us..." The words slipped out, and a part of her acknowledged their lack of truth. Death helped no one.

She didn't want to die.

She just didn't want to hurt anymore, herself or anyone else.

"Luciana," Rayne's voice tightened, and the command in his tone wrapped around her like iron arms, holding her rigid. "Sleep."

One, small, fractious part of her objected to the order, but it was helpless against the rest of her. She obeyed.

Darkness descended on her like bliss.

CHAPTER 12

*R*ayne released a harsh exhale when Luciana capitulated to his order. Relief flickered to life for a half-second before reality crashed in on he and his wolf. The woman hadn't obeyed a single order from him—*ever*. Her dominance in so many ways seemed a league above his own, and the only time she'd ever given in to his demands had been during sex and likely only because she'd wanted the same.

Settling her in the bed, he forced himself to rise. His wolf, barely leashed, snapped within him. A knock at the door warned him a split second before Dani let herself in, bearing a tray. The scents of fresh burgers, soups, fries, and more eddied ahead of her. A step behind her, Mark held at the door. Dani wasn't dominant enough to be remotely a threat to Rayne or his mate, but Mark had already made his feelings on Luciana cleared. No fucking way would Rayne allow he or any of their Hunters into the room.

Fuck, they needed a different name. The random thought drifted out of nowhere. *Another problem for another day.*

"You need to eat," Dani said, hustling the food over to the

table near the fireplace. "I've brought some hearty soup for her, more of a heavy broth, and this was all made by Louis and carried over here by me. No one else has touched it."

His pack shouldn't need to tell him they weren't planning on poisoning him or his mate. Really, they shouldn't. But since Luciana's collapse, he'd been in two modes. Get back to Three Rivers, and keep her safe.

The fact so many of his wolves seemed to want her gone hadn't been something he could ignore. Especially while she was vulnerable.

"Mark's here to report as well," Dani told him, her voice pitched low and when she did glance to where Luciana slept, the younger wolf's expression softened. "I can stay with her if you want to go and talk to him."

It was a two-fold offer, protection for his mate and a way to keep the other male from entering the room. Trapped at the crossroads of no way in hell and get the fuck out of here, Rayne didn't answer immediately. Dani meant no harm. Earnestness rolled off her in waves. She wanted to help, it was a breath of fresh spring air against the cold, frigid terror icing around his heart. Flicking a glance from her to Luciana, Rayne almost told her fine. He didn't want Mark in here at all.

The wolf was decent enough but he'd been one of the more vocal in opposition to Luce staying. *Fuck. You have to get better or I will call you Luce again just to piss you off.*

A dull ache flared behind his eyes. His wolf snapped and snarled within him. "No, it's fine, Dani. I'll talk to Mark at the door. You go back to the diner and tell the gossips she's going to be fine." And maybe he reinforced the words with a deeper layer of command. Maybe he needed her to make it clear he would brook no challenges where it concerned his mate.

Dipping her chin, Dani's shoulders curved against the

force of his order. "I will protect her with my words and my actions." Then she was gone, all but fleeing the room.

Dammit, he'd been too heavy handed. He would apologize to her later. She slipped out of the room and was already down the stairs when he reached the door. Mark stood across the hall, leaning against the wall with his hands in his pockets. The other wolf also kept his gaze lowered, and his shoulders relaxed without an ounce of challenge in his manner.

"We got her car back, but the other vehicle was gone by the time we arrived," he said without preamble. "I know some people at the DMV in Colorado who can run the plates, but it's a rental, so I doubt we'll get much." Mark waited a beat for Rayne to nod, then continued, "Town's locked up tight. Jackson has everyone traveling in groups. Loners call for escort and two go to get them. It's making it a little sticky, but we can handle it. Secondary search teams haven't turned up a foreign wolf…but…" The other wolf held up his hands in a placating gesture. "Jackson and I went out to the rundown house, we found the guy's scent, so we have it and we're not going to let him anywhere near here."

"Good." It was on the tip of his tongue to say thank you, manners drummed into him since birth. Yet, the words died on his tongue. He couldn't forget what Mark had said and right now, he was simply not in the mood. "Keep everyone buttoned tight. You and Jackson split up with the others, go out there in pairs and groups. I want everyone to know that scent."

"You got it." Mark tapped a fist to his own chest twice. "I'll keep her in my prayers."

It wasn't much but it was something. Again, Rayne nodded, then closed the door to allow himself some privacy with his mate. Weariness swarmed over him and he looked over to where she slept uneasily. Lines crinkled the space between her eyes and her lips were pulled away from her teeth. Labored breathing punched the air, worse, the scent of illness and infection grew.

He couldn't take her to a hospital. Willow Bend was the closest pack with a healer...

His phone rang and it took every ounce of his fading control not to growl. Claiming the cell phone before it could ring a second time and possibly wake Luciana, he answered, "Barrows."

"Julian," the Chief Enforcer said by way of introduction. "Hudson River's journeyman healer and her escort landed in Willow Bend an hour ago. They will take a smaller flight to your regional airport, and be in Three Rivers tomorrow morning as long as that's still agreeable."

A distant part of his mind admired the politic way of turning the information over to the Enforcers to share rather than have Dalton call him directly—again. Still, the roaring need to have the healer present immediately drowned out the faint whisper. "Is it possible to have them come ahead or would they be forgoing some diplomatic moment in Willow Bend?" Thank fuck his voice remained even, especially with his gaze locked on his mate.

Julian didn't answer immediately, a measured silence. "What happened?"

Did he tell them? Reveal a weakness? Particularly of the one wolf they all seemed to uniformly dislike? Her arm was so mangled and swollen looking, the scent continued to discolor. If he wanted to save her arm, he had no choice but to gamble the information. Whatever weakness it revealed, he'd deal with it later. "Luciana was injured, and it's a bad break, bone puncturing skin, in her arm."

"Stay on the line," Julian said, the command lacking any sharp bite other than urgency. Quiet permeated the line, the Enforcer had to have put him on hold. Rayne paced over to the food on the table and opened one of the silver lids. Four hamburgers awaited him, each piled with double patties. His stomach lurched, but he needed to eat. His body required fuel and he sure as shit wouldn't be sleeping. Biting into one, he chewed it without tasting and waited.

"Barrows, they're turning the car back to the airport. Dylan Royce is flying them, and he'll make sure they have a vehicle escort right to Three Rivers. He needs free passage to get them in, and then he'll return. Do you need anything else?"

"A lot of fucking prayers wouldn't hurt," he told him, and then blowing out a breath he said, "Thank you."

"Of course." But Julian didn't disconnect the call. The even pacing of his breathing remained audible. "Rayne," he said after the protracted silence. "Do you need the Enforcers for anything?"

The underlying sentiment echoed in every careful syllable. Had this been the result of an assassination attempt? Enforcers could not and would not interfere with internal pack matters, even as a tacit seventh pack and even more newly formed than Three Rivers (though arguable considering how long Julian had led the Enforcers). They did, however, offer protection between the packs, and did hunt rogues.

Not in any mood to play politics or pretty it up, Rayne went with the truth. "Uncertain. It was definitely an assault and definitely by a non-Three Rivers wolf. It happened in Colorado. Male wolf, shifted, and by the name of Rodrigo. That's all I have at the moment, we're sweeping our territory, but if you find him, I want him."

"Done." As simple as that and one of the fists clawing at Rayne's heart eased a fraction. That simple, a sign of faith and trust in a place where none had existed before. "I'll make sure Dylan and Luc are aware of the potential danger."

"I'm sending Jackson and two of my Hunters to wait there, too. I won't see a healer in any danger." Not that he expected the wolf to even know a healer was coming, but then he wouldn't have expected the attack on Luciana to come from an unknown...

Unknown.

Rodrigo.

"I'll have them notify you when the healer is here. I need to go." Then he ended the call with the Chief Enforcer, and stared at his mate for a long moment. Rodrigo sounded Italian. He'd met a number of wolves while in Seven Hills, a wide variety, but most of them hadn't really stuck with Rayne beyond his first sighting of Luciana. The devilish twinkle in her eyes and the teasing little smirk of hers captivated him from the beginning.

He could call Salvatore, but he doubted the wolf would take his call. Not after he'd repudiated Luciana. The siblings hadn't spoken since that terrible night. Of everything that came from the founding of Three Rivers *that* one item was the one he regretted the most.

After consuming the rest of the burgers, he paced over to Luciana's side and took a damp, cool cloth to wipe her forehead. Discomfort radiated off of her, but she remained asleep —or unconscious. The second most likely no matter how much he hated the idea. He paced away from her and sent a message to Jackson with the updated orders. Nothing could happen to the healer.

Done, he paced the room again and stared at his phone. Impotent rage swelled within him. He located the number they had for Salvatore in his contacts and hit connect. The call routed straight to voice mail. Unsurprising, he'd likely declined the call or blocked them all together. He waited until Salvatore's voice instructed him to leave a message and the distinctive beep and the words *Luciana was assaulted. She is alive, but injured severely. A healer is on the way, but she has gone without for hours. I need your help* died unspoken. Instead, he simply said, "Rayne Barrows, Three Rivers, Signore Esposito. I am calling to inquire about a wolf of yours named Rodrigo. If you or one of your Centurions would return my call, I would be obliged." Then he hung up.

Luciana flinched when he said her brother's name and Rayne clenched his free hand into a fist. Politics sucked, but he needed answers and his pride would have to suck it up. His entire body stung as if he'd been raked across broken glass inside and out.

With nothing left to do, he waited for the healer and watched over his mate.

Inside, his wolf hunkered down into silence. They needed her well and safe, and then they had a wolf to kill.

*H*ours dragged by interminably. Rayne ate, but only because it was necessary if he wouldn't sleep. Bruises littered his side, and there were still gouges in his shoulder. Movement aggravated them, but he slapped a bandage over it and ignored it for the time being. Though she had slept for hours, uneasily and sweating, Luciana's groan pulled him to her side.

Her skin was hot to the touch, and dry. The earlier sweat had all but evaporated, and her lips were chapped, and cracking. With a straw, he gathered some water out of the cup, then trickled it over her lips. A drop or two of moisture slipped along the line of luscious mouth, but it wasn't until he dribbled a little more that her lips parted.

"That's it," he told her, keeping his voice as calm as he could make it. Wolves were tough. They healed quickly, and often easily. Wolves had stronger constitutions; common ailments were unheard of... but not complications from

143

injury. Not infection. But they usually didn't suffer from such egregious injuries for very long so they weren't a common issue. Healers made all the difference. Healers could treat the wolf and the person as needed, but healers were rare, and Three Rivers had none.

If they were in Seven Hills still, she'd have a healer already or if they were back in Delta Crescent or any other pack...

Then she wouldn't likely have the injury in the first place. Nor would she be the woman and wolf he'd known her to be.

His phone buzzed on the table, and he paused in feeding her little bits of moisture when she finally swallowed a little. Jackson. He hit answer while he dribbled more water. She was so hot, it was like he sat in front of the fire. The heat radiated off her.

"Talk to me," was all he said.

"I have Hudson River's healer and Second in the car," Jackson replied, his tone flat and utterly devoid of emotion. Even his accent seemed to bottom out, erasing the slow, familiar drawl.

Second.

"Luc Danes is in the car?" Hudson River's Second had traveled with the healer. It could be interpreted a couple of different ways. Either Brett truly didn't trust them or he truly valued the healer. Healers by their nature were valuable, and only a mad wolf would attack one. There was something about this healer, something he should be remembering. But...

He shook his head. It didn't matter. The landing strip was forty-five minutes away. "Bid him welcome and haul ass back here. If they're hungry, call Dani and roust Louis to get a meal made." He'd have to check on the coffee in the house, but that could also wait.

"We're on our way..." Jackson assured him, though the

tempo of his speech didn't change. His brother guarded every word. "How is she doing?"

"Be fast," was all he could tell him. Then he disconnected the call. "Come on sweetheart, just drink a little for me." He dribbled more water between her cracked lips. Everything in him leaned in her direction, even his wolf. The sour undercurrent to her scent tickled his nose. Placing two fingers over the pulse in her throat, he frowned. Her heart raced, her skin flushed a deep red as well as being burning to the touch, and now the scent.

She had to have an infection.

"Stay here," he ordered her, and shoved away from the bed. He was halfway down the stairs when Misty's scent rolled out of the kitchen followed swiftly by the woman herself.

"I put coffee on, and I've got another stew cooking, I thought I'd put together casseroles and heavy meals for company..." She trailed off, her worried eyes searching him briefly before she lowered them.

"I need ice," he told her. "And thank you for what you're doing." He strained for any noise to follow him down the stairs. "Jackson is on his way with our guests." His nose told them there were wolves at his door, literally.

Hunters.

Both of them. Mark had to have left them on guard.

They should be out looking for Rodrigo—or at least getting his scent in case the bastard dared to wander into town. He half-paced to the door, then away again before he followed Misty into the kitchen. She was filling a pail with ice.

"Is this enough?"

He had no idea, when was the last time he had treated anyone with a fever? A part of him wanted to call Amy, the *Traiteur* for Delta Crescent. The healer knew many local remedies and more. But Hudson River had sent their healer —journeyman healer—but what if she wasn't enough?

Taking the pail, he nodded to Misty. "Finish up and go, yeah?" He didn't want anyone else in the house it was about to be grueling with a dominant Second invading and he would most likely not want to be separated from the healer, which meant allowing him near Luciana.

None of these boded well for the fraying ends of his control.

She hemmed a little, ducking her head and sidestepping toward the stove where something meaty simmered. "I thought it would be easier if I could help out while the healer is here..."

"Finish and go, Misty." The order allowed no wiggle room. "They will be here shortly, I would prefer you were elsewhere." Raising his voice, he said, "Dominic, I want you and Trey to escort Misty then stick together."

The wolf in question answered, "We will."

He'd already spent longer downstairs than he wanted. It aggravated him to turn his back on a wolf, even one of his own, in his current frame of mind. So instead of striding up the stairs and back to his mate where he wanted to be, he stared at Misty as she hesitated. The torn look on her face didn't go with the edge of frustration peppering her scent. The wolf was a caretaker, small wonder she ever went Lone Wolf, but sometimes wolves did that. Sometimes they just wandered for a while before they went home.

The sharp spice of discontent wavered as Misty rushed her actions. Some small part of him acknowledged his behavior was not that of a kind Alpha or even a particularly warm and protective one. No wolf of the pack should ever be treated in a way that they weren't welcome. His wolf snorted in derision. They weren't welcoming anyone near their mate at the moment, not while she was gravely wounded.

Instead of being with her right that moment, he had to chase off—admittedly a very well meaning and kind—wolf who had invited herself inside. She shouldn't have even made it through the doors. His wolves *meant* well. But...no. Just no.

His wolf glared out of his eyes as they tracked every movement Misty made. Finally she placed a lid over the pot and rested it on a burner she hadn't been using. "It will keep for hours," she promised in a stammer. "I'll go...and..." Then she was at the door and out.

Rayne waited another beat. Dominic ushered Misty toward Trey, and they lead her from the house. Outside, no other wolves lingered close. Not where he could hear them or smell them.

It was just he and Luciana.

The solitude soothed his wolf; they needed the edge off before the healer arrived. His wolf didn't seem to care. The healer would be there to help Luciana, not harm her. The Second? A necessary evil. Jackson would stay most likely.

The latter idea scraped along his sides like his fur being rubbed backwards. Back in their bedroom, he used the ice to pack the armpit of her uninjured arm, then around her joints. The sour odor of infection had only strengthened in his absence, or maybe his nose had grown more sensitive to it from the break.

A glance at the clock—even if they drove at reckless, crazy speeds, they were still at least ten minutes away. Rayne went for the straw and water again. He wanted to moisten her lips, do anything to try and make this easier for her. But the most impossible aspect of the situation—he didn't dare reach for her wolf. He'd wanted to earlier, call her wolf out, make her shift.

Though she'd been able to refuse, she explained why. He understood the reality of the threat. In her current state, her wolf would likely obey him, but what the hell good was it to be a wolf if the shift would do more damage than it healed? He'd never seen anything like this. Never wanted to see such horrendous injuries on anyone especially not his mate.

With a careful hand, he brushed the hair away from her face. It was tangled, and matted from being heavy with sweat and blood. Carefully, he explored her scalp for any cuts or lacerations. The claw marks scoring her chest were still raw and oozing. The bruises mottling the golden brown of her skin looked like stains.

She wasn't healing. At all.

Or if she was, it was far too slow.

If it were a matter of energy, she should be able to lean on him, but he sensed no pull on him at all. Not even a trickle. As Alpha, he could choose to redirect the energy but that wasn't their bond. She'd never been his alpha and he wasn't hers. A mate was entirely different. But their bond was fractured, fraying, and splintering where it linked them together. Even as he searched along it, all he felt was profound emptiness. Was their bond empty? Or had she fled?

His wolf scrabbled against him, and he pressed his face close to her hair. Breathing in her scent, he listened to the steady thump of her heart. They pushed their strength along the delicate strands of their bond, careful to not overwhelm it. Trickle by trickle, he bled it into her as if he were opening an actual vein to share his life's blood.

The thump of her pulse grew steadier, and the scent of fur tickled his nostrils and his wolf damn near sagged in relief. Beneath the sour taste of the injury, the copper of the blood, and the pain pounded into her skin lay the fur with its kiss of sunshine and hints of the vineyards where she used to roam.

He poured more strength into the bond, determined to give her everything she needed even if he could only do it an inch at a time. The drain wearied him, but he could handle it.

The loss negligible only... the sharp bite of vitality hit him in a wordless pulse. A second pulse joined it. Then a third. And another. Then yet another. The pulses came like beats of his heart. Small, almost as negligible as the trickle he fed to his mate but from more than a dozen sources, and more beyond.

Shock rippled through him. The pulses steadied, replenishing his reserves each time he shared with Luciana. It was the pack. They were sharing with him. The limited network of spider webbed connections tying them together had never quite been strong enough for this and yet, they were there.

Helping him save his mate.

His wolf stretched, head raised. It was what a pack did and perhaps for the first time since they'd settled in Nebraska, Rayne felt Three Rivers come together as a pack. It was a heady experience.

"Rayne," Jackson called from downstairs and his heart fisted. "We're coming up."

The healer was here.

CHAPTER 13

Colby Dalton

*T*he ride from the airport to the small town occupied by Three Rivers could have been nail bitingly tense except for Luc. Sandwiched next to her in the backseat of the SUV, he kept up a running commentary on the various types of snack foods they'd found in one of the old vending machines in Willow Bend.

"Twinkies. It had Twinkies," he marveled aloud. "Now while I think those snack cakes will outlast the human race, I can't think of the last time I saw a vending machine selling them—or Moon Pies for that matter. Didn't think they made those anymore." He held up the one he'd purchased as though he intended for her to inspect it.

The aggravated notes rolling off the two wolves in the front seat made her nose itch and she had to fight a sneeze. Luc was definitely not helping matters. "When was the last time you even ate out of a vending machine?" She pitched her voice low. Even if the wolves up front could hear her if she whispered, polite wolves understood it wasn't meant for them.

Also, if she didn't at least acknowledge Luc's comments, he would never hush. He really was like a wolf with a bone. "You might have a point...did they have them at your hospital?"

"Hmm-hmm. And the school, and most places where people are in a hurry." If she could do one thing right now, it would be to defuse the tension swelling within the car. Jackson Barrows was the Alpha's brother and tacit Second for Three Rivers. He and Luc hadn't clashed precisely, but she also hadn't fully understood all the nuances of their interaction. Neither back off, and neither looked away. When it looked like they might be stuck there in that stare off forever, she cut across their eye line to greet the second wolf standing just to the right and a step behind Jackson.

The mounting aggression perfuming the air bottomed out as she extended her hand and introduced herself. She probably should have done the introduction to Jackson first, considering his rank, but he didn't appear to have time for it. Puncturing that balloon before it went any further seemed a good idea.

Besides, as Gillian told her frequently, the best part of being a healer—*"You can get away with just about anything. It's not about rank, it's about healing."* She would know, she was a hundred percent submissive wolf and she had her mate tied right around her little finger. Brett let Colby get away with a lot, but her mate tended to be far more overprotective and she couldn't blame him considering the history of the pack before she arrived. So planning this trip had been a huge ask, but a necessary one. Since he relented, she'd agreed to listen to Luc on all matters regarding security.

The little stare off didn't qualify, so she justified the choice. Mark seemed relieved at her action and he shook her hand gently. Luc and Jackson both withdrew a step at the same time, as if they'd been shocked by static electricity. The pop was damn near audible.

Luc frowned at her, but she rolled her eyes. No, she was not here for a testosterone match or wolf pissing contest. She came here to complete a portion of her journeyman training, and she was *needed*.

Putting a hand on Luc's to hopefully get him to hush about vending machines and Twinkies—she really had to tell Brett about that later. Maybe they could fill his house with Twinkies. Oh, that was an idea. Brett would do it. It would be hilarious. Mood buoyed above the tension, she focused on the wolves up front. "How much farther?"

"About ten minutes," Mark said over his shoulder. "Rayne wants us to come straight to his house..."

"That's fine, I was just going to say we should go there first." If his mate was as injured as Julian suggested—injured enough to require a healer—Colby just wished they could go faster. Wolves were hardy beasts, but even Luc had required surgery after a vicious accident broke several bones in his body. It was how she'd met him. Though she wanted to ask about the extent of the injuries, she'd avoided it.

Unless they were medical professionals or personally involved, they would likely label it as bad, very bad, or the worst—but that wasn't a barometer for her to judge their injuries. Her phone buzzed as she leaned back, and she pulled it out of her pocket.

Checking in. The corners of her lips curved. Brett had been sending these periodically even when she updated him regularly and she knew for a fact Luc was.

Luc bumped her shoulder, and she grinned at him. He hadn't been thrilled about her desire to do this trip either, but he'd volunteered to be the one to go with her when Brett said traveling without at the very least one guard was unacceptable. All Healers had an escort, period end of story. Owen and Gillian supported him in this assertion so at least it wasn't just his overwhelming desire to keep her completely encased in cotton. The man was sexy, adorable, fierce, and wildly protective, but every once and a while he ventured into the overbearing category.

Still in car. Almost to 3 Rivers. Will be focused when I get there. So may be slow to answer.

No sooner had she hit send than Luc's phone buzzed, and she had to bite back a laugh. With a quiet, almost wordless groan, Luc pulled his phone out and read the screen then gave her a dry look before he turned it so she could see it.

Update me regularly. Don't let her kill herself.

Sinking her teeth into her lip, she fought back a giggle then texted her mate.

Stop growling at Luc. Think about all the reunion sex we'll have when I get home instead. You'll feel better.

Luc didn't bother to hide his guffaw, and it earned her an interested look from Mark, but he didn't ask. Brett didn't answer until the town was in sight.

Woman...that was mean.

She grinned and typed in quickly. *But you love it.*

No. I love you.

Love you more, was her last message before she tucked the phone away. All of a sudden the tension in the car shifted, and it was not aggression but fear—and pain. She still hadn't totally mastered deciphering scents. Her wolf got it, but it still took Colby a moment. The base notes rolling off the pair in front made her lean all the way back in the seat. It physically hurt.

When Luc wrapped an arm around her, she wanted to growl because she was supposed to be able to handle things like this. Grief, pain, and worry were deeply familiar territory. She'd worked in a hospital; she'd seen all types. But this just made her wolf scrabble backward, uncertain of whether they should try to fix it, attack it, or flee it.

Tugging her right against him, Luc dipped his head to her ear. The effect was two fold, he spoke in the lowest of whispers and at the same time his scent surrounded her, grounding her—he was part of home, Hudson River, and Brett.

"Something's happening, just ease back and if you get into trouble I'm right here."

It settled the squirming panic, and she nodded.

"Trust me, sweetheart. You got this." If only she possessed half of his confidence.

Then she squared her own shoulders but she didn't pull away. Wolves were tactile and while she'd never thought of herself as cuddly, she didn't mind Luc for company particularly when Brett wasn't there. Luc had been the one to bring her to Hudson River—well she brought him but that was semantics—and he'd introduced her to Brett. He even worked on training her, particularly in the areas of self-defense. Healers weren't supposed to fight, hence why they always traveled with a guard of some kind. But not supposed to and always safe were two different things and Hudson River had already lost one healer to a mad wolf. Brett and Luc were determined that it would never happen again.

"We're here," Jackson announced as he pulled to a stop immediately in front of an older, but well tended house with what looked like a lovely gabled roof and that was about the extent of her knowledge where architecture went. Luc had his side of the car open and gave her a hand as she slid out. The tumultuous feeling from the car had magnified and it practically buzzed against her skin.

What the hell was that?

Not slowing, Jackson was around the car and jogged up the steps to the door. Luc had a hand on her elbow, but he let her set the pace. The hum had her gritting her teeth, and she shot a sideways look at Luc. "What is that?"

"What is what?" He frowned, but didn't slow. Jackson was waiting by the stairs, and he nodded to them. "Upstairs, second door on the right. *Knock*. He knows you're coming."

So Jackson wasn't going up? She hesitated, then glanced at Luc.

"No, I'm coming," he told her before she could even form the comment.

"If his own brother doesn't think he should be up there with his wounded mate what makes you think he'll tolerate you?" Yet, she was still learning and adapting to the idiosyncrasies of pack life, but one certainty she already understood intimately. Mates were extremely protective, and very dangerous when their mates were threatened or harmed.

"Make a decision quickly," Jackson ordered, and that wild surge of vibration seemed to pulse over her. It was like being right next to a damn power station. All the hairs on her body were standing on end. How did Luc not notice it?

"I'll stay on the landing *outside* the door. Does that work?" Luc asked her, not Jackson.

"I think so, you'll be close enough if I need you." She gave his arm a squeeze. "Get my med kit from the car, please." The medical bag had the most basic supplies in it, and all of her own tools. But she had no idea what she might need when she got up there.

The scent of blood, pain, and...sour...*infection* looped around her like some cartoon vapor dragging her inexorably forward. The smell almost helped her ignore those vibrations that thudded against her like a pulsing base. Almost.

She lifted her hand to knock, but the door opened to

reveal a haggard, and strained wolf with dark blond hair, deep hazel if red-rimmed eyes. She took one look at his bloodshot sclera, then looked past him to the figure on the bed. "I'm Colby," she said, and it took every ounce of her will to not just shove past him. The wolf in that room was desperately injured. Maybe as badly injured as Luc had to have been when he was brought to the hospital and she was no trauma surgeon. "May I please see your mate?"

Some distant part of her mind noted the arrival of Luc, but when her gaze returned to Rayne's, she didn't look away. Power eddied out and spilled toward her, and even as it did, it broke like water over a rock and streamed around her. The humming sensation had her teeth practically humming and she blinked. Her wolf in her eyes and Rayne's eyes flared gold —a split second before they returned to their hazel and the constant thrumming muted.

"Welcome to Three Rivers, Colby," he told her in a hoarse voice. "Please, help me save my mate."

He fell back a step and she pushed right through the bubble of whatever the hell that was in her race to get to the quagmire of pain and infection. Peeling back the blanket, she had to consciously force herself not to inhale through her nose. The stench of illness was hellacious bad and her stomach rolled.

"I need my bag, hot water, plenty of clean soft towels, iodine if you have it, and..." She paused surveying the arm. There was bone protruding through the flesh. She'd set bones—correction, she'd helped set bones before but... "Do you by chance have a portable x-ray machine?"

Movement behind her and the sound of feet moving on the stairs told her people had hurried to do as she asked.

"No," Rayne answered, his voice a rough rasp.

"There's one in Willow Bend...Luc, call—"

"On it," Luc's voice carried. "This is her bag." He hadn't stepped a foot into the room. Rayne moved away from her and then returned. The heavy black bag appeared in her periphery. Colby began to strip off the sheets and blankets. Sweat had collected along her at some point, but her skin was dry and hot to the touch. Someone had packed ice around her but that had melted.

"We're going to need more ice after I get these cleaned up, but what we really need to do is set that arm." A nervous quaver spread out from her belly. She was not a surgeon. That arm could very well need surgery...

Not all severe wounds need surgery," Gillian had explained to her. "You think that way because that's how you were raised..."

"...I think that way because that's how I was trained. *I'm a nurse, not a doctor."*

"No," the sweet little blonde submissive told her urgently. "You're a healer. *And we have the gift to knit bones, mend flesh, and repair damaged vessels. Call it magic if you must, but it simply is—Alphas can call their wolves to them, they can share their power and in turn be powered by them. They stand at the center of the wheel. Omegas reflect the weaknesses—they stand on the rim, their connection as taut as the Alpha, but inverted. Their power is not shared, their power is to reflect because it helps to call out the weakness in the soul, the flaw in the characters, and encourages us to be better."*

"Then what do healers call?" Because that was the point of this, wasn't it?

"We call both, the strength and the power to redirect to the flaw, and we can show the body how to repair itself, we sustain the flow of power to ensure the injury is cleansed, the bones knit, the flesh comes together again. We're neither Alpha nor Omega, but we travel along every spoke of the wheel, and never fear that you will lack strength because the Alpha will always lend you theirs, and the pack will give the Alpha theirs, and you will have it all."

Okay she could do this.

Rayne continued to hover, and the hum she'd noticed earlier surged every time he came close to her patient—his mate. Filing that away for figuring out later, she focused on the problems directly in front of her. Triage time. Assess, identify, and treat in the order of life threatening to least dangerous. She would be a limited resource.

The most dangerous was that arm.

"Julian is flying the x-ray machine directly here, he's going to land on the road outside of town," Luc called. "We need to get some lights set up to create a runway."

"Jackson," Rayne said. "Go. Take whatever resources we have and get it set up." Then he paused. "Luc?"

"Luc Danes." Luc's sober tone carried not a trace of his usual lighthearted manner. "Second to Brett Dalton, Hudson River."

Rayne nodded. "Not sure anyone actually knows how to set up the runway…"

He hesitated; she didn't have to glance over to know Luc's quandary.

"I'll be fine," she said over her shoulder. "Go and help, we *need* that machine."

"Take care of her," Luc said with utter seriousness.

"As if she were my own," Rayne answered.

Colby tuned them back out. Men.

Or more appropriately, *wolves.*

Okay, the arm first but she could clean the areas. Bag open, she glanced around the room. "Can you bring me that table and clean it off?"

Rayne was on the move before she finished speaking. More footsteps on the stairs. "It's Dani," a woman called. "We're bringing the hot water and iodine." The alpha moved to intercept their arrival and soon there were two huge stockpots filled with steaming water. Rayne brought in the iodine and set it on the table as Colby laid out the tools she'd need. They still required the towels, but she had lap pads, bandages, suture kits, and everything else. It was all in pre-sterilized packs. Wolves didn't typically suffer from long-term infections, but the smell alone had her concerned. She kept antibiotics on hand in her bag, and she loaded two syringes. The good thing about a wolf's constitution, it was typically difficult to overwhelm it.

Satisfied she had everything but the towels and the x-ray machine, she flicked her gaze over to Rayne. He was a disheveled mess, blood spattered on his skin, and his shirt had more of it.

"Strip out of that, take all of it out of here. Scrub down, especially your hands, then put on something clean and come back. I'm going to need your hands." It wasn't until she focused on pulling on her gloves that she realized he'd disappeared into the bathroom to do exactly as she'd asked. "I'm probably going to ruin these sheets."

She didn't think he'd care.

"I don't care," he answered. First she cleaned off an area with alcohol, then gave Luciana a shot. Her skin was hot through the gloves. Too hot. Once she got the first round of antibiotics in, she pulled out the forehead thermometer.

110.

Wolves ran hot. But that was too hot.

More steps. Luc was back. She recognized his scent. "I've got the towels," he called and she diverted from the bed to take them.

"As soon as Julian lands, we need that machine up here."

He met her gaze with a nod. "It will be." Then he retreated as she turned away. She added the towels to her table, and soaked one into the hot water before wringing it out some as Rayne returned.

"Gloves," she told him and nodded to the box. "Then

we're going to wash her. We need to get as much of the dirt and debris off of these wounds and everywhere else. Dab, don't rub. When a towel is soiled, discard it and go to another. I'm starting with the chest wounds. You start with her legs. We need to know if there are any other injuries anywhere."

The bandages around the arm were loose, but they were already soaked with blood and what was most likely pus. If there was continuous bleeding, they were in for more problems. *Don't borrow trouble.* Starting with the deep indentions at the top of the lacerations, she began to clean them. Pus oozed from the ragged edges and the smell intensified. The claws had likely had debris on them and it had been pounded into the wound.

She was on her fifth towel and had moved on to flushing the infection when a shout came from downstairs. Rayne swiveled, he'd cleaned her legs and identified two more lacerations, but neither smelled pus-filled so she had him treat those with iodine.

"The plane is here."

Trusting his word, she kept her focus on the first laceration. There were three and it was delicate work to encourage the body to flush out the infection, and debris while soothing the ragged skin. She didn't actually want it to heal over yet.

"Good," she murmured. "When it gets here is the hard part."

Julian's voice drifted over her, as did the awareness of Luc's statement, then both wolves were right at the door and Rayne went to get the equipment.

"Change your gloves," she told him. "We need to keep everything as not contaminated as we can."

The alpha diverted immediately and the sound of his gloves snapping off joined the sound of Luciana's ragged breathing, the little puffs and pulls of air, the stutter of her heart—every time it began to slow, the humming surge would send it back to a steadier cadence. The stutter came, then repeated, and when it happened for a third time. She planted her hand at the heart, eyes closed, and submerged to find the rhythm. The infection had put stress on it, the muscle itself had weakened, but it hadn't been damaged irrevocably—yet.

That would come if she couldn't reverse it.

Behind her came a stagger and thump, then Luc cursed. The hum had all but ceased, and Colby jerked her head up and looked at Rayne. He was down, his face gray and his eyes bruised.

The hum.

The stutter.

Crap.

"Bring him here," she ordered. Rayne had been feeding energy to Luciana. He'd literally been keeping her heart beating, but for how long? The effort had left him depleted. There was a cry from downstairs and Luc jerked his head to the side as Julian set the x-ray machine down, then gathered up the fallen alpha. He set Rayne down on the floor next to the bed.

"There's a problem out here," Luc called.

The faintest of hums rose off Rayne's skin as her hand hovered over him. He was still giving everything he had to Luciana. What the hell? She couldn't break the connection; they were mates. At the same time, the feed trickled over what she could only sense was a static-filled connection. She just lacked the words to do it justice. It didn't matter though. If she let it go at this rate it was going to bleed him dry before Luciana was strong enough to do it on her own.

Julian squatted next to Rayne and within her line of sight, but he said nothing—waiting for her next order presumably.

"Set up the portable x-ray," she murmured, she would

need it regardless but in the world of triage, this problem was far more complicated. Turning her gift within, she sought out her own mate bond. She'd only toyed with it rarely—and usually when Brett had her far more distracted by other pleasures to explore what effect it had on her fully.

There was a sensation of warmth and fur, coupled with surprise. Brett. Yes, she could feel him right there and she pressed into it. For a moment, the sensation of his arms wrapping around her ghosted over her skin. Mate bonds could share more than just emotion; there was power there too.

She'd need Brett's power for this, but she needed to stabilize both Rayne and Luciana's hearts and the flow of energy to balance the fallen pair in front of her before one of them died and the other spiraled to follow. There were no words to frame the request, but suddenly the bond seemed to open and she could feel him and raw energy crackled along her nerves, and it tasted wholly of Brett and pack. Hands settled on her shoulders and she knew it was Luc without looking.

Gathering that willingly shared energy, she twined it around each of those beneath her fingertips. There was the static-filled bond where the energy Rayne shared with his mate seemed to be bleeding off, it was like an artery had been sliced and it pumped out the power faster than he could pour it in there.

Beyond Rayne were more fractured connections, there but only partially formed and they just weren't built for this. And Colby didn't know how she knew, but she knew it. Gillian told her this was what healers were *for*, to find those places physical and not and bring them together.

She could call both.

"It's the whole pack," she tried to tell them. If she did this, it was going to be the whole pack. Even with Brett at her back, he was so far away and this was so much. A second hand gripped her arm and wall of liquid fire seemed to press against her side. It was wild, like the blaze ignited by lightning against dry wood and it tasted of snow and sun. Then another force tempered into the pool, it tasted both foreign and familiar, cool and restrained to the ferocity of the first. Beyond them was the hum of more—deep piney trees, hot sandy desert, mossy green and damp, and cool crispness of the air before it turns to snow. It roamed over her, and swirled around. She could see them all, and there was enough.

More than enough.

She would have to go deep. So many fractures to repair, so many places to piece together, and an alpha pair to keep alive.

"We've got you," Luc told her, and she trusted him. Within her was the fierce grip of her own mate. She had all of his focus. He was right there; he wouldn't let her fall.

Then she plunged into the murky, uncertain field of browned and scorched earth. It was like falling into another place altogether, but she followed the first of the fracture connections and began to fuse it as the rest of her diverted to balancing the alpha pair, syncing their hearts with hers, and distantly she acknowledged, Brett's. As she brought them into balance, another wave of energy slid below hers and equalized as she kept it going. Then she turned her attention to the first of the spiraling connections and pushed up her metaphysical sleeves.

It was just like stitches, only she had to show the connections what to do and once she got them started, the flows would do the rest.

She could do this.

She *had* to do this.

No more doubts.

No more what ifs.

No more questions.

Six different packs shared their strength with her through a complicated network of connections to sustain the pack dying around her, because if this alpha pair went, they were taking them all with them.

CHAPTER 14

$\mathcal{L}$ ight shimmered at the edge of her vision, then faded away again. Twice more it came, then slipped away like the sun dipping behind a cloud. The game of peek-a-boo irked her, but she was too tired to care. The fourth time the light intruded, a spill of water accompanied it. The splash of cool, dampness against her skin accompanied by the tickle of a drop teasing at the edge of her nose. She wanted to scratch it, but she lost her grip before she could reach for it.

The fifth time, it wasn't light waiting for her but varying shadows. Were her eyes even open? The thought itself formed, and on the heels of it came another—where was she? Then another—why did it hurt so much? She attempted to turn her head, but it was as though someone had lashed it down and she couldn't shift even the barest of her muscles. No, she remained in her fixed position staring at...what? A wall? The fireplace?

Gradually, her eyes adapted the longer she held them open. In fact, she managed to keep them open long enough for other sensations to dribble in. Her arm ached something fierce, but it was no longer on fire. Her chest was bruised, but the hot slices had cooled. She could take a deep breath.

Then, as though being aware of her breathing, scents assaulted her. The amount of data threatened to overwhelm her as she sorted them.

The bedroom at the house—the familiar hint of sandalwood beneath the cedar in the floors. The one she'd shared with Rayne.

Her blood. Someone had tried to clean it. Though they'd avoided bleach, because it was caustic to their sense of smell.

Woodsmoke.

Medicinals—alcohol? Iodine?

Rayne…Rayne's blood—and a wolf who did not belong…

She tried to sit up, but her muscles refused to obey her though she managed to turn her head. The effort sent a shock down her body similar to a time she'd touched a live wire.

The woman seated in the chair leaned forward. "Easy. Colby's sleeping and while I'll wake her if you really need her, I think it best you both rest." Dallas Dalton was the last wolf she expected to see there.

Why were the Enforcers back in Three Rivers?

She opened her mouth to ask, but all that came out was a hoarse croak that barely sounded like a voice.

"Easy," Dallas repeated, then reached for something outside of Luciana's line of sight. "This is water, just sips. We've had a hell of a time keeping your fever down."

Fever?

Wolves didn't get fevers. Memory dripped in along with the water as Dallas squeezed a few drops past Luciana's cracked and dry lips. It was heaven and hell as the moisture scraped over her raw and torn throat. Another serving and she blinked slowly before she swallowed. The sensation improved with each small mouthful.

"Let's see if you can drink this yourself." The even patience in her voice seemed to fly in the face of everything Luciana knew about the wolf. Then again, their brief meeting had defied her earlier assumptions. For now, she was helpless and the wolf next to her could have killed her before she woke. She was alive, and the wolf was being kind —so whether a temporary alliance or not, she tried to nod.

"Okay," she whispered, and though rough, it came out intelligible. "Rayne?" She managed to ask before the straw touched her lips. The draw on it shouldn't take as much effort as it did, but the flood of tepid water was like heaven against her parched mouth. She managed to swallow three mouthfuls before Dallas eased it away.

"Let's make sure that stays down, we've been trying to keep you hydrated on IV, but that doesn't help your throat." Now that she'd mentioned it, Luciana lifted her hand slowly. There was an IV in the back of her left hand.

"Rayne?" She asked again, flicking a look back to Dallas' face. The woman's expression didn't shift, nor did her scent.

"He's right over there," she motioned behind her and shifted so Luciana could see him. He was lying on his back, utterly unmoving and if she hadn't been staring she wouldn't have seen the faint rise of his chest. Concern ripped through the malaise in her muscles and she tried to sit up, but her right arm protested.

What the hell had happened to him?

Then Dallas rose, and pressed a hand down on her left shoulder. "Don't, we barely got that arm set and it's not fully mended yet."

Despite the growl rumbling in her soul, she could barely lift her head to snarl at Dallas. "Why is he unconscious? He healed...I saw his wounds close." What the hell had happened to him? Had Rodrigo made good on his threat?

Pain pounded against her arm and twisted up to her

shoulder, but she bit back the cry for the agony rippling along her flesh. The more she thought about it, the more she realized how badly it throbbed. It wasn't alone; her whole body was a ball of hurt. Not struggling against Dallas felt like a betrayal of Rayne, and she hated it.

"Let me go...then tell me what happened to him." She just wanted to see him. The imperious note in her voice probably didn't help, and based on Dallas' dry look, she was hardly impressed. Biting back her pride, she added, "Please. Tell me what happened to him."

It wasn't until she settled that Dallas reset the chair so Luciana could have an unobstructed view of Rayne's slack form. It was like staring at a caricature, still and lifeless when he should fill the room with his aggravating presence. He was supposed to be there, spoiling for a fight after chasing her down in the woods. They could argue, and she would hurl insults and what, walk away again?

Closing her eyes, Luciana curled the fingers of her left hand and tried not to think too much about her right. She needed to calm down. Her wolf barely stirred, it was as though the animal itself had been tranquilized, but the sense of her was there. The sense of fur beneath her skin. Her mate was alive. She searched for the bond, tentative and ragged, but it was there. Though she longed to lean into it, for even just a moment to test whether he would respond she restrained the impulse.

It wasn't her right anymore. Not when she remained undecided, and especially not when it might harm him.

With awareness came clarity. She'd made decisions in those woods, and they all rang hollow in light of her current circumstance. Opening her eyes, she met Dallas' almost understanding gaze.

"Okay, better." The other wolf said, before she leaned forward and clasped her hands together. "I'm going to give you the abridged version, because you and Rayne will need to hear the full version from Colby. To be clear, I will not answer every question you throw at me. Your primary focus should be on resting. We can even try food if you're up for it. You've lost a lot of blood and strength over the last two days..."

Two days?

Her pulse spiked.

"...and the healer needs some time to restore herself before she tackles the very complicated work of your arm. She's optimistic about it." Dallas continued as if she hadn't noticed Luciana's reaction. "I don't have all the details of how you sustained your injuries, suffice it to say that Colby was on her way to Three Rivers as part of her journeyman healer's training. She had just arrived in Willow Bend when your mate asked for her to come straight away. By the time she arrived, you were blistering with fever, your wounds were infected, and you had lost a tremendous amount of blood."

The other wolf's expression remained inscrutable and her tone was kind if a bit blunt.

"In summary, you were dying. Your heart was struggling under the strain, and you weren't even trying to shift. Rayne began to feed you his energy, but you were losing too much for him to sustain long-term." Why that was, she didn't elaborate. "The pack must have sensed his need or he called to them, because they were sharing with him so he could give to you."

Shock rippled through her.

Why would they...? The pack hated her.

Why would they ever?

Dallas gave her a long look, then held the water cup to her lips and set the straw in place. Luciana drank, the long swallow soothing her throat, and she blinked. They stilled hadn't gotten to the part of what happened to her mate.

"I've heard of this type of thing, usually only a small scale —familial bonds are the closest to that of the mating bond, usually it's a bond between parent and child, though sibling bonds can also be powerful. But what Rayne and the pack did was create a loop to sustain you, but they couldn't replenish what bled away from you, what you couldn't use…"

Luciana's gaze went to Rayne. "He was dying." The whole world went a little darker, as though storm clouds drifted overhead leaving the day cast in twilight.

"Yes," Dallas said carefully. "Colby got here in time, and if she hadn't acted as swiftly as she did…we would have lost all of you."

Each nugget of information settled against her like another stone being piled on until the weight easily surmounted any force she could apply against it. Rayne had pulled the entirety of the pack together. He'd done it.

And he'd nearly died for the effort—because of her.

Guilt throbbed along with the pain flashing in her arm. Tearing her gaze away from him, and away from Dallas, she looked at the heavy casement wrapping her arm. There were boards bound to either side, and held in place—a splint, but much sturdier.

Rodrigo had snapped her arm, not once but twice. He'd landed blow after blow, and she hadn't been fast enough or strong enough to take him down.

Then he shifted…

If not for Rayne, she would be dead twice over.

If not for her, Rayne wouldn't be in this miserable state.

The shuffle of a step on the wood, and she turned to find Julian had joined his mate. The noise must have been deliberate on his part.

"It's good to see you awake," he told her, and he sounded ridiculously sincere. "How is she doing?"

He glanced to his mate to answer the question rather than her.

"Far better than I would be in similar circumstances," Dallas commented without any hint of judgment, even if Luciana felt judged and found wanting. Not that she could blame her. Resentment bubbled below it all, but she swallowed it along with her pride. She had failed their child, though she had no idea that Chrystal was their daughter at the time, she'd failed the little Omega and that was her everlasting shame. Yet, here she could barely lift her head, and yet the Enforcers were looking at her... kindly?

Julian's only response was a slow nod. "We debated calling Salvatore," he told her, as frank as his mate was blunt. "Then we debated at least notifying Margo in case we were not successful."

Her heart gave a little nervous jerk and it took everything she possessed to fight reacting to that statement. Flat on her back with her arm locked into that splint as the Chief Enforcer commented reaching out to the brother who repudiated her about the possibility of her dying left her in too vulnerable a place to dare respond. The only saving grace was he wouldn't possibly frame it that way if he'd called Salvatore.

"Thank you for choosing not to," she said, then swallowed. God, she wished they would back up. Having them loom over her even at the slight distance made her want to be able to react and she couldn't.

It was horrifying.

Yet they were here, and they could prevent Rodrigo from getting to Rayne. She tracked her gaze back to him. They had to have moved the bed in from the other room. It was the bed she'd been sleeping in since she'd moved out of their room. The bed she'd retreated to after the challenge and her subsequent loss.

Yet even if she'd won—she would have gone to it anyway.

He'd betrayed her in that moment, and it left a cut so deep she didn't think it would ever heal. Then he damn near loses his life to save her. What was she supposed to do with that?

"You need to rest, Luciana," Dallas said quietly.

Not bothering to respond to the well-meaning advice, she moved on to what else she needed to know. "Is the rest of the pack down?"

"They are...recovering," Julian answered, his choice of words careful. "Some were hit harder than others. Even those hit the lightest require some recuperation. They are all being tended."

Tended. If the whole pack was down...

"The Enforcers are here, along with healers from Sutter Butte, Delta Crescent, and the Yukon. Willow Bend sent Hunters to split territories with the Enforcers as we sweep for Rodrigo." So they did know his name. "Rayne was only able to tell me he was a foreign wolf—I'm assuming Italian?"

"Yes," she answered, then glanced at Dallas. "May I have a little more water?"

She held the cup and straw for her. Swallowing while lying flat on her back was uncomfortable, but better than the alternative. "If you keep doing this well," Dallas told her. "I'll ask Colby if you can have some tea."

If there were other healers present, she had to wonder why they had to wait for Colby, but she didn't want to try and unpack that now. "Thank you," she told Dallas, before looking to Julian. "Rodrigo Mazzanti...he's a Seven Hills Centurion. Apparently he was sent to watch over me, but not by my brother. I think he has taken his duty to mean something else altogether."

"If he's attacking you, I'd hazard a guess that you were right." The barest hint of a smile and she almost laughed. If the situation weren't so horrible and she were able to, she just might.

"He did not take rejection well." Shame curdled in her stomach and the water settled as though it were stones. She had done *nothing* wrong. The idea of entertaining his offer had been anathema. Her differences with Rayne aside, she wanted no other wolf. For better or worse, he was her mate and she doubted breaking that bond would change her desire —if the bond could even be repudiated. Any explanation on that front would go to one person, and it would not be to either of the two listening to her at the moment.

"The last time I saw him before he followed me to Colorado," she said instead, and there was no doubt in her mind that he'd followed her to Colorado. "There's an old house a few miles east of here, follow the crumbling farm road, it turns to a dirt track. That was the first time he approached me...a few days ago. I don't know how long he's been in the area, but he seemed to have been here a while."

And once she'd healed, if they had not found him, she would go hunting for him herself. He'd caught her off guard, he'd damn near beaten her—it wouldn't happen again. Ever.

Weariness swept through her and she very much wanted to close her eyes, but she looked over at Rayne. More she wanted to go over there and just see for herself he was all right. She wanted the scents of all these other wolves out of her house...but she needed them to keep Rayne safe.

He was going to hate this when he woke.

At some point, she blinked and her eyes went heavy. When they opened again the light had changed in the room, and a different wolf sat next to her. Long black hair with a hint of blue at the tips hanging over one shoulder, she tapped away on a cell phone. The distraction gave her time to study the girl—she was a girl. Younger, Asian, or at least some Asian blood, and definitely a wolf with an unusual scent.

Colby.

The healer.

The woman in question darted a look at her, then smiled. She didn't try to lock gazes with her, but she didn't look away. "Ready to talk yet or do you want to keep trying to figure me out?"

"How is Rayne?" she said, her voice strained again as if she'd never had any water. After setting the phone aside, Colby moved to bring the same cup Dallas had used earlier and put the straw to her lips. She drank because her throat hurt and she needed the moisture, but she wanted an answer.

"He's woken once, and that was good. He's in true sleep now."

The water went down wrong, and she coughed and God it set everything on fire. Colby rubbed her shoulder and gave her a minute. She must have done something else because a cool rush of water seemed to quench the fire and ease her back from the ledge of pain.

"Better?" the healer asked, studying her.

"Yes, thank you," she sighed, her eyes still watering. They were watering from the coughing, they had to be, but her gaze tracked to where Rayne lay, and instead of being flat on his back—he was on his side angled toward her. A lock of hair had fallen over his forehead, and the rest of his hair looked shaggy and uneven. He hadn't cut it recently. Stubble lined his cheeks, and though they were a little sunken, his color seemed improved.

Licking her lips, she looked at the healer, "He wasn't in true sleep before?"

"No, I had to put him into a healing sleep to sustain him. I had to do it for both of you, and you woke first. You're regaining energy and the more I stabilize you, the more he stabilizes."

"What do you need me to do?" She wanted Rayne stable. He shouldn't have risked himself for her.

"Well, cooperation is a great first start. My experience with wolves is you are all wretched patients," she said the last with a small smile. "I'll warn you, I've dealt with some real bastards..."

There was a snort from the hall, and her grin widened.

"...so I'm rather used to it all. But I would like to do is spend some time on your arm. You had a lot of injuries, and I had to triage you. We have the bones aligned thanks to the portable x-ray and I was able to repair the vessels that were bleeding, but there is still a lot to be done."

She made it sound easy, but the truth beneath her words suggested it was far from as simple as she described it.

"As for the rest, there is much I need to discuss with you and your mate, but it is better to handle that when you are both awake. To that end, he will be more likely to listen if you are better when he wakes. I had a hard time convincing him to stay put for the time being." The firm, yet bright chatter went a long way toward soothing her unease. The perfectly no nonsense approach wrapped in kindness eased something uncomfortable within her.

"Okay, are you well enough to do this? Dallas mentioned you'd had to save the whole pack. I don't want to strain your resources..." She hesitated, because she'd worried about it back on the mountain when she'd seen the bone jutting out of her skin. "I can shift?" Maybe. It was by no means a definitive. Her wolf still seemed very much asleep. Was that the healing sleep, Colby mentioned?

"I'm fine," the healer said with another easy smile. "I'm much better than you at the moment." Then her expression turned almost apologetic. "I'm afraid that this will be painful and I need you to feel it to let me know if it goes wrong at all."

Not comforting, but she preferred the straightforward approach. "How do I let you know if it goes wrong?"

Colby scraped her teeth over her lower lip as she studied Luciana. "That's the challenging part. What you should feel is tremendous pressure, there will likely be a sensation like stitches...and the fusing of bone can be hot, almost burning."

Those were all sensations she currently experienced on some level. "It's throbbing right now, like I can feel it beating with my pulse. If I focus on it all it–it's very unpleasant."

"Oh, you are an improvement on my patients. You're actually telling me the truth." She grinned, radiating approval and Luciana smiled by reflex. It had been quite some time since she was around a healer. She'd forgotten how soothing they could be, and the sensation of water rolling over her in gentle eddies added to the relief. "You still have a lot of trauma and the bone isn't fused yet, that will likely help, I have to work from the deepest injury out. While shifting can help eventually, you shouldn't—not yet."

Disappointed, she had to settle for a nod. "All right." She closed her eyes. "We should do this before I fall asleep on you again. I'm assuming you can't do this while I'm sleeping?"

"I wish I could—do you think you can hold still for this or should I ask for someone to come in and help?" Someone to come in and hold her still if necessary. A fair question. Though if Rayne woke to seeing someone restraining her, he might react badly. She would if she saw someone doing that to him before she understood why.

"Let's try me holding still. I have some discipline...if it becomes too much I'll tell you."

"Okay," Colby murmured. "Give me a moment." She reached for her phone, and typed in a quick message, then set the phone aside. After circling the bed to the other side, she brushed her hand gently against the fingers of Luciana's right hand. Oh that wasn't remotely pleasant, even the light touch sent a jar through her rioting nerve ends.

The air in the room shifted, a kind of indrawn breath—the quiet in the eye of the storm. Even as she tried to focus on what the healer did, she found it easier to be lulled and she let her eyes close to half-slits.

"I'm going to start slowly," Colby murmured. "Ready?"

"No," she attempted to go for the joke. "But let's pretend I am."

The healer met the comment with a soft laugh. "Here we go…" Then her fingers tightened on Luciana's and the rush of water poured up her arm and the rapid cool turned into fire as though it were as combustible as gasoline.

Too much.

The pressure and the pain locked in her jaw as she held herself still and curled the fingers of her left hand into her palm.

Too much.

Her claws bit into her flesh, but she held herself rigid even as her wolf roused. The one holding them, stroking the hell across her senses was a healer.

Oh hell, too much.

They would not move. They would not harm her.

Her thoughts splintered.

She didn't have time to tell her it was too much. She blacked out when the bone in her arm sizzled.

CHAPTER 15

*B*etween one moment and the next, Rayne erupted from sleep as though he were emerging from the middle of a lake. He drew in a deep gulp of air. His muscles burned, his chest ached and at the center of it all was a wild desire. Twisting, he jerked his attention to the bed where Luciana had been sleeping, still nearly as broken as she'd been when the healer arrived.

The healer in question sat on the far side of the bed, Luciana's hand in hers. Colby's bowed head and closed eyes betrayed her deep concentration. The hum of her tranquility filled the room and belied the very real strength the *journeyman* healer had demonstrated.

Swinging around and setting his feet to the floor, Rayne took measured breaths. His head felt like someone had split his skull with an ax and forgot to take the damn thing out. Yet, simultaneously, an entirely different sense of vitality buzzed beneath his skin. Even his awareness seemed expanded, if still a little hazy around the edges.

Once he was certain the spinning brought on by sitting up had passed, he pushed off the bed. His muscles protested, weakness invading every limb and he staggered more than walked to the bathroom.

His appearance gave him pause. If someone told him he'd gone several rounds with multiple wolves and barely survived, he'd believe them. Leaning forward, he frowned. His skin had a sallow tone, his eyes were red rimmed and bruised. Rubbing a hand against his chest, he grimaced at his own smell and then nudged the door closed so he could empty his bladder.

Every breath ached like shrapnel shifting in his chest. By the time he finished, and opened the door again, he needed to lean against the doorframe to stay on his feet. But no way in hell would he collapse. Two days. Two days he'd been unconscious according to Julian—fucking Julian and his Enforcers were all over Three Rivers along with a dozen other wolves Rayne didn't know because the whole pack was down. They were recovering, or so Colby assured him, but he needed to get out there and see for himself.

The woodsy notes of cedar combining with jasmine, black pepper, and hints of amber teased his nose. Gone was the sour scent of infection, though the heavy tang of sweat and salt lingered. The copper—the copper was still there, but only faintly. It might just be on the linens or the towels.

Pushing away from the doorframe, he made his way to Luciana's side. Her eyes were closed, the thick dark lashes like closed curtains refusing him access to the sweet brown eyes. Ignoring his own stench for a moment, he eased onto the healer's abandoned chair and reached for Luciana's left hand. They'd inserted an IV, and there was a bag delivering fluids to her system. The bruising along her neck and chest seemed to have diminished, though it was still streaked in blackish-green. The deep slices inflicted by Rodrigo's claws across her torso were less inflamed, but they remained open.

With his lips against her hand, he kissed the knuckles

gently. Beneath the thunder in his skull, the mate bond lay quiescent, but still very much there even if it was as bruised and battered as the woman in front of him. Her heart beat, her breath filled her lungs, and she was healing.

Slowly.

But he could wait forever if he had to.

"She's doing better," Colby said, her voice quiet and a little fatigued. "How are you feeling?"

Well at least she didn't order him back to bed, which was what she had done when he woke earlier. The journeyman healer and mate to the Hudson River alpha had walked into his house, up the stairs, and to the door of his room and for a split second when he'd opened that door—all he could scent was her mate. His wolf and he had both been leaning in to keeping their mate alive and classified her as a threat before the fact she was a healer slammed into him. It didn't matter that his dominance hadn't rolled over her, he'd behaved poorly and he would need to apologize for that.

"Like someone hit me with a truck," he admitted. "But I'm on my feet and alive. And she's alive," he added, reaching up to smooth the dark hair away from her face. It was greasy, and heavy with sweat, oil, and dirt. They had cleaned her as best they could or he had tried before he'd collapsed. "Thank you," he said as he met Colby's quiet gaze.

"You're very welcome," she murmured, then glanced down at her patient. "I've begun to fuse the bones in her arm. There were many vessels ruptured and torn muscle, so I had to work around them all while I got the bones re-aligned, but I didn't want to fuse them until I was certain I wouldn't need to rebreak them."

He grimaced, then nodded. "Has she woken at all?"

"A little while this morning, and again a short bit ago. I think that's what woke you. The process is not comfortable, but she didn't make a sound of complaint." Disbelief filtered into her tone. "I don't think she wanted to disturb you."

Maybe. More likely she had not wanted to show any weakness, not even to the kind healer. Luciana despised weakness in herself, despised failure even more. Too many years of being told she could not be or do something because she was too delicate had forged a very, very stubborn woman —and probably far more powerful than she realized.

"As you say," he murmured. Though she'd been discussing leaving him

"I needed to figure out who I was...am...can be." Anguish discolored the words. *"I don't like hating you."*

"And I'm not even sure I can hate you."

"But I don't think I can love you anymore..."

"I...I don't know where to go from here, but I do know we can't keep living the way we are."

"Not much about me you could love anymore."

Every word played out in his head and he scrubbed a hand over his face. "Something is different..." he didn't mean to say it aloud, but the words slipped free. A part of him just wanted to talk to *her* to his mate, but her eyes were closed as she slept, hopefully far away from the pain. "I need to see my pack."

Days, days he'd been away from them and days he'd been unconscious. There were so many outsiders present because his pack had been left vulnerable.

A hand touched his where he held Luciana's and he glanced across her to the healer studying him. The cool swell rolled over him, easing away some of the pain in his head. "You are not better yet," she told him carefully. "You will not want to hear this, but you are still very weak and vulnerable."

No. He did not want to hear that, but he couldn't glare at the wolf. She was not threatening him or challenging him. Healers were given leeway, and they could override an alpha in matters of health—theirs or the pack's. But Colby was also not *his* healer…exactly.

"I need a better reason than that, because if I'm vulnerable, then so is my pack and the last thing I can afford is to stay here and not protect them." The longer he let others do the job for him, the faster he would be facing challenges from other quarters. Those challenges might not be interested in leaving he or Luciana alive.

"Very well," Colby murmured, withdrawing her hand and settling back in her seat. "I will have food sent up. You can go shower, shave, and put on clean clothes, then eat. If you are able to walk out that door after—then I won't stop you."

A generous offer, and one easily achieved. Yet there was something in the manner of her delivery, which should have warned him. Twenty minutes later, when he sat in the same chair, clean, smelling better, and barely able to lift the sandwich they'd brought up for him, he wanted to swear.

For her part, Colby did not say she'd told him so. Instead, she sat in a different chair delivered by the Second from Hudson River who'd come as her escort. He was never far from the bedroom door, but didn't enter. "And he won't," Colby reminded Rayne. "He only came to help when you collapsed. Then it was a case that I needed everyone who could help."

"I appreciate it," he said, because as angry as he was at the situation, he could find no malice in their actions—no demands or anything to gain from the choices they'd made. If anything, he was beholden to them and may never be able to repay the kindness done. "Can you tell me what happened?"

"Yes," she said. Then she did. She laid out each step of the issues she'd encountered from the moment she arrived in Three Rivers to when Rayne woke up the second time. How he'd collapsed as his energy—life force and that of the pack's

—had been swirling away as they fought to keep Luciana alive. He'd nearly killed the entire pack and if not for Colby, they would all be dead.

There was no repayment for such a gift.

None.

"She would have died had you not acted," Colby assured him. "Her wounds were infected, and her heart was struggling. Wolves are very hardy creatures, but whoever did this to her…they may not have realized how badly they hurt her or that internal bleeding would put such strain on her if she could not shift."

Truthfully, it was one of their greatest strengths and perhaps an even greater conceit. Rayne had seen wolves die in battle; they'd all seen it. But they were usually killed in the course of battle; they did not linger and die of their injuries later. No that happened because they'd had no healer, and he'd had to get her all the way back, and…and…and… The litany of reasons could go on and on.

They wouldn't help him except to give him a roadmap for what changes they needed to make. The first being hiring a real doctor or medical staff if they could not bring in a healer of their own. At the same time, they needed to build a medical facility with the equipment like the portable x-ray that they'd had to wait for.

While he'd been aware of the need for different skillsets among his wolves, the rest had simply never occurred to him.

That was his failure.

One he would not make again.

"And you are certain the rest are recovering?" Every wolf in his pack went down, most collapsing where they stood whether it was in a kitchen or on the street. The Enforcers had tracked down all of them, carrying in those that had collapsed farther out. Foreign healers had flown in, all to treat the affected.

"Yes," she assured him. "It will take time for everything to settle, but the frayed bonds have all been mended."

The frayed...the memory of how they'd begun to splinter as the pack answered his call, how they'd joined together, so many branches of the web feeding one into the other to get to him.

Rayne straightened abruptly and closed his eyes. He thought of Louis and he located him. He was in his apartment over the diner. Though extremely weary, he was awake and the sense of him grew the longer he thought on him. He moved on to Jackson. His brother was downstairs in a guest room. One by one, he tracked each of his wolves.

That was new.

When he opened his eyes, he stared at the healer. "What did you do?" Because despite all efforts, the pack had never really come together—not as Delta Crescent had been. They'd chosen to band together, and they'd committed to Luciana and later to him. The seed of the connection had been present, but it hadn't so intrinsically tied them together. Time, he'd assumed, time had to be a factor. That and the natural emotional bonds that grew between pack mates; it was why he'd been working so hard to involve himself in all their lives—to forge those connections.

But what he had now? It was a strong network, and he could feel all of his wolves. The awareness of them was a present thing.

Colby nodded to his hand, and he glanced at his half-forgotten sandwich then took a bite more to keep the questions from pouring out of him. Then with a tired, if a little smug smile, she said, "I am not sure I can even explain what I did...but your pack bonds were too new, too recently formed or too weak to sustain. The more they pushed to you, and the deeper you all tied into Luciana, it was as though the flow had been stuck into one position, you literally couldn't stop it all from spilling away. I fixed that."

But how?

"Don't ask me how, as I said, I am not sure I can explain any of it. I will attempt to when your mate is awake, because there is still more I need from the both of you to make sure this all holds together. You will be better served to talk to Brett or Julian or one of the other alphas…because what you have now is what you should have had when your pack bonds formed in the first place."

Rayne frowned. Luciana had formed the pack; she'd taken the allegiance of each person and the blood exchange. Had they done something wrong? He had no fans in the other alphas and yet—he had spoken with Mason Clayborne more than once, and it was Brett who'd reached out to him to ask for permission to send his healer—his *mate* to Three Rivers in the first place.

"I did not know healers could do that," he told her honestly. He'd known healers his whole life, and he'd never known that.

"To be perfectly honest, I don't think the healers knew it either. I seem to be something of an anomaly." Her smile was small but genuine. "I've never done things the way others do, so I suppose it's just in my nature."

"I can never repay this gift," he told her honestly. "You saved my whole pack…if I can ever do anything for you —*anything*—if it is my power to grant, I will do it." It was a blood promise he would offer freely.

"Luckily, I only ask that you and your pack thrive. That after she wakes and you are both ready to talk, that you listen to me." If her earlier advice was anything to go on, this would not be as simple as she made it sound.

"I will make sure both happen."

"Good," she said with another smile. "Now finish your sandwich—Luc?"

The door opened behind him, and Rayne spared a glance at the wolf he'd barely registered on their arrival.

"Did someone trip on their way to find fresh coffee?" The question was asked so sweetly, that Rayne found himself eyeing the healer because the glint in her eyes was distinctly unfriendly.

An aggrieved sigh left Luc. "No, but Brett suggested that since you're not sleeping you might want to consider tea."

There was a slow pause and all she said was, "Luc?"

"Just kidding." The either very brave or very stupid wolf laughed. "Dallas said she's bring back fresh from the diner shortly. The wolf who runs it has graciously allowed Mitch and Amelia the run of the place, and they've been cooking all day and getting meals out to everyone."

"Hmm...you're not as cute as you think you are." But her smile tilted towards amused. "Thank you."

"Would you like any coffee, Mr. Barrows?" The wolf addressed him, and Rayne glanced at him.

"Luc...?"

"Danes, Mr. Barrows. Luc Danes. Second of Hudson River. Thank you for allowing us free passage to enter your territory." While it was both the polite way and the expected etiquette for greeting an alpha in their territory when you were visiting, it still seemed almost laughable.

"I think it should be quite the other way around, Mr. Danes. Thank you for bringing the healer here, and thank you for protecting her and by extension my pack when I was unable." He met the other wolf's gaze and sought no dominance, but merely a true acknowledgement.

"It was my honor," Luc told him, then he grinned. "So is that a yes to coffee?"

Colby laughed softly.

"Indeed, it is a yes to coffee." The other wolf gave a little salute, then stepped out again and closed the door. The sandwich finished, he gathered Luciana's hand in his again and waited.

"You should sleep," Colby urged him.

"I will," he told her. "After I see her eyes."

After he figured out how to repair what had been torn between them. After he checked on his pack.

And after he killed Rodrigo.

CHAPTER 16

$\mathcal{I}$t was the fourth or maybe it was the fifth time she'd woken, she lost count, but when she opened her eyes, Rayne sat next to her. His distant gaze snapped to her in a heartbeat. His focus laser intense, and then he leaned forward. "Luciana?"

"Ciao," she managed in a voice more husky than croaking. Well that was an improvement. But she cared less about how she sounded and more about the flush of color in his face. The gray tinge seemed to have receded, and while he looked *tired*, he looked better. "You're all right?"

Every other time she'd opened her eyes, he'd been unconscious. They'd assured her he was fine, twice she'd been told he'd been awake but he'd needed more sleep. Colby reiterated Rayne's health had improved. Sleep was vital to his continued recovery.

Yet still...finding him leaning over her, tasting his scent cleanly without the muddying factors of other wolves, illness, or the stringent stink of cleansers steadied her in the most unexpected ways.

"Those are the eyes I've been waiting to see," he said, his

191

smile softening the tight lines of his face. "Ready for some water?"

Like Colby and Dallas before him, he lifted the cup with the straw to her lips even as he slid a hand beneath her head to support her as she lifted and drank. It tasted nearly as wonderful as it had the first time. He didn't pull the straw away, letting her drink until she'd had all of it, and then she sighed as he let her lay back.

"That might have been a mistake," she murmured, slowly taking inventory.

"Yeah?" His gaze went wary. "What's wrong?"

"I have to pee," she admitted and his expression relaxed into a smile.

"I can help you with that," he promised and when he turned, she spotted the bedpan.

"No," she said, more like she pled. The last way she wanted him to see her as was so helpless he needed to place a bedpan beneath her, it was—undignified, and humiliating. "Please."

He tracked her gaze, then gave her the smallest of smiles and for just a moment it was like his eyes were laughing, but not a sound came out of him. "I wouldn't, I promise. There are just some things no one should have to endure." Rising, he slid his arms under her. "But we took out the IV this morning, and Colby said your arm is improved even if we have to keep it in the splint for now."

In the absence of the sheets and blankets, she was still naked but right now she cared less about that than she did her own smell. It was like it hit her all at once, and she grimaced. Rayne steadied her as he stood.

"Did something hurt?"

"Just my nose," she admitted. "Sorry."

"You smell sweet to me," he promised, and at that, she had

to roll her eyes only it left her a little dizzy as he carried her from the bed toward the bathroom.

"Is the healer still here?" Feeling seemed to be surging into her legs and arms as he moved, and then when he set her down on the toilet proper, the world swayed. All the blood rushing downward.

"Yes, do you need her?" Solicitousness rolled off him in waves. As much as she didn't want him to have to take care of her it was kind of nice.

"No, you might though if you think I smell sweet." All she could scent was her sweat, and blood, and the graduating stink of having failed to wash in days. It had been days right? Staring up at him, she tried to catalog his improvements. Better color. A spark in his eyes. Steady breathing. Strength.

He smelled wonderful.

So much better than her.

"I'm fine," he promised. "Empty your bladder and I'll even help you brush your teeth."

What a ridiculously wonderful offer. "What do I have to do to get a bath?"

She wasn't sure she could stand in a shower.

Rayne cocked his head to the side, thoughtful. Then eyed her arm. "Tell me how you're really feeling."

"I feel…" She'd actually been trying to hold it while he stood there, but since he didn't appear to be leaving, she emptied her bladder. It felt like she pee'd for hours and it was a wonderfully relaxing sensation.

Clearing her throat, she tried to focus on how she felt. Her chest didn't feel so tight. She could take a deep breath. A glance down at her chest and abdomen revealed the lacerations had closed, but they were still very red, and the skin looked shiny—new.

"Tired," she admitted. That was definitely one for the list. "Weak." She cared for the second far less than she had the first. "Really sore." It was wearing her out even talking about it. She'd finished and he offered her the toilet paper.

Thankfully, she managed that part on her own. Once had been more than enough. He helped her stand, and her legs shook like a newly foaled colt. One arm wrapped around her, he held her steady as he closed the seat then flushed the toilet before spreading a towel over it and letting her sit again.

"But I think...I think I feel better," she told him after she'd managed to catch her breath.

"Good." The tension around his eyes lessened. He got her toothbrush—reclaimed from the other bathroom where she'd moved it. In fact, most of her things seemed to have migrated back to their shared bathroom.

It wasn't worth arguing over at the moment. After he wet the toothbrush and added some paste, he handed it to her. It was a little awkward to brush with her left hand, but honestly it felt like she excavated all the days of pain and exhaustion as she brushed. He had to help her stand again to rinse her mouth out, but the whole thing was worth it.

"The rest of the pack?" she asked finally. Colby, Dallas, and Julian indicated they were all recovering, but...

"A little unsteady on their feet...almost drunken in some ways," Rayne told her. "It's damn odd. But there's a bond we didn't have before and it's left everyone giddy. They're still resting and we have a lot of outside help for the time being."

She couldn't read his tone for how he felt about it. But there was an ease to him she hadn't seen in a long time. An ease... an ease she hadn't been able to give him, maybe ever, even when she thought she had.

"I'm going to take you back to the bed, then I'm going to ask Colby about letting you take a bath."

Ugh. The bed probably reeked as badly as she did. Her distaste must have shown, because he chuckled, and knelt down in front of her. "Or I'll just call her, how about that?"

He pulled out a cell phone from his pocket, and pressed a single contact number before putting the phone to his ear.

"Is she all right?" Colby answered, sounds of others in the background along with that of dishes.

"She's fine, sorry to interrupt your meal. She's awake and wants to bathe, do you have any issue with that?" Rayne's gaze steadied her as did his hand on her knee.

"No, not at all. Keep the right arm out of the water though and try not to get the splint wet, but if it does. We can replace it when I get back."

"Thank you, Colby. Enjoy your meal." Then he rang off and smiled at her. "So would my lady like her bath with something sweet smelling in it?"

The fact he called her my lady should not have sent a little thrill through her, so she suppressed that reaction. It was the bath she needed to be excited about. "Honestly, I just want to be clean, and maybe wash my hair."

Fifteen minutes later, thoroughly scrubbed and her hair washed and conditioned, Rayne settled her back into the fresh bathwater and she just sighed. They'd barely spoken while he got her clean, and after the first couple of minutes, her gratitude chased away her embarrassment and humiliation.

"Someone feels better," he grinned, kneeling next to the tub. His shirt had soaked through, and water splashed his jeans, but he didn't seem to care. He'd retrieved a comb and had begun to gently pull it through her hair and she closed her eyes.

"You have no idea," she had to say. "Really, I feel almost like a brand new wolf. Would it be enormously selfish of me to ask not to be put back on the dirty linens?" It wasn't like she got much of a choice. He'd done nearly everything for her, and she was so tired, she wanted to go back to sleep right now.

"Not at all, I'll take care of it once we're done in here." As he had said earlier, he wouldn't leave her alone. Not while she was vulnerable. He preferred to be right at her side, and if she were honest, she actually found that she wanted him there. Yet if that wasn't selfish, what was?

"Thank you."

"You don't have to thank me, Luciana. You're my mate," he reminded her, and though it was the first time he'd brought it up, she couldn't escape the sting of it. "No matter what else has happened, that *hasn't* changed and I don't want it to either."

"Rayne..."

"No," he said firmly, putting a hand on her knee where it emerged from the water. "Listen to me—please." The last word cost him, and silenced her objections. At her nod, he rubbed his thumb over the top of her knee. "I know things have been bad between us. Bad enough...bad enough you might have..." He trailed off, but the pain rippling like flash fire through his scent and darkening his eyes couldn't be ignored. "That part doesn't matter. What matters is that—I love you. That hasn't changed since they day we met. You took my heart then, and I never want it back."

She had to look way from his eyes, her attention zeroing in on his hand. Every brush of his thumb made her wolf stir, and with it her hackles. Biting the inside of her lip, she swallowed back the words to push him away.

"You said you didn't want to hate me or keep living as we have been. I don't want that either."

Swallowing around the hard lump in her throat, she blinked back the tears burning behind her eyes before she met his gaze. "I also said I'm not sure I can love you anymore." Licking her lips, she didn't shy away from the fierceness in his stare. "More I'm worried I never loved you the way I should have."

"There's no should," he told her, firm in his conviction. "There's you and there's me. I think we both forgot about it, but I want to fix that now. I want it to be you and me again."

"When did you forget it?" She didn't want this fight, but here they were and as badly as she ached and as dependent on him as she was in this exact moment, it killed her to hear him say he wanted to fix it. "When you challenged me? When you bested me in combat? When you took the pack away? Was that when you forgot it? Or have I overlooked some other pivotal moment?"

With each question, she burned from the betrayal.

Dropping his chin, he seemed to wrestle with his temper yet it was only pain in his scent. Pain she'd magnified.

"And this..." she sighed the words, as she looked away from him to stare at the tile on the wall. "This is why I went to the mountains."

"Because I challenged you?" The question came out rough and hard.

"No, because I can't look back at that choice, and *not* feel that betrayal. Because I hate you—no I don't even know what I feel about you anymore. But I hate that you did that. I trusted you and you..." She blinked away the tears, suppressing it all. "No, I just...want it to stop hurting Rayne. I want to stop making these mistakes and hurting you. Everyone in this pack hates me, and why not? I was too weak to keep the Enforcers and the other Alphas from quarantining us, I didn't recognize an Omega when she was right in front of me... and I didn't see that the man I trusted the most would be the one who would betray me. So you have the pack. You have earned their loyalty and brought them together in a way I never could. I am very proud of you."

She meant every single word.

"But I went to those mountains to make a decision. To figure out what I needed to do...and not just for me." She pressed a hand to her face, and rubbed at an eye viciously. She did not want to cry. "The pack doesn't want me here. Their feelings are very clear. You will lose face with them if I continue to stay...and after the pack nearly died in trying to save me, I doubt their feelings will have changed much." If anything, they would worsen.

"Well on that part you're wrong," he told her solemnly. "They helped to save you."

"They helped *you* save me." It might seem a minute distinction, but it was most assuredly a potent one. "Do you really want to punish their loyalty with me here? With an alpha pair so mismatched we don't even sleep in the same bed anymore?"

"That was your choice," he reminded her. "You moved to the other bedroom. I didn't fight you on it, because you wanted the distance...you seemed to need it, but that was *never* what I wanted."

"What did you imagine?" She pulled her hand away and stared at him. "What did you imagine would happen after you challenged me to a form of combat that typically ends in the death of the one who loses? Did you imagine that we would come home, have a glass of wine, laugh over what a good time my beating was, then fall into bed?"

The expression on his face wrenched her; denial warred with grief while vying with obstinacy. "I don't want to lose you."

"It may already be too late for us," she confessed. "That's what I figured out in the mountains. It's what I was coming down to talk to you about—I don't know if it's even possible to repudiate a mating after the fact. Maybe if we both choose to walk away..."

"I'll never choose that," he told her, his tone flat and his eyes hard. "Never. We can fix this. If saving you can bring the whole pack together..."

"...it nearly killed the whole pack, Rayne. Killed them. My choices put me in that position and I was alone when Rodrigo attacked and my damn arrogance nearly cost me my life—and yours and everyone else here. That's twice my arrogance has done this. I don't think we can afford a third." A shudder went through her and the water seemed to chill.

Without a second glance, Rayne reached into the water and freed the plug to drain the tub. Then he grabbed a heavy towel and wrapped it around her as he lifted her. Rising, he cradled her close and stared into her eyes. "I don't care. I'll walk away from the pack. I'll let someone else take it once they are balanced again. If you can't stay here then I'll go with you."

"That's a very kind thought, but you can't leave them." If anything, she'd learned something very true about him. A type of truth she should have understood from the beginning and in a way she had, but not on this level.

"Why the hell not?"

"Because you chose them over me already," she reminded him, and the pain wincing across his face burrowed deep into her soul. "You wanted to save them from me, from my mistakes, from what you clearly believed I was doing. Or maybe...maybe what I was doing." If she were going to be honest, she needed to be honest about all of it. "It might take me forever to understand why it went wrong. Why what I thought would happen and what did happen varied so greatly. But one thing I am perfectly clear on, you saved the pack by choosing them over your mate, over me."

He carried her into the bedroom and settled her on the bed he'd been using, then he carefully rubbed her down—mindful of her right arm—before wrapping her in a blanket. "I'm going to change your sheets and stuff."

All but sagging against the wall, she watched as he moved around their room with an economy of motion. He'd stripped the bed, and the pads that had been used to catch her blood. It was all soiled, and now that she'd bathed, the stench was even worse. He set the linens outside the door, spoke to someone and sent them for food.

That finished, he remade the bed. The combination of fresh linens and the removal of the others ease the air considerably. Then as if reading her mind, he cracked open a window. It was chilly outside, but it let in fresh air and she lifted her nose as though she had already shifted. Her wolf stirred, but remained sleepy almost as if exhausted from everything. Awareness of her spread though, the faintest ruffle of fur, and the rub of a head as if to remind her she was still there.

Done, he scooped her up with the same care he'd shown throughout and carried her over to the newly made bed. Only instead of leaving her to lie flat, he propped her up against pillows so she could recline, then he settled more pillows beneath her arm to keep it elevated.

"Better?" he checked with her.

"Yes," she told him truthfully. Sitting up was a far less vulnerable position than on her back with her head so far below everyone else's. "Thank you."

"You never have to thank me," he reminded her. "The fact you feel like you have to show gratitude for something you should expect from me reminds me of how much I've failed you."

She couldn't argue with that, yet... "Not until I failed you first." Because she had to have.

"I'm not ignoring what you said," he told her finally as he took a seat on the edge of the bed. "I promise you I'm not. I know I may have lost the right to your trust, but I am asking you to trust me a little while longer."

Her hand was shaking when he covered it.

"Please..."

"Why? What do you need me to trust you with?" Because that might be impossible. No matter how grateful she was that he was alive, and that saving her hadn't killed him—it didn't magically make it all better. It couldn't erase his betrayal or the last few months.

Nothing could.

"For starters..." he said slowly, the picture of calm despite the riot in his eyes. He'd locked it all down, but his wolf was right there under the surface and he'd never been more alpha. "Tell me about Rodrigo."

"He isn't important."

"Yes, he is," Rayne told her firmly. "Don't make me order you. He nearly killed you. You called out his name when I found you at the old house. Told him to go away. Then you were with him on that mountain."

"No, he followed me. I was alone up there—for three days. Just me and the wind and the snow. I came across him when I was on my way back to the car."

He studied her for a long time as though weighing and measuring her words. "Okay. Tell me about him."

"Why?"

"Because I need to know."

"Rayne—he's dangerous."

"I don't care." His flat tone echoed as much. "Tell me, Luciana. Now."

Licking her lips, she nodded slowly. There was no escaping this embarrassment. He was right. She knew he was right, but she didn't want him to see her as anything lesser than he already had to at this point.

If she was going to leave in the end, what did it matter? Maybe it was time to rip all the blinders off.

Especially her own.

CHAPTER 17

$\mathcal{H}$is mate sat in front of him, and yet she seemed to be slipping right through his fingers. Rayne had never had greater reason to rejoice—she was alive—and to rage—but she didn't want him anymore. His wolf bucked against the suggestion, yet he restrained both it and himself. More, he needed to brace for whatever she would tell him about Rodrigo. Even the name made him want to curse.

"Rodrigo Mazzanti is a Centurion from Seven Hills," she spoke in even, direct tones though her voice remained deeply wearied and weak. The desire to let her sleep vied with the need to know everything about the wolf that'd assaulted her and as yet remained on the loose. "The first time I knew he was here was the day you found me at the old house." Her gaze flicked to him, and he nodded.

Yes, he recalled her off the cuff remark about telling Rodrigo to go away. Holding her left hand between his, he waited her out.

"I go out there to think, and I'd had a run in with Dallas. Which is probably not a fair assessment of our encounter, but I was feeling particularly raw. He approached, and I admit, I was surprised. I had not seen anyone from Seven Hills since the night...well you know when that was."

The memory of that night was not soon erased. Margo had broken his knee, and Luciana had battled her brother, summoning the nascent bond of the pack, and filling it with her own power. He'd never felt anything like it; she filled in all the gaps in those moments—her determination and fiery spirit a brilliant thing. He, like every other wolf in the pack, had begun to shift to answer her.

Then Margo fired that gun.

It had damn near deafened him.

But he had still been able to make out her words and her intent. If Luciana hadn't stood down, Margo would have shot him. At that range, not even being a wolf would have saved him. Enforcers used hollow point bullets designed to explode their exit wounds far larger than the entrance.

The ugly moment, suspended in time, had cost Luciana dearly when she surrendered. She'd chosen him first, and foremost. It had been if not the first, then the first significant blow to the bonds holding them all together. Because pack bonds had existed *then.* The beauty of it, that moment when he'd *felt* her at the center of all that power, and more than just across the vibrant mating bond. His adoration for her had never been stronger.

Then came the moment Salvatore repudiated her and his mate's heart broke. In all of her defiance and determination, he didn't think it ever occurred to her that her brother—the man she worshipped—would forswear her and banish her not only from her home, but also any lingering ties to the pack that raised her.

The months that followed?

No, Rayne did not want to contemplate those. Because sliver by sliver, his Luciana had wasted away and he hadn't realized it until it was almost too late. After the Russians blackmailed her, and after she'd granted them safe passage in an effort to shore up the dangerous tide in the pack—after she'd made a choice that would have brought every Alpha down on her.

She cleared her throat. "I haven't even heard my native Italian since then, and for a moment—a moment I think I wanted to pretend. Yet I didn't understand why he was here. Giovanni, he told me. Giovanni set him to watch. I do not know if he is the only one or even the first. Honestly...I don't even know if it's the truth." The smile on her lips reflected only bitterness. "But he wanted to offer me his service, which is impossible. He is a Centurion of Salvatore; he cannot possibly serve me. He wanted to let me know I was not alone after your betrayal."

Rayne's wolf snarled, but he kept his fist closed tight on his temper at the implicit challenge in those words.

Luciana no longer even looked at him. Her gaze had gone farther away, as if she were somewhere else entirely. "I told him to leave our lands, for he was trespassing. And he told me he would go, but not be far. He can avoid our Hunters, and sentries for he is a Centurion and they can mask themselves. It is a gift my brother possesses and it is shared by many of the older wolves that serve him."

Another sigh.

"He said he would be there if I needed him, but I told him I would not. I just wanted him to go. And foolish of me, but I hoped it would be the end of it. A fool's errand."

"Yet, you didn't tell me about him." That hurt.

The coolness in her eyes stung him further. "You wouldn't have listened. Not then."

In reality, she wasn't wrong. That made the sting even worse.

"And the mountains? What happened there?"

A tiny shrug, then a grimace when the movement ached. He squeezed her hand gently.

"I need to know, Luciana." Especially after he'd all but accused her of sleeping with Rodrigo, of cuckolding Rayne to punish him.

The wolf had touched her. He'd *hurt* her. And what had Rayne done? He'd added insult to the injury for there was no trace of a lie in her words. She hadn't wanted Rodrigo there, and she'd sent him away. There would be no penance too great that Rayne shouldn't face. Fine, the Italian bastard could mask his scent and hide his presence because of his age. Well, Julian was pretty damn old, and there were others scattered among the packs.

"He followed me. I don't know for how long, I didn't actually see him until I'd shifted back and attempted to dress. I was alone for those days. I'm sure of it. Alone until I was on my way back." She wouldn't look at him. "He wanted to persuade me to join him—South America, Asia...elsewhere." That wasn't all he'd done, Rayne would swear it, but she still wouldn't look at him. "I refused. I may not be certain of how we can go on, but I would never choose him much less betray you."

Curling his fingers around hers, he battled the urge to snarl.

"Rodrigo—Rodrigo has only been a Centurion for twenty some odd years. He was often assigned the regions around the vineyards. There was always a reason for him to visit, every few weeks, to dine at Mama's table." A half shrug, and even that sent a flicker of pain across her face. "He seemed to be under the impression that since I'd left Three Rivers, it was an appropriate time to make his offer. I refused—rather violently."

Then she looked at him, and he couldn't read the emotion in her eyes. The flicker of gold around the edges of her irises suggested her wolf roused at the distress eddying beneath the surface. His own kept lunging forward.

"Why did you have to react violently?" Because Luciana had a temper, of all people, he knew her fiery nature. She could be loud, and fierce, and temperamental, but she'd never been overtly violent. The most he'd ever seen was the night she faced off against her brother. Even then it had cost her dearly.

"I don't really want to keep discussing this, I was close to losing that fight as well and I think that's enough humiliation." It wasn't quite a plea, but it lived there nonetheless.

"Sweetheart," he didn't try to disguise his plea. "Tell me. I don't blame you for any of this. I will not think less of you, but you've been carrying so much pain." So much of which he'd helped to cause. "Let me help shoulder this for you."

"He wants *me* Rayne—or the idea of me. I am not sure which nor am I sure why he thinks it's even a possibility. I barely spoke to him in Italy beyond the pleasantries one greets guests of your mother." With every word, she lifted her chin. Pride kept it up, and her eyes glittered even as the discomfort in her scent increased.

The wolf had done more than just *hurt* her. He'd actively tried to pursue her and she'd discouraged it—violently. And if Rayne hadn't arrived when he did? Truthfully, he hadn't believed it possible to make him angrier than he was.

"Luciana...did he?" Fuck him, he couldn't even say the words.

Her eyes narrowed for a moment, then she bared her teeth in a way that made mockery of a smile but promised very real physical harm. "I'd have ripped it off."

That was his girl. "Good."

Finally, he bowed his head and pressed it to her hand. How the hell had they let things get so bad? He'd made a choice, a hard one and one he never thought he'd ever have to make, but he had to protect her. And in doing so, he'd harmed her more than he'd imagined. Worse, he'd focused on the pack and not her—because she'd pushed him away and he'd let her do it.

When she tugged her hand from his grasp, he loosened his fingers. No matter how much he wanted to hold on, he wasn't going to force her to accept it. Then she carded her fingers through his hair. It was a gentle, almost tentative motion.

"I didn't say thank you," she whispered.

Not this again.

"No matter how much you do not want to hear it," she continued. "I have to say it. We have both behaved poorly, perhaps me more than you—yet you came for me regardless. You came and you were there when I needed you most —twice."

His heart fisted.

"For that I will thank you if I wish it."

Choking on regret and self-pity, he whispered, "I will always come."

But she made no sound of agreement or acceptance. When he dared to glance up at her, he found her staring at the window.

"Luciana…"

Before he could finish the thought though, a quiet knock on the door interrupted and he straightened. He wanted *time* with her, but there were already too many pressing issues. "Come in, Colby," he called, rising to block her view of Luciana to give his mate time to compose herself.

The healer stepped in with an apologetic smile. "I was trying to give you both some time, and I've pretty much kicked everyone out or at least downstairs with the TVs on."

That was kind of her. Living with wolves made privacy a precious commodity. While he had no interest in sharing their intimate details with everyone, he also didn't care what they heard as long as Luciana heard and listened to him.

"Thank you," Luciana said before he could and she touched his arm. It was enough for him to shift slightly and he settled his hip against the bed near her to free the chair up for the healer.

"You're welcome," Colby studied them both.

The wolf was young, and there was something very different about her. It was more than she was the mate of an alpha or a healer who could apparently affect an entire pack's bonds—bonds that had apparently been formed incorrectly which made less sense the more he thought about it. Except, he hadn't truly experienced the sense of the bonds themselves until the night he'd tried to keep Luciana alive.

"You have both been through so much, and I'm only going to be able to keep Julian and the others at bay for so long. They have a great deal they want to discuss with you."

"They can wait," Rayne told her bluntly. "Until Luciana is fully recovered and able to move with me, I'm remaining here." Once said, he couldn't disagree with the sentiment. Nothing would part him from her side, not until Rodrigo had been dealt with. A wolf willing to do what he had done despite his supposed allegiances to her *brother* and caring for *her* in the first place would be too dangerous an adversary to risk exposing her again.

"I was hoping you'd say that," Colby told him with a small smile. "But I also have business with the two of you, including an update on your arm." The last she said directly to Luciana.

"It feels somewhat better," she admitted. "Though I'm exhausted and it's very sore."

"I still have more work to do, but we're having to take our time. That was truly a lot of damage done, and I can go into detail or I can simply say we need another twenty-four to forty-eight hours—and then I think you will be ready to shift. I'll need to monitor that shift because I want to make sure everything holds up."

That was good news, and practical advice.

"I can be patient another day or two," Luciana said. "Thank you, Colby."

"You're welcome," she murmured. "Now for the more uncomfortable discussion." She moved over to sit in the chair, the clasped her hands together as she studied them. "I have only told one other wolf the explicit details of what I did for you. That wolf is my mate, and we will tell no others unless you expressly give permission for the information to be shared. I told him for three reasons, I needed his strength and relied on it heavily, I needed his understanding as an alpha, and relied on his knowledge, and I needed him to anchor me so I was not lost in my efforts."

It was hard not to frown, but Rayne could not fault the healer for her reasoning or her choice. She had every right to tell her mate, and while Rayne might prefer to keep something of the intimate knowledge of how badly the pack had floundered to themselves—it would hardly be possible with all the visitors in town. "I appreciate both your discretion and candor, I'm afraid there are already a great many wolves here who likely already know."

The healer tilted her head, and then shook it slowly. "You misunderstand me." Something in her tone sent a frisson of warning along his spine. Luciana put her hand on his leg and he covered it with his own. "How so?"

"First, let me apologize—you may not know this, but I wasn't raised in a pack."

"You are a latent wolf, a rarity to be sure." That much he already knew, but Luciana seemed surprised or perhaps she had forgotten.

"Exactly." The healer seemed relieved she didn't have to

explain. "So I am not always the best at wolf politics. In fact, I think most of the rules are pretty stupid. As Brett often likes to remind me, I should possess a better bedside manner than that, and I do—but I also know that dancing around subjects can make you overlook the things that are important."

She looked from him to Luciana and then back.

"Accepted," Rayne drawled. He'd been raised to observe a certain amount of decorum in all his interactions, not just those of pack. By that same token, he had the advantage of traveling through Europe, and he'd encountered all different kinds. Sometimes blunt was simply better.

Though she said nothing, Luciana nodded her head.

"Good. I explained to both of you about the damage to the pack bonds? And the way you were all tied together? The drain it put on the pack and the threat?" She waited long enough for them both to nod, before pressing on. "I've had some time to process what I did, and if I had not had the power of all the packs coming to me, I don't think I would have been able to fix what had been done—and again, I didn't tell anyone, not even the wolves who were in the room helping me, they knew I needed power, that was it."

The unease in Rayne's wolf slid through him. The build up the healer was giving the topic worried him on a funda-mental level. What had broken?

"I have never seen a pack formed, but I have encountered one that was deeply wounded. Every pack has a soul for lack of a better word, and for some reason, I can feel the flow of that soul. You might call it a character or a culture deeply associated with the pack itself. You were both in packs before, so you know the feeling of belonging in those packs, the life you had there—the way it felt. Does that make sense?"

"Yes," Luciana answered before he could. "In Seven Hills, Salvatore always stood at the center, no matter how the world swayed, he kept us stable. It was a fair bond and a balanced one. But the pack took its direction from him. Always."

"Exactly," Colby exhaled another long breath. Her nerves agitated his wolf. Healers should not be this unsettled and it made him very much want to deal with the cause so she would be serene once more. "Pack bonds are strengthened and weakened by a wide variety of factors, and every pack is different. So what may strengthen one, may not another. But at the heart of all packs is an alpha. The alpha."

Luciana's nails dug into his thigh, and he stroked his thumb along her hand accepting the discomfort.

"Your pack has been in conflict for some time, the bonds formed—or at least the ones in place when I arrived—were unequal, in some places disintegrating, and in others just half-formed. Think if you will of a road construction project where they block off an entire lane for miles, but there's no actual work going on because either they ran out of money or something broke. The surface might be cracked, filled with pot holes, you can make your way on it, but it's going to wreck your car eventually and it's definitely not a comfortable ride."

"What a horrific comparison," Luciana murmured.

"It's the closest I could come to explaining something I *knew* and *understood*, but I'd never seen before."

The explanation didn't soothe Rayne's concern. If anything, it suggested there was something fundamentally wrong with him.

"I can't tell you what caused it, not definitively. Again, my only exposure to anything similar was a wounded pack and it was wounded because the alpha was wounded. It couldn't heal until he healed." The careful selection of words suggested she discussed her own pack, but did not want to draw too much attention to it. Out of respect for her discretion of their issues, he wouldn't press her on it.

"Which of course, brings us full circle to the two of you—and your mate bond."

Tension jerked through him, and he narrowed his eyes on the healer. "What about our bond?" Too raw from the earlier discussion, he'd found his limit on how intimately he was prepared to let this wolf probe into their lives. It was only Luciana's relaxing of her grip, but not pulling away that kept him grounded. They may be unstable, but she was still with him and in this, she seemed to be if not fully committed, at least allied.

"There is something wrong with it, and I think you've already discovered that for yourself."

As much as he wanted to deny the charge, he'd had a difficult time pushing more than a trickle through the bond. What should have been wide open and flowing both ways had been gnarled and weak. The strands twisted, misshapen, and withering. What it said about their relationship didn't bear contemplating.

"Can you fix it?" Luciana's question startled him. "Or is this something we must do ourselves?"

Colby turned her gaze to his mate. "That bond is so intimately formed between you, that even were I to attempt a repair—I don't think it would take without your full and willing cooperation." The dubious note in her voice said she didn't think she'd have that from either of them.

Could a mating die? Was that even possible? Rayne scowled. "We have to be able to undo the damage."

"Perhaps," Colby said, spreading her hands. "Perhaps not, and in this I don't know how to advise you. If we were talking strictly relationship issues—then you two need to be talking more. You need to confront whatever grievances you're holding onto and find a way to let them go or forgive them. But that's almost a simplification. Mating is—mating unites two wolves as much as it does the two people involved. It's a bond you form out of love, respect, admiration, need, and desire—like a pack itself, the bond is a complex symphony of emotions. There's a synergy to it—and that's not to say discord won't happen. Hell, I fight with Brett all the time."

A flash of a smile appeared and then as swiftly vanished.

"Conflict can be healthy, especially if it helps to clear the air and dispel the tension." She eyed them both.

"Clearly, our conflict isn't," Luciana sighed. "I haven't exactly been the most cooperative or accessible person of late."

"You've had no reason to be," Rayne told her, shifting his full focus to her. "This is not your fault." If anyone's it was his —he'd challenged his *mate*, how could their bond be anything but damaged after that?

"Assigning blame won't fix it," Colby observed. "In my experience, the more uncomfortable a truth is, the more likely we are to avoid it. No one is perfect. We're all flawed. We all have weaknesses. We also have strengths."

It wasn't really advice, not that he could parse enough to make sense.

"So you don't know how to fix it, and you can't tell us what went wrong—what is the point of saying anything at all?" Luciana demanded, and the ache in her voice raked through him.

"Because that bond is at the center of what went wrong with the pack," she warned and it was a harsh slap in the face. "That bond has the potential to warp it again, because the alpha stands at the center, and the pack takes its soul and direction from the alpha. You don't have an omega, someone who can point you to the flaws, who can reflect them so you can see what needs to be shorn up."

They'd had one. And she'd been so unstable she kept

disappearing off to Willow Bend. Maybe that should have been their first clue.

"And you don't have a healer who would be helping to stabilize the pack as well…something we apparently do because we're just here. We're part of the bonds, and while I can see them, and feel them, healers give packs something they need."

So, not only was their mating bond a problem—their lack of the right wolf types was also an issue. Rayne scrubbed a hand over his face.

"Having a healer or an omega won't fix everything, and repairing the mating bond might not either. But it's like Luciana's arm," Colby said, giving her an apologetic look. "It isn't just one problem that needed healing, it's multiple ones and you have to repair that which needs it most before you can heal the rest."

"Do you have any other bad news for us?" Rayne asked, barely keeping the snap out of his voice.

"Rayne," Luciana admonished him, and the silken threat tangled with her accent on the single syllable of his name raked down his spine like the feeling of her nails that he'd never have again.

But he didn't have it in him to yell at her. He'd done enough to his mate. More than enough—the fault in all of this lay squarely on him. It was up to him to fix it.

"I wish I had better advice," Colby told him and he believed her. She meant every word. "I will stay and do everything I can, for as long as I can."

He nodded, then glanced at Luciana and found the same troubled expression in her eyes he was sure had to be reflected in his own. "Heal Luciana, that's all I ask. I need to figure out how to hunt a wolf who can disguise his scent."

And he had a good idea of who to ask about that.

Maybe he could do one thing right.

215

*C*olby wanted to resume with another check of her arm, but Luciana asked for her to step out instead. Rayne hadn't moved away from his perch on the edge of the bed. He'd continued to cover her hand with his, but the tension cording him turned his thigh to granite beneath her fingertips.

"You should let her look at you Luce," he told her and while she'd never cared for the nickname, his use sent a shiver up her spine. He was also the only one who had ever called her that—or frankly she'd ever allow to shorten her name in such a manner.

"I will, I'm tired though—really tired." She'd been trying to hold out for food, but she wasn't even sure she could eat at the moment. Especially not after learning that their mate bond had potentially poisoned the pack. It was like every ugly word said about the mission to form Three Rivers had been proven right—worse, that Salvatore's mate had been right about her.

"Then sleep," he said with a frown, twisting to look at her. The wolf flickered in his eyes, shifting the color to gold between one blink and the next. Her own wolf barely lifted her head. She'd barely responded when reciting Rodrigo's actions. Maybe the damage to the bond went deeper—maybe it came from her in the first place.

Shaking off the melancholy thought, she focused on his troubled gaze. She'd placed enough in front of him to have to repair. It was time she offered some assistance. "I'm going to call Giovanni. Salvatore won't take my calls, but Giovanni might."

"No," Rayne said, with a firm shake of his head. "Giovanni is who sent that bastard here in the first place. I don't trust him. The last thing you need to have to do is swallow your pride and ask any of them for anything." The set of his mouth and shoulders declared he would not be persuaded on this point.

"Rayne, to hunt a Centurion, you need another Centurion." It was just how it was. They were the most powerful wolves in Italy. She would argue they were stronger than many of the alphas in Europe. Their power and ability to hold their power was what reinforced Salvatore's position. From the end of the war to the present day, he'd had a singular focus—empowering the Seven Hills pack to never face such devastation again.

"Maybe in Italy, chére, but not here. I won't ask that pack for a single damn thing." His expression darkened. "Not your brother, not his Centurions. None of them."

"I can do it," she offered. "You don't have to, I can swallow my pride. I can be the one who—"

"*No.*" The single syllable came out a growl. "You will not." The command rolled over her, but even as tired as she was, her wolf stirred and Luciana met his steely gaze unflinchingly. "Luce—no. We made choices, and we made those together. You don't have to go to them hat in hand. They aren't the only older wolves in the world. That little trick is one that comes with age and technique. As it so happens, there's at least two Alphas I know who can do it."

"Julian," she answered swiftly, but there were five others. It wouldn't be Mason, he was strong but still young. Serafina perhaps, but even she did not seem to have the age behind her and Luciana was almost certain she was older. She knew next to nothing about the Sutter Butte Alpha Cassius. But that pack seemed to have relatively low life spans. That left Dalton from Hudson River or the reclusive Yukon pack leader. "The Yukon Alpha, but I find it hard to believe he would offer assistance."

"Well I don't think he'd offer, but I can ask him. I'll start with Julian, if nothing else he might be able to tell me how to track someone like that. The point, is we have resources here. Resources we can take advantage of to accomplish what we need to do. We do not have to go begging for your brother's scraps."

The level of hostility in Rayne didn't match with his earlier behavior at all. He'd once urged her to make peace with Salvatore, to reach out to him. They were still family even if they weren't pack. But at the time, Luciana had seen no way to reopen those channels of communication without prostrating herself to her brother. She'd quite literally burned bridges, and she'd known she would be. From the moment they began gathering wolves, she'd known she would have to face Salvatore at some point or other. She'd only hoped that she would have significantly more time.

So much more time... she'd wanted the pack secure and thriving before he noticed. Childish on her part, probably and she'd likely have been better off telling him directly. Salvatore had never been able to stand a liar or deception. There was nothing deceitful about him, but those wounds extended back to the war. She'd known it, but she'd also bargained on her position as his treasured baby sister.

Well, she'd always wanted him to treat her as an adult and a wolf in her own right. She should be careful what she wishes for.

"Why does asking him bother you so much?" She studied Rayne, looking for any clues to his reaction. "You wanted me to make peace with him—even after what happened. You encouraged me to write Mama and to Salvatore, when I was too angry to even consider it."

He raised his hand toward her face, then hesitated a moment. It hung there suspended between them as if he'd directly reconsidered his whole idea until finally he put his hand to her hair and smoothed it away from her face. "You adore your family. The three of you were so close," he told her, his tone almost gentle. "Even with Salvatore in Rome often, it was like the house was entirely different when he came to visit. You and your mother were so much more animated. I didn't want you to lose what you have with them. Rifts can be mended...even the deepest of family squabbles can be repaired. You were pining for them, Luce."

His gaze fixed on hers and she blinked rapidly, fighting against the tears welling there.

"You were pining. If I thought he would have taken my calls, I would have done the prostrating myself then. As it was, I nearly called Margo twice to ask her to intercede."

Surprise speared her. She'd had no idea. Then again that she-bitch had pointed a gun right to Rayne's temple. She could have ended his life right then and Luciana wouldn't have been fast enough to stop her.

It marked her first true failure as a mate and as an alpha.

"Margo and I may not have parted on the best of terms, but I knew her for a long time. She's not an unreasonable wolf."

"What made you not do it?" Because she never wanted him to be in that position either. He didn't deserve to have

OUTLAW WOLVES

to humble himself for all the critical errors Luciana had made.

"I couldn't force you to reconcile with them, no matter how much you missed them. I wanted to fix it for you, but I couldn't. Jackson and I fight, we've fought many times. It's always on us to make it right again." He trailed his fingers down her hair to the tips of it, then dropped his hand back to cover hers.

"Since then, you've changed your mind? Even if I want to reach out to him to solve this problem?"

"Outside of the fact it was one of your brother's Centurions who sent that bastard here?" The words came out a pure rolling growl. "Has it occurred to you that *Rodrigo* was acting under orders to get you back home?"

The question sent a shockwave through her. "No, not even once. Salvatore would never and Giovanni, I trust him. He and Salvatore are more than Centurion and Alpha. They're friends."

"Your brother repudiated you," he reminded her as if she needed it. "He washed his hands of you and your choices, doesn't that stand to reason that it also extended to his Centurions?"

"In the sense that they wouldn't come to my aid or protect me, yes. But Rodrigo insisted Salvatore did not know, that it was Giovanni sending Centurions to watch over me. I do not think Rodrigo was the first. Which means they have been here since Salvatore's visit..." Which numbered in years not months. "More—I told him he would never be able to bring me back to Seven Hills, Salvatore would kill him. He would kill him for the assault alone whether I was his sister or not."

Even using the word left a bitter flavor on the back of her tongue.

"So you think he's broken with Salvatore, too?" Rayne

curled his fingers around hers. It was just the lightest of touches, and yet it offered a wealth of comfort.

"I think he's broken period." Just recalling the way he glared at her, the twisted light in his eyes. The claim he'd always wanted her, and that Rayne had stolen her away was ludicrous. "You have to be careful of him. I know he wants to eliminate you."

At her warning, Rayne smiled. "Oh I hope he tries."

She disagreed, but she felt like something of a hypocrite in warning him off. Now and again, she forgot amongst his gentler manner that before he met, mated, and then later betrayed her, even before he'd been a Lone Wolf, Rayne had been a Hound of Delta Crescent, a powerful wolf in his own right. He could have challenged for the leadership of that pack, but he'd declined and stood on the sidelines to support Serafina, leaving only after she had secured her place.

"You should rest," he told her. "I need to check on the pack. Colby will likely want to work on your arm some more, and we need to let her finish so she can return home. She's already stayed longer than her original intention."

"We can never repay her..."

"No," Rayne agreed. "We can't. But you can take care of yourself for now. You can let her heal you, and then you can sleep."

Even leaning back, propped up in the bed, it was a fight to keep her eyes open. "What are we going to do about..."

"Us?" He seemed to understand without her explanation. "I don't know chére, but we will figure it out together—that is I would like to figure it out together."

How were they going to do that?

"Don't run from it or me. Stop avoiding me. I will give you your space, but I need you here, with me. I need you safe. If we never talk—if we're never in the same place, we're never going to resolve this."

"Even if the resolution is for me to walk away for good?" Because she had to know. If she could not find it within her to forgive him, and to trust him again—her staying could truly wreck the pack.

"I won't accept that outcome."

Stubborn wolf.

"Rayne..."

"No," he repeated firmly. "Just no. I *love* you. That didn't go away. It will *never* go away. Mating is for life, it doesn't just end on a whim."

A whim? "Mates don't challenge each other for pack leadership either..."

"I had to dammit," he spit out the words. "The other alphas would have killed you. You helped the Russians, you gave them a place to land. Once they learned of your complicity—they would have come for you and no amount of bargaining would have saved your life. I took the pack because if they came for anyone it would be me."

He rose, his expression thunderous and his wolf damn near shimmering in the air around him.

"The very last thing I wanted to do was hurt you. But I could not allow anyone to kill you either. You are headstrong, impetuous, and impossibly impulsive, and I love every part of you and it. You are so passionate and driven, you never let anyone tell you no. You made what should have been an inconceivable dream possible. There's only a pack here because you believed it could be done. You didn't let anyone tell you anything differently—those wolves down there? They're here because of you."

But those wolves hated her now.

Lifting her hand to his lips, he kissed the knuckles gently. "We are all here because of you. So no, I do accept that you will have to leave or that we cannot make right between us what has gone so wrong. It is okay if you don't believe me yet. I haven't given you cause to believe me and if it takes the rest of my life, I will earn your trust again, I will earn back the right to be your mate."

Then he pressed the lightest of kisses against her lips, before rising.

"Now rest." His posture firmed. "That is an order. When that arm is fully healed, you may resume your rebellion where I am concerned. Until then please, you will stay *here*." Though he layered it with command, he pushed none of it at her. Only the quiet little please in the middle.

Even if she weren't so exhausted, she would have acquiesced. After his declaration, she couldn't challenge it or him. He was breaking her heart, and she still couldn't. "I'll stay," she told him.

His relief was palpable. Another kiss, this one to her forehead and then he was gone. The door closed behind him. Weariness blanketed her. He challenged her because she'd let the Russians in. Because she'd let the...

A little laugh wound up through her, one almost borne of hysteria and she had to press her good hand to her mouth to keep the sound contained. Her mate had betrayed her and taken the pack because she let the Russians in and he wanted to protect her from the other alphas—from the sure retribution they would take.

The soft knock on the door alerted her to Colby's arrival. The healer slipped inside and gave her a smile. "I saw Rayne downstairs, so I thought I'd come do this so you can sleep."

Biting the inside of her cheek to get her irrational reactions under control, Luciana nodded. Colby made her way around to the far side of the bed.

"You do look much better," she assured her. "You were so very pale the last couple of days, but there's color in your cheeks—and that spark in your eyes is a great sign."

If she said so, but still, Luciana couldn't say anything. If she opened her mouth, it would all come pouring out. She would lose what ragged pieces of her sanity she had left.

The healer paused as she eased away the splint. Her arm was crisscrossed with thick red marks and heavy bruising. Where the bone had penetrated the skin it had closed, but it look fragile. The striations in the bruising had spread down the whole of her arm, as though trying to lessen the pressure from the internal bleeding.

All were likely true.

"And this definitely looks better, and since it looks horrible that should give you some idea of how it looked before as well." But she didn't move to take her arm or to begin her work; instead she studied her. "You're upset."

"It doesn't matter," she managed to say, because if she didn't find the words then it may truly worry her and the healer would call Rayne back. He had his work to do. She could handle this for now.

"I know I dumped a lot on you..."

"Colby," Luciana said and tried to keep her voice kind. "We owe you a debt we can never repay, but you and I are still relative strangers and I am very tired, very sore, and I apologize for this, but if you don't hush—I am likely to start snapping at you and you do not deserve it."

No healer ever did and it was an affront to consider bellowing at one.

"Hmm," Colby let out a little laugh. "Would cussing someone out help you feel better? Because I tell you what, I can take it. Bigger wolves than you have growled and scowled, and stomped their feet. I promise, you can rage against me and I will let you get it out."

"No," she assured her, though her smile this time was genuine. "It would be better for everyone if I keep it to myself."

"If you're sure…" Though the healer sounded very skeptical.

Of course, she wasn't sure. She was certain of nothing except the universe or God or the devil or something was having a great joke at her expense. The wicked little laugh bubbled up in her again, but when she looked away from Colby the wolf sighed and began her work.

Luciana fought to concentrate on the healing, on the spider web of pain latticing through her as Colby did her work. It helped to choke off the inappropriate laughter.

She had to keep it back because if it escaped it would bring all her tears, her rage, and her howls with it. He challenged her, ripped out her heart, and betrayed their bond to save her life.

And she had only let the Russians in to save her pack's life —his especially.

CHAPTER 19

The last thing Rayne wanted to do was walk out of that room. He'd decided much earlier that he wouldn't leave her until she was completely healed, but the more she told him about Rodrigo—the better picture he had for the problem. If she were fully healed, she'd want in on the hunt and no way in hell would Rayne give that bastard another shot at her.

Not when her confrontation with said bastard had rocked her confidence. Confidence Rayne had damn near decimated in his challenge. The last remaining shred of his conscience convinced they could just put the challenge behind them died an ignoble death. He would win her back if it took the rest of his life, but he'd made a choice to save her life by crushing her and he had to accept she might never forgive the action or him.

Chewing the bitterness of that pill, he strode down the stairs and took inventory of his home. It smelled of multiple wolves, many who didn't belong. Enforcers. Hunters. Healers. All wolves from other packs who'd come to help. A part of him resented the hell out of their presence, but it was the territorial side that only saw them as invaders. The rest of him, the friend, the mate, and the wolf who had sworn to protect his pack—that one was grateful.

And he would be equally as grateful as soon as they were gone. In the kitchen, he found Colby's escort, kicked back in a chair his eyes half closed and cup of coffee in his hand. "If you want me to fuck off, I can go upstairs and sit in the hall, but man—your floors suck."

The droll comment alleviated some of the negative pressure humming around Rayne. From the moment he descended the stairs, his wolf had risen and begun to pace within him. The restless rustle of fur brushed against the inside of his skin. "It's just Colby and Luciana up there. You can continue to fuck off right where you are."

"You're all right," Luc said with a laugh. "There's more coffee. I carried another urn over. Colby can drink it by the gallon when she's in heal mode and she's a real bear without it." Something about the sentence made him laugh, but since Rayne had zero interest in criticizing the woman who'd saved his mate and pack, he let it go. She could have coffee imported straight from South America if she wished and he'd find a way to foot the bill.

While pouring a cup, he made a mental list of everything he needed to do. First on the agenda was to make a sweep of the pack. He needed to make a point of visiting every single one of them. He owed them more thanks and care than he could ever admit. While performing that task, he would track down Julian and his wolves. Hopefully the Enforcers had something for him. Third, he would find the son of a bitch and gut him.

He would prefer to skip to number three on the list.

In fact, he might just work on number three while taking care of number one and two. Who the hell did this damn wolf think he was? Even if he'd had a flirtation with Luciana, which Rayne doubted ever existed—he'd seen her in her native element. He'd watched the other wolves tease her and be solicitous, but none of them stepped a foot out of line with her. She was Salvatore's sister and the Centurions acted like another set of older brothers.

It had made their trysts all the more titillating—because Rayne hadn't been scared of her brother. He also hadn't dragged her into bed, no matter what the rumors said. They'd actually spent time together, a lot of walking, talking, and she'd pulled out every story he had for living in America, for being part of Delta Crescent.

"If you loved it so much, why did you leave?" They were sitting under a tree on a little hill overlooking the vineyard. Honestly, there was no part of this place that Rayne hadn't found to enjoy. It was peaceful and settled the disquiet in his soul.

Or maybe it was just the wolf with him.

"Because I didn't want to be an alpha, and I didn't want to serve anymore...it's strange, because I love Serafina. She was an amazing Hound and has proven to be a great alpha. When I left the pack, I wandered. But I never found what I was looking for..."

"...what were you looking for?"

Her. It took him a while to get there, but it had always been her. The restlessness—all of it faded with her.

Memories rolled over him like thunderclaps in a summer afternoon storm. The gradual rising crescendo inciting his anger to burn hotter, and his wolf thrashed against his skin. He could almost feel the fur prickling as it rippled over him, and yet all he did was lift the cup to his lips to drink. A low sound pulled his attention, reminding him he wasn't alone.

Luc's relaxed posture had stiffened. Though he hadn't straightened from his slouched position, he studied Rayne with quiet, sober eyes. "They haven't found him yet," he told him, straight edged and blunt. "We're running teams day and night, and we've been moving out in graduating circuits.

Dallas has located at least two of the places he had been staying—two different vacation rentals about thirty minutes away. But he's cleared out and not returned to those."

That was something.

The front door opened, and Julian's scent announced his arrival, and that of three other wolves with him. He recognized Dallas' scent, but not the other two.

"Mitch and Amelia," Luc said, his voice low. It wouldn't carry, but Rayne couldn't miss it. "Mitch is Julian's Second."

Not altogether certain why the other wolf was being so accommodating, but appreciating it nonetheless, he nodded to him. He took another drink of his coffee and waited for the wolves to arrive in the kitchen.

"Glad to see you're up," Julian said without ceremony. "Luciana?"

"Is healing still, her arm was severely damaged and Colby wants her to take another day or two before she shifts." Normally he wouldn't be so swift to share his mate's condition with anyone, but these wolves had earned his respect and were due some greater measure of politeness beyond grudging.

"I'm glad to hear it," Dallas said, her tone conveying nothing more than that exact sentiment. "Rayne, this is Mitch Jackson and his mate Amelia. Amelia's been working at the diner, and getting meals out to the pack, and the visitors. Mitch has taken point on watching the town while the rest of us hunt."

"Thank you both," he said, though the formality of it all sat on him like an itchy wool coat.

"Glad I could help," Amelia answered with a small smile. "Louis is back today though and he kicked me out of his kitchen." That was excellent news. Her smile grew at the last and she held up a canvas bag. "He also sent me with gumbo for you. It's sealed in a thermos so it stays hot."

His stomach rumbled a response that even made Julian crack a smile. "Would you mind eating that while you and I talked?" The question was well-phrased, because Julian had to know the last thing Rayne wanted was to sit and talk to him. He needed to check on his pack. While Louis' gumbo wasn't New Orleans quality, it was still damn fine and he'd only made it for Rayne on a few special occasions.

"If necessary," Rayne told him, accepting the bag from Amelia with another quiet thanks in her direction. "We can use my office." He added a spoon and bowl to the bag, then refilled his coffee before leading Julian to his office.

Had it been only a little over a week since he'd last hosted the man in here? The fireplace was cold, and dark. No foreign scents marked the leather or rugs. So they'd been in the house, but they hadn't used this room.

Having had to tolerate the smell of other wolves even in his bedroom, this proved something of a respite. Circling the desk, Rayne pulled out his chair, and then set about preparing his gumbo to eat. As soon as he finished, he wanted to check on his wolves—starting with his brother, who was conspicuously not present along with Mark.

"We haven't tracked down Rodrigo Mazzanti as yet. Dallas located at least three bolt holes for him now..."

"Luc only mentioned two," Rayne commented between bites.

"We located the third today. It was a campground, probably hasn't been used since the weather turned, but he kept a bag of gear there stowed in a waterproof canvas. Including his passport. So unless he has a private way out, he's still in the country."

His wolf went on point. "You have someone watching the campsite? He'll want that back."

"I have two of my best there. Neither John nor Hadley will let him slip by." The Chief Enforcer went quiet as Rayne steadily devoured the gumbo. The moment he tasted it, his whole being seemed to wake up to the fact he was hungry. He'd eaten pretty much anything they put in front of him, but he hadn't tasted it.

The world lack flavor, substance, or color when his mate struggled to survive. Even if he had not earned her back, she still lived and the color could bleed into his world, albeit in a washed out palate.

"I have refrained from reaching out to Salvatore or Margo." The quiet admission pulled Rayne's attention back to the older wolf. Julian wore his displeasure close, and didn't make it an issue. "Amelia is also familiar with the mate of Giovanni Conti, the wolf who sent Rodrigo here. We have not reached out to her either." Though clearly he wished to.

"Say what's on your mind," he told Julian. He didn't have time for games or to parse the hundred different meanings of his words and actions. They were not that close, and God willing, they would never need to be.

"It is a mistake to not utilize all the resources at our fingertips. Rodrigo is one of Salvatore's wolves—for good or ill—as Alpha he is responsible for the wolf's choices and actions. Just as you would be for the actions of your wolves, and I am for the action of mine." As Julian always had been though the Enforcer pack was even *newer* than Three Rivers.

"Salvatore is no friend to this pack," he kept his tone even, dispassionate. Salvatore was no friend of his nor of Luciana.

"He's not an enemy either," Julian countered. "And he is still her brother…"

"*He* repudiated her. Disavowed her of any claim to him or his pack. Tell me again why you think he'd even answer a call?" Because as yet, the wolf had not returned Rayne's message. Granted it had been cryptic, but if the man had even a curious bone about his sister he'd call her.

"I can understand your reluctance…"

"It's more than reluctance," he told Julian as he set aside the empty bowl. The gumbo had warmed his stomach, and given him some clarity as it dulled the sharp edge of hunger. "The wolf claimed he was sent here by Giovanni. Giovanni answers to Salvatore. Ergo...Salvatore sent a wolf here that ultimately assaulted my mate and tried to kill her." He'd tried to do a hell of a lot more than that, but that was between Rayne and Rodrigo. "Tell me again why I should reach out to someone who put her at risk in the first place."

"Honestly, I can't. Salvatore will need informing one way or the other, when this is over. But...it is your call." He didn't sound like he cared for it too much but at least he was letting it go.

"We can inform him when we send him the body bag. If there's enough left for one." That wolf was not walking away. Period. It was well within his rights and Luciana's to demand that satisfaction. As old fashioned a concept as it might be, even the most modern among them wouldn't fault the demand that blood required blood. "Is that all you needed to discuss with me? I don't intend to be short, but I have several things I need to do before I get back to Luciana."

"Nothing that can't keep. As of now, the Enforcers and other guests are here at your pleasure. We can send home anyone you wish to remove from the territory as your pack regains their footing."

"Appreciated. And for now, if I can extend your goodwill to a few more days, I would be obliged. In particular, I would like to extend my thanks to all who came, in particular the healers. But my focus has to be on the pack, my mate, and hunting Rodrigo." Not necessarily in that order.

"Not a problem. We'll keep running it as we have. I haven't had them coming to you with any issues, do you want that to change?"

"If it's basic supplies and demand, I'll leave that in your

hands. If it directly ties to one of my wolves, I'd appreciate the heads up." It was a tightrope to balance control between two alphas. A little over a week before when Julian sat in the office, Rayne hadn't experienced the kind of confidence thrumming through him currently.

That wasn't the right word for it, even his wolf seemed more settled and less disturbed by the ally in the room—even if he was a powerful dominant and alpha in his own right. Rising, Rayne extended his hand. "Thank you again."

"Not a problem," Julian said with a nod as he clasped the hand. "It is literally why the Enforcers exist. We protect the packs. All of them." He didn't have to add *even yours* and there was no element of judgment in the proclamation.

"I still appreciate it…I do have one favor to ask though." This one would be a favor.

"Name it."

"I need to see my brother, and check on my pack in person. Can you and Dallas remain here until I return?" He didn't have to include the why, nor did he expect Julian to ask.

"We will keep her safe." He hesitated a beat as he straightened. "And may I offer you one piece of advice?"

Might as well. "Name it."

"The other alphas have all been where you are right now at some point. While it may not seem the same, they have been. They're also a resource. Talk to them."

"I'll keep that in mind."

After Rayne cleaned up the dishes from his lunch, he left the house with the Enforcers to keep watch. The sensation of leaving his mate under their protection rubbed his fur the wrong way, more unsettling than distressing. Outside, the cool air rushed against his too tight skin.

He paused as he descended the two steps from the wrap-around porch and looked down the length of their Main

Street. They'd been gradually reclaiming the buildings, refurbishing them inside and out. The town, like the pack, was a work in progress.

The fresh coats of paint with their varying colors brightened the town despite the gray skies and looming rain. They'd survived. The whole pack had come together and they'd survived. It had taken help—a lot of it—but they were still here. Glancing back at the house, he sought the sense of his mate via the fragmented bond. Sending a wordless pulse along it, he tried not to lean in to it too hopefully. But the answering pulse told him she'd at least sensed him, she knew he thought of her.

It wasn't enough to tell her. He had to be more active in how he showed her. Determination renewed, he pivoted and headed down the block to the apartment Jackson had claimed.

He didn't even make it to the top of the stairs before his brother's door was open, and Jackson greeted him with a hard hug and a pound on his back. "Don't you ever scare the hell out of us again, brother. Cause I will kick your ass." Jackson laughed in the middle of the threat, and then eased back to study him. "You look like hell."

"I feel a hell of a lot better." Luciana was alive. It could have been so much worse. "Mark up and about?"

"Yeah, as of late yesterday. He still looks like he went on a ten day bender to Sin City, but he's on his feet."

"Good. Call him. I want him here. I want every one of the Hunters who are on their feet, here unless they're looking for that Rodrigo bastard."

Slinging an arm around him, Jackson led him into the apartment. "I'll get then here, and then have Louis send over some food. You need anything?"

"Whatever he sends for the rest is fine." Jackson's apartment was basically one wide-open floor space with some columns to break it up. He'd knocked out all the walls, and it gave him a generous sprawl and was perfect for his oversized sectional that was only slightly outmatched by his enormous television.

"Rayne," Jackson said, phone in hand.

"Yeah?"

"I'm glad Luciana made it," he told him, the words ringing with honesty.

"Thought you weren't a fan." Though he kept his tone even, one of the items on his discussion with the Hunters today was a clear cut stake that Luciana was his mate, and she was staying—if they didn't like it. They could leave. No more doubt. No more prickling. No more whispers about him getting rid of her.

"You know...I didn't think I was either. And then I felt you call. Felt why, too. Not the whole picture, but enough of the gist to understand the urgency. Wasn't going to let you lose her if I could help it." Then he gave him a wry smile. "Besides, no one ever said we have to like our family, did they?"

A fresh layer of relief buffered him. "No," he told his brother, accepting the pledge for what it was, an open acknowledgement that Luciana was family and therefore someone he should and absolutely would protect. "We definitely don't—been plenty of times I couldn't stand you."

"Feeling's mutual bro," Jackson winked. "Definitely mutual. Now let me get the text sent out. Then I hope you have a plan, because I'm liking all these strangers and not pack around less and less every day."

"I get it, but we need their help and I'm grateful for it." It wasn't about his pride; it was about his pack and his mate. "But we have another matter we have to deal with first..."

CHAPTER 20

*T*hree days later, Luciana made her way down the stairs. She'd successfully managed a shift, and even though it exhausted her, the triumph had buoyed her mood. Hudson River's healer needed to go home; she'd been with Three Rivers for over a week when her original visit wasn't supposed to last two full days. Luciana would miss the healer, but she welcomed the reason why—she no longer required her care.

Her first shift the day before had failed miserably, and with Rayne in the room. Too much pain, and the soreness in arm had been distracting. Or maybe it had been Rayne who was too distracting. Either way, she resisted the shift until she sagged, soaked through with sweat and panting for a breath. Rayne ordered her to stop, then begged her.

Relenting seemed too close to failure, but she couldn't argue with the pain reflected in his eyes. Though he spent as much time as he could, he'd also spent a growing number of hours outside of the house. The limited range of motion in her arm worried him to the point, she'd stopped arguing about staying in the master bedroom. Thankfully Colby had helped her air it out, and they'd brought in fresh bedding and more. It smelled less like a hospital chamber bathed in her blood, and more like a bedroom.

But the moment he left earlier that morning to hunt—as if he thought she didn't know—she'd gone for the shift again. Alone, and without an audience, she'd gritted her teeth and made it happen. The snap and reformation of her bones nearly had her blacking out. Once it was done, however, once it was done, she took her first real deep breath in a week and stretched the muscles along her frame.

No doubt, she'd lost muscle and she would be weaker on one side for a while. That didn't mean she couldn't correct it. The first step was no more lounging about. Luc and Colby had both stared at her in surprise when she appeared. The wolf Luc Danes, she'd seen very little of him. Rayne hadn't allowed him in the room and if he'd been in there when she was unconscious, she likely wouldn't remember him.

"Luciana," she said by way of introduction.

"Luc," he answered…then made a face. "That's for Lucas, actually, but most people call me Luc. I didn't put that together before."

She chuckled, nor had she really. "It's fine." Turning to look at Colby she met the healer's measured stare. "Yes, I shifted."

"You did it alone." The accusation carried no heat, but a great deal of recrimination. "That was dangerous."

"It was necessary. It was painful, but I expected that. And as you can see," Luciana said, flexing her arm. "It's much better now."

Colby had pulled her long black hair back into a braid off her face, and she tugged on it as she considered her. "You still need to have care for the next few shifts. Each one will improve the strength in that arm, leg—you know what I mean. But you need to be careful not to overdo it. You will probably be more prone to injuring it for a time."

"So you told me," Luciana assured her. "But for now, I'm sick of that room and that bed. If you try to send me back there, be prepared for very strenuous objections, followed by my ignoring you."

Luc hid a smile, but he couldn't quite contain a chuckle. "Sounds like you're definitely better to me."

"I agree," Colby told her, then rose. "I'm not sure if you do hugs. I was never much of a hugger, but the damn wolves are always hugging and I feel like you could use one."

While Luciana couldn't say she was much of a hugger, she took a step toward the healer and accepted the swift, if careful embrace. "I will never be able to thank you for what you have done," she told her. It bore repeating.

"I'm glad I was here," Colby admitted as she stepped back. "I wasn't really sure I was ready for this journeyman trip, but everyone—except Brett said I was."

"Brett just didn't want you that far away, he always knew you could do it," Luc reminded her, and it sounded like an old and familiar argument.

"I know," she said to him over her shoulder. "But I still had my doubts and I was rather enjoying the fact he kept blocking it until I fought him on it."

It was Luciana's turn to smile. "He knew you were ready when you fought for it. That's pretty common with alphas. When you can fight for something you want, something that you need, they usually understand the difference and can support. Otherwise, the default is simply to protect—doubly so for healers."

"Triply so for healing mates," Luc tacked on. "But if you're really doing better, then I want to start making arrangements." He rose from his seat, and though he contained all that dominant male wolf, it unfurled with his interest in getting Colby out of Three Rivers and back to their own territory.

"You haven't had an enviable position, have you?" She could only imagine the pressure on the single wolf to protect his alpha's mate being thrown into the middle of a pack collapse.

"Not really," he said giving her a comical look, his eyes wide and his jaw set. "No."

"Luc," Colby objected, but Luciana waved her off.

"You have to understand, healers are a treasure in all the packs, and we were not in a position to protect you, which meant the full burden fell to him." Meeting Luc's gaze, she had to surmise there had been times he would have wanted to just remove her lest she risk herself. "You both stretched yourselves for us—and I appreciate it."

"I'd say all a part of the job, lady," he actually made the last endearment sound like a compliment. "But I'm ready to show this town our backs and get Colby home to her pack."

"Are you absolutely sure?" Colby hesitated, her dark eyed gaze a deep well of concern. "This is your first day downstairs."

"I am certain. Rayne is on his feet; the pack is on their feet and by all reports recovering. We have support from the Enforcers…your work is done, Colby. You should go home, and rest." Because the shadows beneath the other wolf's eyes weren't lost on her. They had diminished some over the last few days, she still seemed more than a little pale, and her eyes shadowed and reddened. So much of herself had she poured into all of them, and so much work she'd done to rebuild and save Luciana's arm.

"Okay," she smiled, her whole expression lightening and even the atmosphere in the kitchen seemed to lift. "I'll call Brett."

"I'll call the plane." Luc offered his hand to Luciana as

Colby headed into the guest bedroom on the first floor—likely where she'd been sleeping during her time here when she slept. Luciana grasped his hand carefully; a little wary of how her right arm and hand would feel. "Thank you for that," he told her in an almost sub vocal tone. "She wouldn't leave you until she was absolutely certain you would be fine."

"I understand." No, she didn't, not fully but she was beginning to. The healer owed Luciana nothing, and didn't know anything about her. Yet she'd committed so much of her energy to Luciana's recovery, to saving the pack as a whole, to restoring Rayne, and to explaining to them the damage done to their mate bond. She'd been in a precarious position, and likely no one would have faulted her if she'd balked at the inherent danger in what she'd done. "Take care of her."

"With my life." Luc gave her hand a gentle squeeze. "And for what it's worth—you definitely seem like someone who was worth saving."

She laughed. "Thank you?"

"You're welcome," he said with a wink, then he pulled out his own phone before stepping just outside the back door.

They seemed to be the only two wolves in the house. After pouring herself a cup of coffee, Luciana made her way up to Rayne's office—her former office. A room she had refused to enter since the day he challenged her. Even standing in the doorway sent a hot-cold chill skating over her skin. Her wolf roused, as weary from the shift as Luciana had been, but she was no longer shirking. They stared into the room as the next obstacle they needed to cross.

Three days since Rayne had begun to re-gather his mantle as alpha. Three days since he'd resumed his leadership by meeting with every member of the pack. He'd left early each morning and returned late each evening. Once he'd come to see her at lunch, but then he'd been off again.

Three days since he'd begun hunting for Rodrigo. They hadn't found him yet. There had been no word from any of the wolves. If anything, she'd heard notes of frustration in the voices discussing it as quietly as they could downstairs in the hopes that she would not hear.

What they couldn't understand was it had been a week since he'd tried to kill her and threatened her mate. It didn't matter what secrets they sought to keep. She would not withdraw from the hunt. They'd had the time she was recovering to find him.

Now it was her turn.

Shoulders set, she stepped into Rayne's office and moved to the desk. There was mail stacked in the inbox—bills generated by the town, invoices for supplies, purchase orders, and other items that all required review. Next to that was a couple of thin boxes. They had the scent of other wolves on them, and one had the seal of Delta Crescent— likely a gift from another alpha.

She left those alone.

The laptop was sleeping, but two keystrokes and she had the password screen up. His password used to be *San Gimignano* for the region where they met. Clearing her throat, she typed it in and the screen opened to a local map of the region. Rayne had been studying the topography. There were notes added, little x's—probably for places they'd eliminated—some houses were noted, these were several miles way, but in isolated spots. They were circled, then X'd through. Entering the addresses for those places, she frowned. They were rentals of some kind.

Rodrigo would need a place to stay that would give him relatively easy access to their territory. He must have had a vehicle to follow her to another state... how close had he been to her to even know that was where she'd gone? She'd left town directly, and run—not driven—to the storage facility. No one had been close to her. As desperate as she had been to get away, she didn't forget to pay attention to her surroundings. She had not been so foolish as to not check the path behind her and in front, even if she'd been half blind in her desire to put distance between she and Three Rivers.

To track her in town would mean Rodrigo had to *be* in town. Leaving the desk, she crossed to the windows. The blinds had been slatted open, but they were angled for privacy. The sun had come out after days of rain and gloom, but it was a watery kind of sunlight.

There were three buildings with good line of sight on their house. He'd appeared atop one that first night after revealing himself when he'd stared in her bedroom. She should have recognized the danger then. Still... those buildings were all occupied by Three Rivers wolves. They already worked and lived in two, and were working on the interiors of the third daily to rehab it.

Even as stressed as the pack had been, they would not miss someone unknown being there. The back of the house opened onto a green area, but it lacked trees. There was no cover. No place to blend in out of sight. The only place Rodrigo had approached her previously was the old house.

She went there often enough, he could have spent time watching it. But still, he had to have shadowed her at some point in order to follow what was going on in town, to know Rayne challenged her, to know she'd lost her position. No wolf could mask themselves so much they would be missed by everyone in closer quarters.

Not even Salvatore had done that. He'd masked himself, he and his Centurions when they'd gone to meet Margo, but Luciana had known he was there. She just didn't know where.

Studying the street, she narrowed her eyes. Three Rivers had been comprised of Lone Wolves, wolves used to being on their own, wolves aware of the subtlest of changes. It had made for a difficult bonding, because they were so used to being solitary. Adapting to a pack atmosphere, one so radically different from the packs they originated in had been a frequent source of conflict. In some ways, it had weeded out the troublemakers, the ones who would never truly bend or adapt. It had elevated others as they created a place for themselves.

And in some cases—it ostracized, highlighting their differences and making them feel alone. Like Chrystal. The little omega had wanted so desperately to fit in, to belong, and she'd floundered because she had no idea what pack should feel like and the rest of them were fighting to bind ties while simultaneously holding back to protect themselves.

And that's on me. I failed to recognize how difficult it would be for everyone. I assumed that pack meant exactly the same thing to each person, and we would all be on the same page. I worked from that perspective, and tried to just endure the moments where it became clear it wouldn't. That's on me.

Yet even amidst all of that, they would have known an outsider was in town. There was a frenetic energy to the pack at the moment, an agitation brought on by outsiders in their midst. They weren't afraid or angry, but unsettled and her awareness of their unease coated the back of her mind like an aftertaste. They would be happier when the outsiders were gone, but they endured.

They'd found equilibrium, finally. That confidence existed beneath the rest. Confidence, and perhaps a little frustration. Still...

She pivoted and paced the room. How had Rodrigo followed her to the mountains? How had he known where she'd gone? The car was in storage, she hadn't used it since settling in the town. She rarely went to the storage facility, seeing it had jogged loose the memory that she had items there...

The storage facility.

They rarely went there.

Hadn't in months.

It wasn't so far, she couldn't run the distance.

But it wasn't in pack territory.

Yet, she paused and stared into the cold hearth. It was the perfect place to lie low, and to disappear amongst so many other conflicting scents. A place they would avoid scenting too deeply if they went at all. But it still didn't put him in a position to observe the town...

Observe.

Whirling, she returned to the window and she stared at the buildings. Studying everything from the shape of the windows, to the angle of the roofs, to the wood struts supporting their porch coverings. The watery sunlight gleamed off one window, a slight glare that stung her eyes if she stared at it too long.

Would he have been so bold?

Could he...

Pivoting, she stalked out of the office, and down the hall to the front door. Luc called something, but she waved him off as she stepped outside. Mark glanced up from where he leaned against the railing on the porch—his phone in hand. "Mrs. Barrows..."

"I've told you to call me Luciana," she informed him, and then jogged down the steps and across the street. He hurtled after her, but she barely heard him as she focused on where she'd seen the glare.

There were other wolves on the street; they stopped as she moved around them. To each greeting, she murmured a response, but she and her wolf were on a mission and they needed an answer.

"Luciana," Rayne's voice came from down the street, but she only half-glanced to her mate as she reached her destination and stared up at the lip of the porch roof, how it tucked in, but had a different brace along the inside, a kind of windbreak.

She sensed more than saw Rayne's rapid approach as he jogged up behind her. A rush of anger swamped her before it cut off abruptly. It wasn't fury exactly, it was—concern. "What are you doing out here?" The contact of his hand against her lower back silenced her answer and she nearly staggered under the heat of it.

Turning her head, she caught sight of his eyes. The pupils were blown; gold bleeding into the color, but his attention was riveted on her. And it hit her, all the worry and concern that she was just outside and on the street. Why wasn't she inside and safe? Where the hell was Mark? Below that, *need*. Need to get inside, and hidden away again—protected and shielded.

Shaking her head slowly, she tried to clear away the drunken sensations. "This is important," she told him, grasping his forearm and tugging his hand from her back so she could turn and point. "I came out here because of *that*."

There, nestled against the wood, tucked strategically was a camera.

Rayne glared at it. "Son of a bitch."

"And I bet there's more…"

She didn't have to say another word, the wolves around them scattered. Belatedly she realized most of them had been their Hunters, though there had been Enforcers in the mix, too. A shout came from down the street. Another camera had been found.

And another.

By the end of the day, a dozen different cameras in varying locations giving the widest view of the town from day to day. None had been inside, likely because the wolf or wolves who installed them could mask their scents outside, but it would be a damn sight more difficult to cover up their presence on the interiors.

Sitting on the desk in Rayne's office, Luciana let him pace back and forth. There had been debate about what to do with the cameras, but she'd said take them down. Anyone monitoring would have seen her pointing it out, so that cat was long since out of the bag.

"They didn't have long range, but they were sending to a server they'd installed in one of the empty apartments we weren't likely to get to for months." God, he was furious. It was a damn good look on him, all that barely contained power vibrating as he stalked back and forth. "That server then sends it off to God knows where. And they've been spying on us...*for months.* Your brother..."

"Not Salvatore," she said, her tone firm. No way her brother had anything to do with this particular piece of trash. She highly doubted Giovanni would have either.

"You don't know that, chere." He stopped and stared at her. "He was very angry with you..."

"That's how I know," she admitted. "He repudiated me, Rayne. Whether he still cares about me as his sister or not, he *severed* his ties to me. Severed me from Seven Hills. Salvatore is an *honorable* man and an *honest* one. I'm not saying he wouldn't lie, cheat, or steal to protect what is his—but that day—that day I died to him. That out there...those cameras, that's not him."

He considered her for a long moment, then nodded. "What about Giovanni?"

She shook her head. "Giovanni is...he's a charmer. He's a diplomat. He wins more with his skilled gift of words and sentiment than he does in straight combat. But never mistake how strong he is, or how vicious a fighter. It would be the last mistake. Those cameras are...they're invasive. They're an act of war. Rodrigo insisted Giovanni sent him to protect me. Those cameras...they don't protect. And if that's how he knew you challenged me..." Since it happened in broad daylight in the middle of town where everyone could be front row to her humiliation, she didn't doubt it was. "You would think that knowledge would have sent them rushing to my aid."

"But he didn't even show himself to you for months."

"Exactly. Whether Rodrigo did it or one of the other wolves Giovanni sent, I know it wasn't Salvatore. I'd stake my life on it."

"Even now?"

She nodded.

Blowing out a breath, he crossed to where she sat and settled his hands on her knees, a light touch, a grounding one. "Then not him. But we still don't know where those cameras are transmitting."

"I think I know," she told him, more certain than ever. "But when you go after him—I'm going with you."

"Luciana..."

"Together or not at all, Rayne." She zeroed in on his gaze, his wolf shining out at her and hers rose, her eyes shifting and changing her perceptions but she never stopped staring at him. "This isn't just your fight."

He didn't want her there. The resistance was like a palpable wall pushing her away, but his fingers curled and tightened against her legs. The wolf in front of her wanted to lay down his life for her, but she'd much prefer he lived.

Finally, the pressure eased and he blew out a breath. "It's our fight."

Yes.

It was.

ogether, or not at all Rayne. The declaration staggered him, not in the least because the force of her will had met his head on. Stalemate was one thing, but it was the sizzle of energy lighting him up that had his wolf rousing. A rightness he could barely define, and though the very last thing he wanted was her in danger, it would be impossible to leave her behind.

No—it would be *wrong* to leave her behind. They'd had enough wrongness. His agreement didn't surprise her as much as he'd thought it might. Instead, she'd merely smiled and then turned the laptop screen around to show him the picture of the storage facility.

"That's where we kept your things and your..." He trailed off, and anger scorched his belly a flash fire threatening to turn everything to ash. "That son of a bitch set up in there? That's how he followed you."

She nodded slowly. "I couldn't imagine any other scenario for how he tracked me to those mountains. And if he'd been here—in town regularly enough to track me the day I left *on foot*, I would have noticed. You would have noticed him.

Salvatore is the only one who can mask his scent so perfectly I couldn't tell he was there—but that erasure doesn't mean their scent won't linger on something."

"The cameras?" It had been like chewing ground glass since she pointed it out. Their placement was an invasion he couldn't overlook. It was even worse than the monitoring they'd endured due to the other packs and the Enforcers. At least they'd known who was watching them, and why. There had been negotiation and information exchange.

This? This was just plain invasive.

Luciana remained perched on his desk, her feet dangled as she kicked them lightly. The rhythmic movement something she did when she needed to focus and she had too many thoughts running through her head. The familiarity in the action made him smile. It had been a while since she'd fidgeted so openly in front of him. So much better than the unnatural stillness and distance she'd affected for months.

"The only thing I can think of are the first weeks after we were discovered here. We had so much construction going on, and we were all pulling a lot of hours—we had materials coming in, and we were coping with the first wave of Hunters and Enforcers arriving to monitor..."

"You think they slipped in during the chaos."

"One more wolf amidst many who were still relative strangers to each other, while having actual strangers here? Yes." She nodded slowly, her dark eyes thoughtful. "I think it would have been simple enough to make these adjustments, install the cameras, set up the routers. We had *so* much happening." She frowned. "That's a failure on our part."

"Agreed," he said, aligning with her fully. "But this is a failure we can recover from, and make sure never happens again." Then he exhaled because as much as it was necessary, he wasn't fond of the next point. "We need to head to the storage facility. If Rodrigo is smart, he may have already left since we found the cameras."

Her gaze zeroed in on his, and she nodded slowly. "He's too arrogant to run. We found the cameras—you and I are at odds, we are not terrifically friendly with the other packs, and we're facing possible invasion with so many foreigners here and our pack seemingly down."

Rayne's jaw dropped slightly. There was something exquisite about her conniving mind. "You want to play to his arrogance because you think he'll be there."

"Yes," she said succinctly. "He's been there for months and we never noticed. We haven't had any cause to hunt there. You've been looking for him for days, and now even the Enforcers are involved, and no one has found him."

Though aware of the fact, it still raked him the wrong way for her to point it out so baldly. Narrowing the distance between them, he settled his hands on her thighs and stilled her legs. "You want to play to his arrogance," he repeated even as he turned the idea over in his mind. She wanted to bait him, bait the wolf who'd tried to kill her.

The memory of her blood on the snow, the pain rippling in her expression, the awful image of the bones protruding from her arm overlaid by the stutter of her heart as she slowly wasted away in their bed upstairs.

Lashes dipping, she met his gaze from beneath them. "Yes. He's beaten me once," she kept her tone light, and spread her fingers against his chest when he growled. "He beat me, Rayne. If you hadn't been there—he would have killed me. No matter what his intentions were, he won that fight."

"No," Rayne argued, dipping his head so he could hold her gaze. "He didn't. You're still here, and with me. He didn't take you away."

The corner of her mouth curved upward. "But until today, he didn't know that."

The information rolled over him like the Mississippi rising to burst her banks. "He didn't know. He couldn't have known—you were inside the whole time. It was raining when I got you back here, and all he would have seen..."

"...was you carrying in my body." Her eyebrows lifted and she curled her fingers against his shirt before she pulled her hand away and he mourned its absence. "Until today, he thought he'd killed me."

"Luciana—that is a dangerous game to play with him."

Her shrug was so careless, he wanted to spank her. "It doesn't matter. What matters is we lure him out, we force the confrontation—but we do to him, what he's done to us...to me."

The ambush. Use his feelings against him. Manipulate him. On one level it did not sit well with him, this wasn't how wolves fought. But on the other—she was right. Rodrigo had abused whatever affection she may have had for Seven Hills, her loneliness, and her own grief. He'd abused it, and turned it against her. Then he'd tried to force himself on her...the wolf in him just wanted the bastard dead. The man in him wanted him to suffer. The alpha said he needed to be eliminated, expediently and within pack laws for the U.S. But the mate?

"You will not go inside his little bunker if it is indeed there," he told her, his decision had been made when she'd declared her intentions. He couldn't deny her this, he had no right to do it and more, he didn't want to. The mate in him wanted her to succeed. She had the greater claim in this fight.

The true claim.

"All right," she agreed, almost too easily. "You will not interfere until I've drawn him out."

He didn't like it, but he nodded. "Then we take him together."

"That defies single combat etiquette." It was the etiquette of most wolf on wolf combat, the battle was to be one on one. The rules were more explicitly stated for alpha challenges, but most wolves respected it in their other conflicts. It kept them civil.

"I don't care," he admitted. "You're my mate. No mate would *ever* stand aside…"

"Except in an alpha challenge. You know as well as I do—the mate must stand aside then." But they never had.

That was the crux of it.

"I don't care," he repeated. "When Salvatore and Margo came for you—I would not be removed from your side. When we left Italy, we did it together. When we built this pack, we did it together…"

"When we broke this pack, we did that together, too." The quiet charge lashed him, opening the barely scabbed wounds of betrayal stretched between them. At least when they bled this time, they bled clean. Maybe they needed to be bled.

"Yes," he said slowly. "That we did." When she covered his hand on her thigh with one of her own, he glanced at the picture her more delicate fingers made against his squared and blunted ones. "We're better together, Luciana…" He very nearly whispered the words. "We've been better together from the beginning. I left Delta Crescent, and wandered for years before I went to Europe, and I wandered there until I came to Italy—until you."

The rush of her indrawn breath pulled his gaze upward.

"I'd been looking for something for years…I found that with you. I don't want to lose it again. I don't want to lose you. We do this. We take care of this together—and after… after we decide together our future. If that means we leave Three Rivers, then we go. But we do it together."

"The pack needs you," she said carefully, as if doubting his every word and he couldn't fault her for that. He needed to earn her trust again.

"The pack needs *us*." The correction rang with truth. "They need *us*, Luce...they need *us* and even if they didn't, I *need* you."

She licked her lips, and her heartbeat jumped in pace. "I loved you," she said quietly and his own pulse stuttered.

Past tense.

"I really loved you," she continued. "But I don't know if I loved the idea of you or you yourself."

The pain of it garroted him, but he forced himself to stay still.

"We've both changed since coming here." Instead of pulling away, she curled her hand around his. "We've both... had to change. Do you still love *me*? Or the idea of me?"

"Both," he said, without hesitation or pause. "You give me reason to breathe. I would do anything for you...I would endure anything for you, for the chance of you. Do you think you can forgive me? And love me again?"

"I don't know."

He died a little.

"But I'd like to try..."

Then he had his arms around her and crushed her to him. More, she wrapped her arms around him. Closing his eyes, Rayne buried his face against her hair. He inhaled her scent, and just wanted to stay there and roll around in it. "Thank you," he whispered against her.

"Don't thank me yet," she replied, but her voice had gone husky with unshed tears. "It may not work—I'm not sure how it will work, but I don't plan to make this easy."

"Yell at me, berate me, put me through my paces," he pledged. "I've been wanting you to do it since this happened." Pulling away, he cupped her face in his hands, then stroked away the tears from her cheeks. "I *love* you, Luciana. My wolf is yours. I'm yours. Give me the challenge, and I will meet it."

She sniffed, then traced her thumb over his lower lip. It was the lightest graze of a touch and it sent shivers through his whole system. God he'd missed this, just the casual moments of careless skin-to-skin contact without demand or fury. All those months of hunting her down, seeking her out just to be near her and the fact she kept pulling further and further away from him.

"You're really beautiful," he told her, sliding his fingers up to caress her dark hair. "The most beautiful woman I've ever known—ever will know."

"You're biased," she told him bluntly, and he grinned.

"Damn straight, but doesn't make it any less true." Then he focused on her lips, and his own felt dry, and chapped by comparison when all the moisture fled his mouth. The desire to kiss her threatened to overwhelm him, but he leashed the hunger. Pressing his forehead to hers, he soaked in her presence.

"You ready?"

"Not even close," he admitted, but she was right. They needed to do this. Straightening, he took it one step at a time to slide his hands off her thighs as he backed away. Then he extended his hand to her. "Are you ready?"

If there was even a shred of doubt in her, they would not do this. The precarious nature of her recovery continued to haunt him. Even having her standing before him, her eyes bright and color flushing her pale cheeks, he couldn't shake the unsettled feeling when she'd collapsed on him, when fever wracked her body, and her heart struggled so fiercely.

"No," she said quietly, taking his hand and gripping it. "But I will be when we get there. I have to be."

He frowned. "No you don't."

"Yes," she told him firmly and he had to bite his tongue. "I do. Together, remember?"

Yes. He did.

A knock on the door interrupted and he didn't loose the growl building in his chest. They'd been lucky to have this much time uninterrupted. "Yes," he murmured to her, then lifted her hand to kiss her knuckles, before he faced the door. "Enter."

Jackson's scent announced him even as the door opened. Rayne settled against the desk, leaning next to his mate, and he threaded his fingers with hers. To his surprise—and plea-sure—Luciana settled against his side, her hip brushing his.

His brother glanced between them, and for a split-second, his gaze dipped to their joined hands before rising to study their faces. A smile spread across his face, lightening his expression. When the smile became a smirk, Rayne shook his head.

"Yes, Jackson?"

"Pack's gathering outside." He nodded to the windows, and Rayne followed his glance. They were indeed filling the street out front. Most wore jackets, some were in sweaters, and still more were just in t-shirts and a handful in dresses or skirts. They were leaning on each other, or at least toward one another. Little pockets had formed, they were chatting, some laughed, and others looked thoughtful.

On the whole though...

"Everyone?" Luciana asked, a hint of wonder in her voice. When was the last time they were all together? The first few nights after they'd settled in the town? There had always been outliers, how could there not be in a pack formed from Lone Wolves who preferred their time to themselves? There had also been the troublemakers, like Patrick DuMonde who'd challenged Serafina, and Chrystal, who didn't feel confident in her place, and even their humans—those humans who had helped them so much before they too, drifted away.

"Yes, even Louis is out there. They've been gathering steadily for the last hour or so."

Since he and Luciana settled inside to talk? Rayne frowned.

"They know something is happening," Jackson told him. "We can all feel it. We know about the cameras, and you two are talking—planning. The Enforcers are still here and some of the other outsiders, but they've all kept their distance from this. This is about Three Rivers." Jackson shifted his attention to Luciana. "And the wolf who challenged us all when he hurt you."

Rayne winced at his brother's choice of words, but Luciana merely tilted her head. It was exhilarating and terrifying all at once, how utterly her moods could consume him. Yet there was no distress in her scent. "You would fight for me?" The doubt there, however, the very question threatened to cripple him

His brother had made his feelings plain on this subject, but before Rayne could fill the silence, Jackson touched a hand to his chest. "We've always wanted to fight for you. We just thought you'd given up on us."

That stunned her more than him, though. It echoed through the mate bond, the ragged sensation growing clearer by the moment.

"I didn't think any of you wanted me anymore," she whispered, and her pride lay bare and exposed. Rayne squeezed his mate's hand, determined to anchor her and yet, he needed her to ground him as much. She was real.

They were real.

Jackson's expression gentled far more than Rayne would have expected. "We're a bunch of cantankerous bastards," he said with a resigned air. "But we're your cantankerous bastards. You may not always be the most likeable of wolves with your foreign ways, and arrogant mannerisms—"

Rayne glared at him, but Jackson ignored the heat.

"—but you're ours. If they are coming for you, then they are coming for all of us."

Luciana laughed and suddenly Rayne could breathe again. Marveling at the sound, he glanced down at her. "Arrogant mannerisms and foreign ways? Because I prefer wine with my meals, and for company to actually dress for dinner?"

"Sure," Jackson drawled. "Let's go with that." But there was a glimmer of amusement in his eyes. He was teasing her.

What the hell was happening? Even as the question dawned on Rayne, he decided he didn't care as much about the what so long as it would last. Outside, the pack gathered, waiting for *them*. Not just him, but his mate as well.

"Shall we go and see our pack, Luce?" Their pack.

Not just his.

Not just hers.

Theirs.

"I think we should, but we can't stay long," she reminded him, her voice dipping to sub vocal on the last few words.

"I know," he assured her. But he wanted her to feel the waves of affection, curiosity, and protectiveness coming from those fiercely independent wolves. He wanted her to experience it all.

He nodded to Jackson. "Let's go."

"With pleasure," his brother declared, and he pushed open the doors to lead the way.

Luciana paused just before they exited the office and said, "Does this feel—a little crazy to you?"

"Yes," he said with a firm nod. "But I like this kind of crazy."

Her smile lit up her eyes. "Me too."

CHAPTER 22

The time spent with the pack left her with an almost surreal feeling. It wasn't until Dani hugged her, and then one, after another, the rest of the pack closed in to hug her sometimes in groups, sometimes solo that the change hit her. She was a wolf, but she'd never been overly affectionate. Maybe it was a flaw in her character, but she'd never sought the same kind of tactile comfort so many around them seemed to need.

Sitting in the passenger seat of Rayne's SUV, she stared into the distance as the landscape around them rolled by. Her brother was tactile enough, he always had a shoulder grip or hug for his wolves. Yet neither she nor her mother had been especially affectionate. It hadn't truly occurred to her until today that when she'd welcomed those wolves into the pack, she'd done so through an oath, a blooding, and a personal pledge—but she'd not hugged them to her or wrapped an arm around them.

A glance at her mate had her rubbing below her lower lip in thought. He did those things. He shook hands, slapped backs, and wrapped his arms around any wolf who needed it. It was as easy as breathing for him, but not her.

"You're thinking very hard over there," Rayne said into the quiet. They'd changed before leaving, and Rayne had spent some time with Julian and Dallas before meeting her at his car. She, in turn, had spent time with Colby for one last check up before the healer left. Two Enforcers would be escorting she and Luc along with two Hunters from the pack including Mark, to the plane Hudson River would be sending for them direct. Her prior trip to Willow Bend had been rescheduled. Despite Colby's dry wit and snarky comments, there was an air of tiredness around her she couldn't hide and Luciana was deeply grateful to send her back to her mate and her pack in one piece. "Luce?"

"Woolgathering," she said with a blink. "Trying to sort it all out in my head."

"Can I help?" They had a little under forty-five minutes to get to the storage facility. Jackson would take care of the pack until they returned, while they went after Rodrigo on their own.

"I was thinking I don't hug very much," she admitted. "I never really thought about it today, but when Dani hugged me, she looked vaguely surprised when I returned it. And then—they all wanted hugs."

"Is that a bad thing?" Amusement touched his voice and she glared at him.

"Don't make fun of me."

"I'm not," he said, but there was still a laugh underscoring his words. "Truly, Luce. I'm not."

"Yes you are." She made a face at him and stuck out her tongue, before resuming her study of the horizon. "And maybe you should..."

"Hey." All traces of mirth erased under the tenderness in

that single syllable, and he laid his hand on her leg. "No maybe about it. I'm not making fun of you. Nor do I want to. Talk to me."

"I'm just not a hugger," she admitted, then settled her hand over his. His touch burned right through the denim to warm her leg. "I've never been particularly affectionate. Not with my mother—not with Salvatore."

"You were affectionate with me." The soft observation tugged at her.

"You were different," she admitted. Rayne had appealed to her on so many levels. Hell, he still appealed to her even when she struggled against what he'd done, when she'd struggled with her conflicting emotions. "You are different."

"You don't have to be a hugger Luce, not all wolves are...I mean have you ever looked at Julian and just said the word snuggle to yourself?" The dry, dry comment pulled a laugh from her. "Seriously—not someone I would look at and say, he gives great hugs."

"You're ridiculous," she chuckled with the words. "It's not the same thing though...I'm sure Dallas finds him snuggable —they have a child together."

"Yeah, not something I want to picture. Thanks." The gagging look entertained her. "Still, there's nothing wrong with being selective about who you touch."

"But maybe that's the problem—another one that I didn't see that I had."

"It's *not* a problem, Luce." He squeezed her fingers. "Seriously, it's not. Yes, as a whole we're a boisterous lot who thrive on gossip, hugs, food, sex, and a good run. But those are generalities. We're not all artists, we're not all thoughtful, we're certainly not all interested in listening to the problems of other people. Some of us are hermits, some of us are easily distracted—some of us pick fights rather than talk."

"Fighting can be easier than talking."

"Sure," he agreed with a careless shrug. "And sometimes you get ninja hugged by a five foot healer who won't take no for an answer and she squeezes your life story out of you like you're a tea bag that needs to be wrung out."

"That's oddly specific." And fascinating.

"Well, it happens. We're not identical, if we were—it would be damn boring or you'd look just like your brother and no offense Luce, you're hot—but he's so not my type."

Just the image had her covering her mouth as laughter tore through her dissolving the tension in its path. Rayne cast her a grin, and she shook her head. "Fine," she conceded. "Point made. I'm not a hugger, and that's okay."

"Damn straight."

She licked her lips, and blew out a breath. "I still can't believe they like me—more that they've forgiven me." Nor did she truly understand it. After the challenge, after all of it, they'd all seemed so cold and remote.

"Luce, we used to say you didn't get to choose your family, but you did your pack—we chose them, but more, they *chose* us."

Us.

The choice of pronoun resonated.

"We let them down," he continued, his focus on the road in front of them. They were getting closer with every moment. "We failed them—not you, not me—we. We did this. They were there for us—and we're going to fix it."

He had already fixed it. Tilting her head, she turned her attention from the rolling landscape to study her mate. The last few days had weighed heavily on him. He'd lost some weight in his face, and some color. But the tightness in his jaw had eased, and there were laugh lines at the corners of his eyes once more. His smile never failed to warm her, and now was no exception.

As if aware of her scrutiny, she felt the wordless, if staticky pulse along the bond. It accompanied the swipe of his thumb against her palm. "We're going to be all right, Luce."

Oddly, as much as that nickname used to get her hackles to rise, she relaxed more each time he used it. "Rodrigo first. We remove the threat." Because as much as she wanted to latch onto the romantic notion they could overcome everything, they lived in a very real, and very dangerous world.

She'd let her own arrogance defeat her twice. No more. Rodrigo was a real, and visceral threat. A threat she should have dealt with the day he stalked her at the old house. Another mistake to add to the cobblestone path she'd bricked with them.

"That's why we're heading to the storage facility, but we have to face facts he might not be there." Rational. Reasonable. Perfectly logical.

"Then we keep looking," she stated. "Even if he decides to return to Italy, I'll fly there myself if I have to." She would follow him, and she would kill him in front of Salvatore if that was what it took. Her brother had repudiated her, and she would be risking her life...

"You will not," Rayne said sharply and she gave him a small smile.

"You can't command me."

"Fine, please don't make me tie you down." The immediate snapped response made her smile. He'd probably do it, or at least want to do it.

"We will never have any real peace as long as this sword hangs over our heads—hangs over mine." Dammit, let her embrace it for what it was. "I've made mistakes. I let the Russians blackmail me into landing in our territory. We were struggling, the whole pack was, and I wasn't sure how to fix it and the Volchitsa were haranguing the other packs—

hurting them. But it wasn't a Russian who threatened us, Rayne. It was a British wolf, and he'd been damn familiar."

The fear she experienced at that first meeting had been unsettling. She'd been too young to remember all of the war, but she remembered the stories about the British wolves. About their push to take Italy from them as they marched in with the Allied armies...

"I won't make a lot of excuses, but he guaranteed me if the Volchitsa turned their eyes on our pack, you would be their first target. One wolf? I could take him. A host of them, coming for us as they were for the others?" Then she shook her head. "When I was growing up, we would tell stories about the wolves of Russia. They were our boogeymen, they were the wolves you never wanted to anger. Because they were mad dogs, one and all. Even their most civilized was mad."

Mad was the kind word her mother would use. Fucking insane was how Salvatore usually referred to them.

"When they left Russia to venture to other territories it was because they were hunting fresh territories of their own and they only knew one tactic—destroy everything in their path. Leave no survivors to challenge them." The threat had been very real. "So I made a decision to protect you, and to protect them."

The vehicle didn't slow but the air inside the car seemed to go torpid. "Why didn't you tell me?"

"Because I wanted to protect you. As alpha, it was mine to protect the pack. The decision is not one I'm proud of. It was dishonorable...and cruel. It demonstrated an absolute lack of faith in the other packs." If she were to be perfectly honest... "One I felt they deserved considering their treatment of us. I'm not making excuses. At the time, it was the only choice I could make."

The choice led him to challenge her, driving a fissure right down the middle of their bond and their pack.

"Luce..."

She dared a glance at him. Dared to let herself look at the raw pain on his face.

"You...you should have told me."

The corner of her mouth kicked up. "The same way you should have told me why you challenged me that day? Why you were suddenly compelled to betray me? To betray us?"

He pulled his hand from hers, and hit the steering wheel once, his knuckles white. The vehicle bucked under the rigidity of his grip.

"We both made bad calls—for the same reason. Ironic, isn't it?" Yet she found no humor in it. Would likely never find humor in it.

"No," he told her, his tone flat. "It's tragic."

Silence ballooned between them as the storage facility came into sight. The pressure of it turned oppressive, threatening to strangle all the air from her lungs. "Rayne..."

"I said together," he said, though the words had teeth. "I meant it."

The plan called for Rayne to drop her off, and she would walk in—much as she had the day she came to get her car. A muscle in his jaw ticked as he slowed, and pulled over to the side of the road twenty feet from the facility. The tension was almost unbearable, and she gripped the latch to open the door when he caught her arm.

"Luce..." The demand in his voice, the need of it had her turning to look at him. His pupils were so large they seemed to swallow his eyes and gold bled in around the edges. Wolf and man regarded her with equal ferocity.

She recognized the next movement before he made it, and she had time to resist, to pull away, or even to shove him back. She did none of these things as he slid his hand up to her hair, and then closed the gap between them. The first touch of his lips to hers and she dragged him closer. The first taste of his chapped lips, salty with a hint of sweat and tasting of dark brewed coffee intoxicated her.

Something inside of her unlocked, old dreams she'd banished, and unforgettable passion she buried. Everything his challenge transformed into impossibilities, because how could she ever want him again?

God, how could he ever want her?

Then he gasped into her mouth, a harsh, terrible sound that has her toes curling inside of her shoes. One lick of his tongue and her reticence morphed into desire. Then she swept her tongue against his, tasting him and for a moment, he stiffened. Uncertainty corded through her. Had she read him wrong? Had she stepped too far, too fast? But then he unsnapped his seat belt and hers, before dragging her to him, his arms locking around her as he devoured her as hungry and desperate as she had become.

A voice in the back of her mind whispered frantically. They weren't ready for this. It was too much. It was too soon. It was dangerous and foolhardy. Too much lay broken between them, and she sank her fingers into his hair as if bound there.

When he finally dragged his mouth from hers, it was only to press a line of kisses to her throat, and she tilted her head to the side, granting him access. When his teeth scraped over her pulse, she fisted his hair and pulled his head back even as she froze.

No.

His lashes revealed eyes of pure gold gazing at him and her wolf had long since roused to stare back. The kiss had ignited her, but they were not ready for his teeth at their throat.

"Be careful?" he demanded in a husky voice brimming

with the dark promise of passion and pleasure. "Do you understand? Be. Careful."

"I'd rather be deadly," she told him. "But I will be cautious with it."

Licking the taste of him from her lips, she released him as he freed her to sit back in her seat. His gaze pinned her there, but neither of their wolves—neither of them backed down.

Together, she reminded herself. They were doing this together.

"Be close?" It wasn't a command.

"As your heartbeat," he whispered, then brushed his knuckles down her cheek. "Go get him."

She found a smile for him, then slid out of the car. Before she could close the door, however, he said, "And Luce?"

"Yes?"

"Kick his ass."

This time her smile spread of its own accord. "I very much intend to."

After closing the door, she headed down the road and didn't track the SUV as Rayne pulled away and continued on. He would park a mile away and jog back. They wanted Rodrigo to believe she was alone. He seemed to prefer to approach when she was alone and *vulnerable*, so she would use the weakness in her he'd exploited before against him.

But she wasn't that vulnerable. Not this time. Her lips still tingled from Rayne's kiss, a reminder that not only was she not vulnerable—she wasn't alone. The awareness of him was a staticky hum settled in the back of her mind. This near each other, she had no doubt he could close his eyes and turn himself blind in her direction.

She could him.

Still, she had to appear susceptible.

To that end, she strolled rather than hurried. Affecting a bad mood wasn't at all difficult, though she lacked the bleak depression of before—just the prospect of dealing with Rodrigo set her blood aflame. The idea he'd been this close, that she'd likely gone right past him the last time she was here aggravated her like an open scrape on her flesh.

His expression in the woods flashed in front of her eyes. The wildness in him, the possessive fury—his obsession made no sense. They were barely acquaintances and yet he wanted to her to runaway with him like a pair of illicit lovers.

She was seething by the time she reached the gate to the storage facility and plugged in the security code. It rolled back with a rattle and hum, and she strode inside. Since she couldn't look like she was here for him, she made a beeline for her storage unit. If he were here, then he had to have been on that route to notice her—unless he had cameras all over the place here. The storage place had security cameras of their own, but they were clearly posted.

Head angled slightly down, she kept her ears open and tested the air with every step. Rodrigo could mask his scent. But even a wolf with a mask scent will leave traces somewhere he was regularly. It was simple biology, and it overcame even the most skilled.

She was almost to her unit when the taste of orchards in summer, and the vineyards in spring—a heady cocktail and the source of some of the best wines—made her nose itch. Beneath that familiar scent, was something more cloying and wet, like a rot for grapes left too long on the vine.

For a brief moment, nausea swam over her and her vision split. The all too recent memory of pain sent a spike of fear through her. But the staticky hum in the back of her mind expanded. She wasn't alone. No matter how discordant the connection, how fragile, she wasn't alone.

The shuffle hush of a step against the gravel pulled her

around, and she had her expression under control before her gaze met Rodrigo's.

"Hello, Principessa. I am so happy to see you looking well."

He wasn't going to be happy for long.

CHAPTER 23

*A*llowing Luciana to walk into the storage facility unescorted didn't sit right with the man or the wolf. She was not alone. He parked a mile away and came back overland; aware that every second it took him was a second she could possibly be confronting her assailant.

The only wolves he informed of the plan were Jackson, Julian, and Dallas. Jackson he'd ordered not to share, and as for Julian—he'd only asked he come looking if they failed to return or call within a few hours. If the unthinkable happened, he would pull that bastard away from her so they could find her.

It was the only way he could live with her decision. He made no mistake of believing he'd allowed her to do this. She asked him to do this together, and if he'd refused her—if he'd challenged her right to stand up for herself, she would have left him to face Rodrigo alone.

Of that, he had no doubt.

Yet, he couldn't fault her. The trepidation quavering through him came straight from the mate bond, and he stilled to focus all of his attention to the worry echoing along the damaged connection. Leaning into it, he poured his faith and confidence into the channel. Luciana was more than strong enough to do this, she had to not doubt herself.

He would be there. She was not alone.

She would never have to be alone.

Not as long as there was breath in his body.

Then nearly as soon as he'd conveyed the sentiment, the connection buzzed like a nest of bees hummed beneath his skin. The sting of her agitation ramping up, and he could almost taste the anger wreathing the air around her. It would be spice on his tongue, because Luciana was fierce in her fury and she'd always had a temper.

"You got this chère," he murmured to himself as he approached the storage facility from the northwest. The ripple across the bond and his wolf was on point. Luciana wasn't alone. The wind continued to come from the southeast. He would be downwind, and he could already taste Luciana on the breeze. He could find her blindfolded in a hurricane.

The second scent broke, as if the breeze punctured it, but the notes were right. Rodrigo was indeed there. He leapt the fence and cleared it to land on soft feet on the far side. Luciana's storage unit was one building over from him, but he went up the side of the building to the roof.

They were thirty feet from him, and he was still downwind. The Italian wolf towered over his Luciana, and Rayne's wolf thrust himself forward, glaring out of his eyes. The desire to rush him, to systematically break every bone in his body and gut him rolled over him like a hot wind.

"Hello, Principessa. I am so happy to see you looking well." The urbane voice, the heavy accent, and the smirk just pissed him off more.

Lying sack of shit.

"Happy or surprised?" Luciana dared him; she didn't back

away or cross her arms. The swell of her displeasure vibrated the air around here. Only a fool would see welcome in her chilly regard.

"Of course, I'm happy Principessa. The last thing I wanted was to harm you." He reached out to touch her, and she slapped his hand away with enough force the other wolf actually flinched. It was a small jerk, but present.

"I see," she said, raising her eyebrows. "I must have missed the chapter on protruding bones as a courting technique."

"You were very aggressive, *cara ragazza*, what else could I do but prove myself to you?"

Rayne's eyes were slitted and his wolf rumbled within him, but the purely cold fury rising in his soul wasn't coming from him. His anger was far hotter. In front of Rodrigo, Luciana looked composed, her expression neutral, and her scent hadn't changed an ounce. If he could see her eyes, he'd bet they were golden—or maybe not.

Despite her tempestuous nature, she possessed a poise he'd seen in few others. The calm despite storm raging within her—it was that calm or seeming indifference that irked him when she'd walked away from him. How could she not fight for them?

What a fool, how could she do anything but fight for herself when he isolated her? Yet instead of turning the pack on him, she'd withdrawn behind her walls and given him the room to grow even as she bled internally. His fist clenched.

"Rodrigo, you're an ass," she said with all the sweetness of a freshly squeezed lemon juice. "And a bore. You're also tres-passing on North American territories without leave to be here."

The wolf barked a laugh, and put his hands on his hips. "This again, *bella*? Come now, we have more important things to discuss." He reached for her again, but Luciana reared back and she struck him in the center of his chest with a leap kick and Rodrigo staggered backwards, but her second kick sent blood flying from his mouth as he tumbled over.

Rayne grinned. There she was—his mate.

Instead of closing the gap though, Luciana circled away from him maintaining her distance from Rodrigo's greater reach. "Luciana," the other wolf warned. "Don't be a fool. You can't beat me."

"I don't have to beat you." The soft words carried and Rayne frowned. That wasn't what she'd told him. Fur rippled beneath his skin, the need to shift a violent force closing in on him. "I don't have to do a damn thing. You are a dead wolf walking."

After Rodrigo spat blood off to the side, he stalked toward her. "We are done with this game, Principessa." And power rolled off the other wolf and went crashing toward his mate. The kind of power Rayne tasted the night Salvatore challenged them all. Where Salvatore's had been wild and unrestrained, a force of actual nature striking like a wall, Rodrigo's peeled away from Luciana like a rip current, unable to hit the shore.

The hair along his arms stood up, and the feeling cascaded over him as if the current tried to strike him and broke like water crashing against rocks. The slash and slap lost momentum and force. The hell of it was, his wolf exulted at the sensation. But Rodrigo didn't even know he was here, unless...was he playing them?

Even as the thought crossed his mind, the Italian wolf had gone dead still, all of his attention on Luciana. Though he'd tried to close the distance, she shifted her stance and moved away, never truly retreating as she instead circled him. Then her back was to Rayne, and he had to drop lower as Rodrigo continued to face her.

"How are you doing that?" The Centurion demanded.

Rayne wasn't sure what he was asking, but the look of shock on the wolf's face gave him a savage pleasure.

"I'm not freshly shifted after three days of running," she answered him. "I am not caught off guard by a supposed ally threatening to kill my mate—to take me and *make* me his. I am not entertaining the ideas of a mad wolf who should know by now even if he managed to run, his alpha would still hunt him down." The choice of words held a specific power, his wolf lifted his head sharply. Luciana understood Italian wolves, what had she said once about the alpha challenge?

Why would any alpha who was valued by their pack have to face such a challenge alone? Why would not every single wolf stand in the challenger's path?

Because it was the law, Rayne told her. It was honorable.

"That's the foolishness of the same wolves who believe wolves can run alone. We are never alone, mi amore. Wolves who are alone are unloved, unvalued. If even their pack won't defend them..."

If even their pack won't defend them.

Her shock when the pack stepped in to save her, and their embraces outside the house. His poor Luciana, she'd believed herself abandoned by all of them. No wonder she'd shut down, and shut him out.

The woman facing off against Rodrigo wore her power like the crown she deserved. The mate bond flared, the hum of it vibrating in his bones.

Together, or not at all Rayne.

Together.

Rising to his feet, he stared at the wolf beyond Luciana and smirked when the wolf spotted him. Thunder filled Rodrigo's expression. "So you didn't come alone."

"I'm never alone," she reminded him, pride filtering through her tone. "Your mistake was believing I wanted you in the first place, much less needed you. So I will tell you one last time Rodrigo—because we were once pack, you will leave the States—return to Salvatore, don't return to him, I don't care." Truth resonated in those words. Rodrigo's fate interested her very little. "But you will leave."

"And if I don't?" Rodrigo hadn't taken his gaze off Rayne, idiot. The danger was right in front of him, and he would regret his choice very shortly.

"Then we're going to kill you."

Emphasis on the "we."

Rodrigo laughed. "What happened to your so-called honor system? Do you not believe in single combat challenge in here? Were I to declare Alpha Challenge, you would have to stand aside while I took care of your mate for you, and brought your pack back to where it belonged—then I could lay it at your feet."

"That system is not mine," she said with a kind of slow satisfaction, the sounds of the trap closing practically rattling in Rayne's soul. "I am not American, I am Italian, and I was raised by the fiercest wolf in Seven Hills—and while I may not have been a good sister, I was an excellent student. You want to issue an Alpha Challenge, feel free *pezzo di merda*."

Rayne took three steps forward and then leapt off the roof. Rodrigo's gaze flitted to him, then to Luciana, then back again. Something dark and unsavory shifted in his expression. "Are you prepared to risk everything, Principessa for the fool who didn't even know the treasure he stole before he so carelessly discarded it?"

"Hey asshole," Rayne said by way of greeting. "Luciana is a treasure, and treasured, but she isn't a thing to be taken or stolen or possessed—she's something far more precious than that. Now answer her question—you leaving the easy way or the hard way? Do me a favor. Please pick the hard one."

He was a half step behind his mate, and for the first time

in months in perfect sync. His wolf leaned toward her and hers toward him. It was like a gradually shrinking band, pulling them tighter together.

The invader snarled. "You do not deserve her."

"Well on that, we can both agree. Luckily for me, she seems to like me. So you're just shit out of luck."

"And I tire of this conversation," Luciana's tone was as arch and arrogant as it had ever been and his heart swelled at the sound of it. She sounded like *her*. "Choose Rodrigo, or we will choose for you."

Yes, they would.

The protracted standoff needed to end. Rodrigo's right eye twitched, a barely perceptible motion, but a telling one. The wolf turned partially, as though he would walk away, but Rayne lunged forward as Rodrigo spun, claws extended to swipe at her. Partial shifts were a talent of only a few, and while Rayne didn't have it—he'd fought the fuckers who did.

The arm lock pushed Rodrigo's arm up and away from Luciana. He didn't waste time grappling; he stepped into the wolf, then wrenched his arm backward until the joint gave with a sickening pop. Vicious pleasure speared him as he shoved the wolf backwards.

Luciana hadn't moved a muscle, her entire focus lasering on Rodrigo as the wolf spit. Pain creased his face and Rayne didn't follow. He could lay into him, slam his fists into him until he'd extracted his pound of flesh but his vengeance wasn't why they were there.

"Are you done?" Luciana asked the Italian wolf, extending an olive branch he did not deserve.

Rodrigo didn't deign to answer. He wrenched his shoulder forward trying to pop the joint into place as he charged her. In that instant, he was a step closer to Luciana than Rayne was, but she curled her fingers as she struck and raked claws across his face in a spray of blood. At the end of her arc, she was on the far side of Rodrigo, once again out of his arm's reach and he staggered, barely able to lift his wounded arm to put a hand to his face.

This wasn't about beating him. The other wolf needed to understand something. More, they needed to demonstrate it. They didn't need to defeat him, they'd already won. They were still together, and he was the outsider—the interloper. Any wolf could kill him and many wolves were hunting him. Sooner or later, he would fall.

His death wasn't the point.

But damn would it feel good.

Luciana gave him a reproving look and Rayne shrugged. The bastard hurt her; he didn't get a second chance.

"Rodrigo Mazzanti," Rayne used his full name. "Tired yet?"

Of course he wasn't, this time when he lunged he aimed for Rayne but altered direction at the last moment to close on Luciana. The speed at which she avoided the blow even when she wasn't directly facing it gave Rayne the opening to ram his fist right into Rodrigo's kidney, one strike, two, and on the third the man went to one knee, and Rayne locked his arms around his throat.

The wolf froze beneath his grip, and they were both left to stare at Luciana as she regarded them with a near unreadable expression. But Rayne didn't need her emotions on display, not when the disappointment rang clearly through to him. Rodrigo's demands and actions had gone beyond the pale.

"Do it," Rodrigo demanded. "Then send me back to your brother as the act of war it will be."

It wasn't a lightly offered threat, but Luciana didn't even react. She flicked a look up to meet Rayne's gaze. Were they in agreement?

He nodded once.

"Ciao Rodrigo."

Rayne didn't give him the grace of another response; the bastard already burned too many opportunities. He wrenched the wolf's head in a vicious twist until the vertebrae snapped and his body went limp.

Luciana followed the descent of his body's collapse, then sighed. "I'd hoped he'd make a different decision. Even as angry as I was…"

"I know, Luce. But you can't save everyone. He crossed the line long before he walked into those mountains." He'd done it with his first approach of her. "You know this isn't on you, right?"

A little shrug, and she looked away from the body and toward the storage units. "We need to find the one he was using. And delete whatever security footage they've recorded here."

It all seemed rather anticlimactic, but Rayne didn't give a damn. The wolf who'd hurt her would never be able to again. "We will." Then he stepped over the body and caught her hand when she would have moved off to begin her search. "Hey…"

She let him pull her to him. "Yes?"

"You're all right, aren't you?" He couldn't get any read off of her, nothing. The sudden absence crushed him.

"No," she told him simply. "I'm not all right."

The fist around his heart squeezed. What happened? What the fuck had he missed? They'd just…

"It should never have had to come down to his death," she said quietly. "I'm not upset with you or even with me." She studied the body. "But he was one of Salvatore's and right now, he's feeling the loss of his Centurion, and he won't know why. It's going to hurt him even more when he finds out the why—and that feels like my fault."

"Oh sweetheart," Rayne murmured, wrapping his arms

around her and to his utter relief she burrowed into him and let him hold her. "That's not your fault. Something was wrong with him. He made bad choices. You told him no. You told him no and he didn't listen to you, so that's all on him. You came here today and you gave him the chance to walk away, you gave him the kind of grace he did *not* deserve. He spit on that. So all of this—whatever pain has been inflicted on your brother and definitely the pain he inflicted on you, that's on him."

"You make me want to believe it." The absence of her began to fill in again, like shading filling in a sketch with texture and nuance. "Why couldn't he just walk away?"

"We're never going to know why. What matters is you tried—what matters is that we did it together." Then he rubbed her back slowly. "And I get it now, Luce. I get what I did and why you pulled away and I am so fucking sorry that I hurt you. I thought I had to do it to save you and I don't know if you can ever forgive me..."

"...I already did," she admitted, and the shock of it rocked him. Pulling away a fraction, he met her gaze and her watery smile. "You wanted to protect me and all I wanted to do was protect you—somehow—we failed at that pretty miserably."

They had. "But we did it together." The cold comfort that it offered pulled a wet laugh from her and he smiled as he thumbed away a tear from her cheek. "I love you, you know that right?"

She nodded slowly. "I do."

"Yeah, I need you to show a bit more confidence in that, so I'm going to spend the next few decades making sure you know how much." The flare in the bond pulled another smile from her. The sense of her was stronger than it had ever been, and he pressed his forehead to hers. "I love you."

"I know," she whispered. "But I'm not kissing you next to a corpse...so can we go find his stalker unit then go home?"

His mirth at "stalker unit" paled in comparison to the pleasure of the word "home." "As you wish, my love."

Hell yes.

Home.

She made a rude sound and gave him a gentle shove, but she couldn't erase his grin. Pivoting, she marched away from the body and he pulled out his phone as he followed. They needed to clean this up, but he couldn't pull his gaze away from the sway in her hips or the bounce in her step.

The sooner they finished, the sooner he could steal her away and prove his love to her. As many times as he could.

With fervor…

"You know, the unit isn't going to find itself…and you staring at me like that is not going to make my clothes spontaneously burn off."

There was an image and he was still grinning when Jackson answered.

CHAPTER 24

*L*uciana should be giddy, and some part of her was, but the rest of her remained absolutely focused. The storage unit with Rodrigo's equipment, and more were vital to the case to present to the Enforcers. With Rodrigo's execution, they had no choice but to inform Salvatore.

Her heart ached for her brother. It had taken her too long to understand what her actions had done to him. To taste the betrayal from one she'd loved, to have her pack seemingly turn their backs on her. She'd been a damn fool. In gathering this pack together, she had always been an Italian wolf and they were always Americans. What they thought and believed did not always mesh with her own beliefs—Rayne was the glue, the bridge between she and them, but only because he was so like them but loved her.

A shiver raced up her spine.

Love.

Her mate loved her.

And she'd had reason to doubt for far too long.

He paced her on the opposite side of the blacktopped

pavement between the rows of units. Hers was still one back, but Rodrigo had already been back here when she'd walked in, he had to have come...

She stopped. The scent familiar. "Here."

Pivoting, she faced the metal door. There was no lock. Gripping the lip, she rolled the door upward, half-surprised it didn't make a sound as it rolled neatly into the unit, revealing a wall of monitors, a server, a laptop desk, a bed in the corner, and more. Rodrigo's scent was everywhere.

Beneath it, she could taste a couple of other wolves, but they were faded and indistinct. Rayne glared at the equipment. "I'm liking Giovanni less and less."

"I can't say I'm his biggest fan at the moment. But I have the most difficult time believing he would have supported *any* of Rodrigo's actions." It was disconcerting. To see it set out before her. Even after Rodrigo's words and the attack itself, a part of her simply did not want to believe anyone in Seven Hills could have done this.

"We don't have to do this..." Rayne told her.

"There is one thing we have to do." One thing they would do before she allowed anyone else in here. "The recording of the challenge."

His harsh exhale and the plummet in his scent wrenched at her. Without a second thought, she took his hand and threaded their fingers together. "Someone else will be reviewing all of this. They might even return it to Salvatore..."

"No. The fact it exists at all is all the proof we need and the Enforcers saw the cameras. We're destroying *all* of the footage." The savage vehemence in his tone thrummed through her. "No one gets to spy on you—to spy on us. No one is going to try and dissect us or our pack."

In truth, that result would absolutely be her preference. "How do we know which ones to destroy..."

Rayne faced her, squeezing her hand. "Trust me?"

Searching his eyes she found not a hint of deception in them and more, she gazed into the eyes of both wolf and man. The mate bond hummed like its own living entity, and it said yes. He was worth it.

More, it told her what she already knew…

"Yes."

With a smile, he dug the keys out of his pocket and pressed them into her palm. "The others are on their way. Go get the car, and come back. It's about a mile past the turn in the road, parked at the old dilapidated fruit stand, behind the ripped billboard."

She glanced at the contents of the unit, then at him again. "Are you all right to do this alone? Because you don't have to."

Together meant in everything.

"I know, and you're right—together is better. I will never forget that again," he swore it to her, and something twisted and knotted inside of her unlocked. "But I want to do this for you, I need to do this. You never have to see that again if you don't want to. No one will ever see it again."

"Then why do you have to?" She had to understand. If this was just his pride needing to shelter her…

"Because I need to own my mistakes." The solemnity in the declaration smashed any other resistance from her.

"For what it's worth," she told him, lifting their joined hands to her lips so she could kiss his knuckles. "You already have."

"So have you. But I need to do a little penance."

She shook her head. "I don't want a martyr for a mate."

"Trust me, you won't. You're going to have the man who is worthy of you, who will be able to look himself in the eye because he knows the depths to which he slipped once and will never allow himself to do again."

That was truly sweet, and it definitely made her heart pump a little faster, but she narrowed the distance between them. "You take care of my mate—or you'll answer to me." His pupils flared at the declaration and the answering pulse along the mate bond pleased her.

"You have my word," he promised, and then his mouth closed on hers or maybe she lunged to capture his. Either way, they collided together and she drowned in his scent as his mouth fought to claim hers, but she wound her fingers into his hair and tightened as she bit down on his lower lip.

The answering growl made her smile, but she laved her tongue over his wounded lip.

"Be careful," she admonished, echoing his earlier words back at him.

"Be close," he responded, then licked another kiss against her lips, this one slower, and sweeter. It amazed her how much she'd missed him, even when she hadn't allowed herself to consider it.

Even walking away and passing the corpse of the wolf who'd made the last week bordering on hellish, she didn't try to contain her smile. She leapt the fence and landed on the other side still walking on light feet. A sense of purpose and rightness she hadn't experienced in far too long hummed in her veins. It wasn't just about Rayne it was—everything was back where it belonged.

Everything.

Luciana stopped dead and concentrated.

Everything was back where it belonged.

She whirled and looked back at the storage facility—what had Rayne done?

The whole of the pack branched off around her, a cascading awareness. Her pack.

The pack she was no longer alpha of, yet—she could sense them, the bonds settling where they *had* been. Beyond that, the mate bond—damaged and crumbling—surged with new life and she touched at it, and the answering pulse was a caress against her soul.

What did he do?

How was it even possible?

The topic haunted her over the next couple of hours after she returned to the facility to find Jackson had arrived with two Enforcers and two of their Hunters. Though they all greeted her, she kept her distance—just watching them. Jackson pressed a kiss to her cheek before he left and Mark settled in at her side and stayed with her until Rayne finished up with Julian. Even her sense of Jackson, and Mark seemed to have expanded. It was even stronger than before. Not that she couldn't read their scents—that had always been possible —but if she closed her eyes she could have identified which was which without being in close enough to scent them.

"Louis has sent dinner to your house," Mark said when Rayne joined them. "Hudson River's healer is safely aboard the plane sent for her along with Luc. Julian and Dallas continued on to Hudson River, though they indicated they would be returning within the week."

The lack of animosity in his tone discussing the outsiders coming and going suggested the pack had grown more comfortable with their presence. "Thank you, Mark," she murmured, testing a theory as she squeezed his hand.

"You're welcome," he said, then nodded returning the quiet affection before nodding again to Rayne and moving off to finish the work of clearing out the storage unit. Rodrigo's body had already been dealt with thanks to the Enforcer John.

"You okay?" Rayne's took her hand, lifting it to kiss her fingertips.

"I am," she assured him, then studied him closely. He seemed—more and not remotely diminished. "Are *you?*"

He gave her a quick smile. "I'm fine—ready to go home now, if you are…"

Even studying his eyes, she could detect nothing off. He seemed just as he had in the car on the way here. Maybe even more settled because of the ride—the confrontation—and the sense of unity.

Sobering, he raised his brows. "Luce?"

"Nothing," she said slowly, uncertainty threading through her. She could feel the pack. That level of awareness hadn't even been present when she woke after the pack had bonded with Rayne to save her. Then as she recovered—her sense of Rayne had been there, but not this. Not this all consuming perception of the pack. Behind them, Jackson had snapped something at John, but the Enforcer only laughed despite Jackson's actual irritation. The humor settled him though.

Rayne looked past her, his attention on his brother briefly but he relaxed as Jackson did. "C'mon," her mate murmured. "We should get going before they start something that needs me to stay to settle it."

"They'll be fine," she assured him as she fell into step, hand-in-hand with him. "Jackson can handle it." Rayne's brother had risen amazingly well to the task at hand as surprising as she found it. He'd never seemed incompetent, but she hadn't thought him this capable.

The drive back to town passed swiftly, but her mind wandered. Her attention lingered on the landscape, though she saw none of it. Once they were back at the house, Dani left the diner to come out and greet them. She wasn't alone. There were call outs from other wolves making their way along the street and still others who stepped out or opened windows to wave.

The surge of affection bordered on inebriating and she couldn't hold back her smile even though the public displays of affection were just not her thing. When Dani gave her a ninja hug, she even laughed and then grinned wider when Rayne caught her eye.

It took several minutes to extricate themselves but finally Rayne shooed the wolves off and shepherded her inside. Once he had the door closed, he leaned against it and closed his eyes. "I love you all, but if you are not me or my mate and you happen to be in the house, you need to be somewhere else—now."

Command rolled off of him, but they were safely alone. The corner of her mouth quirked upward.

"Yeah, yeah. You wouldn't think it was so funny if you had a houseful to entertain."

"True," she soothed him. Even as she puzzled over the changes, she couldn't help but marvel at how at ease and wound up Rayne was. Yet, he was so clearly him—balanced and grounded. "But I've never seen you so eager to escape them before."

Eyes narrowed, he shook his head. "Not eager to escape them—just to be alone with you."

"Really?" Challenge arched through her. "And what do you plan to do with me now that we're alone?" Hell, a week ago, she would already be spitting with fury and ready to rip into him. But in that moment, all she wanted to do was provoke an entirely different kind of reaction.

Faster than she could react, Rayne snatched her up and carried her up the stairs. More amused than startled, she clung to him and laughed. Once in the bedroom, he kicked the door closed and strolled over to their bed. In a single smooth motion, he had her on her feet, and her shirt off over her head. Next went her bra, then her jeans and when even her panties vanished. Her knees bumped the edge of the bed as he folded his body around her. The speed and precision with which he had removed her clothes overwhelmed her and left clutching at his broad shoulders.

"*Santo cielo,*" she whispered.

He steadied her against the broad expanse of his chest, his hands gentle but his eyes? They were all predator. "All right?"

"Very," she promised him, then dragged his mouth down to meet hers. It had been eons since she'd been in his arms and the kiss in the car had only lit the flames. Rayne seemed quite eager to assist as he licked his way past her lips and cupped her breasts in his rough palms. There was no hesitation in his touch, and she arched her back as he rolled each nipple with his thumbs.

The heavy weight of his cock pressed against her belly, the denim doing little to disguise his erection. He was all teasing hands, soft lips, and sharp teeth. If overwhelming her was the goal, he'd more than exceeded it. Everywhere he touched her, he left goosebumps in his wake. He'd always stood taller than her, and broader, but it was entirely different to be completely surrounded.

She knew this man, she'd kissed him, danced with him, made love with him, fought with him, run with him, and everything she thought she could possibly do with a mate and at the same time he was utterly devastating every one of her defenses. It was like discovering him for the first time.

Locking a leg around his waist she pulled him off balance and they crashed together against the bed. His weight settled against her pelvis and the roughness of his denim rasped across her skin. It was delicious in its discomfort and his hips pumped twice as if he couldn't help himself.

Heat speared right up through her and she dragged at his shirt, yanking it out of his jeans and forcing him to let her go long enough to pull it off. Pupils blown and bleeding gold into the iris, he let out a choked gasp when she rolled her hips, deliberately grinding against his erection.

"Fuck Luce," he hissed out a breath as she worked her fingers into the catch of his jeans and jerked down the zipper. His teeth clicked together as if snapping off whatever he'd been about to say.

"What do you want, Rayne?" She ran her hands up his sides, gliding over the smooth, heavily muscled flesh to his hair. It was thick and soft. She arched against, rubbing her breasts to his chest. The contact sent an electric pulse through her system, and she clenched her thighs against his hips, desperately wishing he'd move. "Just say it—tell me what you want."

"I just want to push these jeans down and be inside of you...fuck I've missed you Luce."

"Then do it," she encouraged him.

He shook his head. "I want to do this right."

Fisting his hair, she angled upward, her legs locked on his waist and her eyes fixed on his. "Rayne Barrows—any way you touch is doing it right. You aren't the only one who has missed this—missed you. We've got all the time in the world to play, but I need you." It was like a heavy pulsating wave, growing stronger with every surge. The need skyrocketing until every part of her was oversensitive. Nothing mattered but this—them.

For a moment, she squirmed at the relentless demand seeming to radiating out of her. She couldn't possibly be in heat; it wasn't anything like this. This was so base, primitive, and fuck, if he didn't get those jeans off...

She released his hair and his hands collided with hers as she went for his jeans. It took them a minute, and his jeans tore in their efforts and she had to disentangle her legs from him long enough to set him free. Then he was there, and gloriously naked.

Kneeling on the bed between her legs, he sank his hands into her hair and plundered her open mouth as he licked, sucked, and devoured her. With a shaking hand, she grasped his cock and stroked it once, then twice and he moaned against her mouth, then she lined him up against her slick entrance...

"Luce...are you...I don't want this to hurt you."

"You're not going to hurt me." She was shaking with need, couldn't he feel that? It seemed to vibrate all the way through her. Finally he eased forward, slowly pressing inside and she nearly screamed in frustration. She was so empty, and needed him so badly—needed to feel the thick heavy weight of him inside of her.

But the look on his face as he settled on his elbows with his forearms bracketing her, silenced her objections. Pure relief filled his eyes, something hot and coiled that had wound through both of them since the challenge came undone as he sank into her. Hurts. Desires. Enmities. Needs. Lies. Secrets. All of it boiled to the surface, and washed away.

Then he was seated in her with an abortive little thrust as if trying to drive himself even more impossibly deeper and it pushed the air from her lungs. Wrapping her arms and legs around him, she cradled him as he bottomed out.

"I've got you," she whispered, her wolf surging to the surface. He needed her so damn much, and she'd missed him. He was hers, he'd been hers and then she thought she'd lost him. Never again.

"Luce..."

"I've got you," she whispered. "I'm here...we're here."

His eyes seemed to roll back into his head as he pulled all the way out, then with a curl of his powerful hips he thrust again. "Can't lose you."

Tightening her fist into his hair, she tugged until he looked at her. "Not going anywhere. I'm here." She squeezed him, her whole body rolling up to meet his thrust as she flexed her legs. "I'm here..." She didn't want to be anywhere else. Their teeth clacked once as they fused their mouths together and then they caught a slow, sinuous rhythm his tongue matching his body as he thrust into her. She dragged her nails down his back, gripping his ass to urge him deeper.

It was like that first time all over again, the need to have him pound his scent into her skin and for her to mark him with hers. The bite of her claws left marks on his back, he was hers and she wasn't letting him go.

The embers of desire flamed to life as he pumped in and out of her, the concussive pace striking just the right spot to drive her spiraling higher, and higher.

"I need you to not leave, Luce," he whispered against her mouth in between biting kisses. "I need you to never leave. You have to be here."

"I will," she swore, understanding the request and needing to meet it. "I need you, Rayne."

"I love you," he said, before dropping his head to rest against her collarbone. His thrusts picked up speed. Each one hammered out a high-pitched cry from Luciana as she clawed to pull him closer. As if the two of them could possibly be any closer than they already were in that moment. Whispers in the quiet gray of the room. Flesh meeting flesh, and kisses that scalded and healed where they fell.

Luciana was past words at that point. Her whole body felt incandescent, sparked to life by the ceaseless rhythm of his cock. But Rayne's voice seemed to come unhinged and unleashed. He talked without ceasing... kissing promises into her skin as he pounded into the hot clutch of her body.

The edge of her climax neared at a rapid pace. "Please," she begged, the words muffled against the pulse in his throat. And he didn't. He pistoned into her over and over with exacting precision until her vision whited out and she bit his shoulder, her teeth piercing his skin. Hers. She marked him, even as she squeezed around him when her orgasm crashed over her. Rayne followed her; his back bowing as he thrust deep, and his teeth sank into the juncture of her throat and shoulder. The world shifted around them, a rubber band snapping back into place, a joint fixed to where it should be —the exquisite pain of returning.

In an instant everything turned soft, and hazy, and slippery. Claimed. Hands that had been insistent and almost bruising before turned gentle and soothing. Bonded. Their lips melted together and they thrust languidly against each other, wanting to wring every last bit of ecstasy and togetherness from that moment, before Rayne's softening cock slipped out of her. Mated.

He carefully rolled them both to their sides, pulling her close and twining their legs together. They lay like that for a long while, sweat cooling and breathing slowing as they took in the sudden change of circumstance. He pressed his forehead to hers as his hands wandered, caressing the swell of her hips, the bend of her wrist, and the hollow of her throat.

It was—everything.

"That was..." He paused as if lost for words, but his gaze worshipped her as if she were the most precious thing in the world.

"Everything," she offered, drunk on the feel of it. The sense of the pack rolled in, the knowing of Rayne, and the rightness of being in the center, balanced perfectly once more.

"Yeah..." He agreed, pulling back a fraction to study her. "Luce...do you feel that?" The wordless pulse vibrating into her and the echoing back to him. She could feel it coming and going.

She nodded. "Rayne...what did you do?" A little bewildered by it all.

"I didn't do anything—" He panted softly, as if the fight to catch his breath wasn't as important as talking to her. "But it feels..."

"...different, yeah. I know. The pack...I can feel them again. *All* of them."

"So can I."

How could they both?

"But the alpha...stands at the center." How could they both feel the whole pack... "You didn't before, right?"

He shook his head. "Not even—not even after I claimed it from you. Not until..."

Not until the night he'd fought to save her. When they'd all united. Rayne's eyes softened. She licked her lips, savoring the taste of him. "Can a pack even have two alphas?"

The breadth and brilliance of his smile hushed her. "Yes," he said. "Because *ours* does. I never wanted to take this from you—and we're *better* together."

Together.

A laugh escaped and she was blinking back tears. Yes they were. They were so much better together. Even their mating bond seemed better, more solid, and sunk so deeply into her bones it wasn't going anywhere.

"I think we need to call Colby in a few days," she suggested. "After we let this settle..."

"A few days," Rayne agreed, his cock already stiffening against her. "I have so much more we need to work on settling."

"Together," she whispered and she swallowed his answer with his kiss and then they didn't need words.

EPILOGUE

A month later, Luciana and Rayne hosted the anniversary celebration for the founding of Three Rivers. Every member of the pack was present, along with a few honored guests—the humans who'd helped them settle in the first place including Shiloh who had become a wolf herself after her mating.

Three of the five of other alphas attended—Serafina, Mason, and Brett. They'd all brought their mates. Julian and Dallas brought a gift, but they had stolen away with their granddaughter not long after Chrystal had arrived with her mate Dylan.

A true honor, because it was the first infant to be in Three Rivers, and rather fitting that it was that of their former Omega. It was a rare celebration, and one where old enmities were being laid down, and new alliances forged. Colby confirmed what he and Luciana suspected; they were both Alpha. It should be impossible, there could only be one, but their devotion to each other and their reforged mating bond cemented it.

Three Rivers was rather fond of their unique position,

even if it stumped the other alphas. Luce hadn't wanted to make a fuss. For dealing with the other packs, Rayne would stand as alpha, but as she reminded all of them—he didn't stand alone.

He spent a solid hour with Serafina, discussing old misunderstandings and repairing a friendship they'd let go fallow. She in turn told him that Amy had requested to move to Three Rivers for a time, to be a healer on loan until one of their own came up. She would be welcome home whenever she wished, but she asked Rayne to look after her. It would be his pleasure.

Luciana apologized to Mason, though Rayne didn't think she needed to, but she said she'd wanted to. They'd been building bridges with the other alphas, and she expressed her naiveté with how different the States were from Italy. But she had involved his humans, making them complicit, and for that she owed him an apology. The other alpha had merely smiled, shaken her hand and said that was the past. Now they worked toward the future.

From the music to the bonfire to the renewal of old friendships and the cementing of new ones, it was perfect. For an anniversary gift, the whole pack announced the old house Luciana loved so much would be ready for them to move into in the spring. Jackson and Mark with help from the Reagans had already gotten to work on tearing out all of the rotting wood and replacing it.

He'd never seen his mate nearly cry in public before, but she didn't try to stem her tears and she was the one giving them hugs. His wolves were thrilled and his mate content.

Though he couldn't ask for much more, there was still the issue of Rodrigo. Julian had taken care of sending his body back to Italy under escort. What word, if any there was from Salvatore, he'd not heard. Luciana didn't ask, but he'd seen her staring off into space now and again. If she had any regrets, it was about him.

It was late, and many of their guests had begun to make their way home while their own wolves slipped off into smaller groups, leaving he and Luce alone to sit on their porch. It was cold, but clear. The town was lit up, and full. It had taken them a long time to get to this spot, but damn if the payoff hadn't been worth the misery. "You ready to go in?"

She'd drawn a shawl over her shoulders, and when she glanced up at him, he caught sight of the cell phone in her hand. "Not yet—I want to call Salvatore."

Stilling, he searched her gaze. "You sure?"

"Yes." She gave him a tremulous smile. "It's time."

"He may not answer," he warned carefully, not wanting her to be hurt.

"Then I'll keep calling...I'm his baby sister, and I know how to annoy him until he listens. But all I want to do is to tell him I'm sorry, and that I get it now. That I was wrong to treat him as I did, and even though I don't regret you or what we did, I regret *how* we did it."

Brushing the hair away from her face, he nodded. "You want me to stay?"

"Please."

Settling in, he wrapped his arm around her, and pressed his lips to her hair as she dialed the number.

ABOUT THE AUTHOR

USA Today bestselling author, Heather Long, likes long walks in the park, science fiction, superheroes, Marines, and men who aren't douche bags. Her books are filled with heroes and heroines tangled in romance as hot as Texas summertime. From paranormal historical westerns to contemporary military romance, Heather might switch genres, but one thing is true in all of her stories—her characters drive the books. When she's not wrangling her menagerie of animals, she devotes her time to family and friends she considers family. She believes if you like your heroes so real you could lick the grit off their chest, and your heroines so likable, you're sure you've been friends with women just like them, you'll enjoy her worlds as much as she does.

Keep up with Heather
www.heatherlong.net
heather@heatherlong.net

Always a Marine Series

Once Her Man, Always Her Man

Retreat Hell! She Just Got Here

Tell It to the Marine

Proud to Serve Her

Her Marine

No Regrets, No Surrender

The Marine Cowboy

The Two and the Proud

A Marine and a Gentleman

Combat Barbie

Whiskey Tango Foxtrot

What Part of Marine Don't You Understand?

A Marine Affair

Marine Ever After

Marine in the Wind

Marine with Benefits

A Marine of Plenty

A Candle for a Marine

Marine under the Mistletoe

Have Yourself a Marine Christmas

Lest Old Marines Be Forgot

Her Marine Bodyguard

Smoke & Marines

A Man Called Wyatt

Going Royal

Some Like It Royal
Some Like It Scandalous
Some Like It Deadly
Some Like it Secret
Some Like it Easy
Her Marine Prince
Blocked

Lone Star Leathernecks

Semper Fi Cowboy
As You Were, Cowboy

Madison, The Witch Hunter

Every Witch Way But Floosey's

Magic & Mayhem

The Witch Singer
Bridget's Witch's Diary
The Witched Away Bride

Mongrels

Mongrels, Mischief & Mayhem

Space Cowboy

Space Cowboy Survival Guide

Wolves of Willow Bend

Wolf at Law

Wolf Bite

Caged Wolf

Wolf Claim

Wolf Next Door

Rogue Wolf

Bayou Wolf

Untamed Wolf

Wolf with Benefits

River Wolf

Single Wicked Wolf

Desert Wolf

Snow Wolf

Wolf on Board

Holly Jolly Wolf

Shadow Wolf

His Moonstruck Wolf

Thunder Wolf

Ghost Wolf